STALKING LOVE is a romantic thriller set in St. Petersburg, Florida during the current real estate crisis. With a serial killer targeting people involved in the real estate business, and a potential love of a lifetime in the works, it takes all of the strength and courage of a woman thought to have it all, but lacking everything that really matters to grow and develop into who she is destined to become.

As Rachel Contino, a proficient, thirty-eight year old realtor, attempts to avoid the real estate meltdown caused by her main client, developer Jonathan Harrell who had died in an apparent suicide, new evidence surfaces that it wasn't a suicide but murder. This is soon followed up by the murder of Jonathan's partner. These murders inside a condo complex hosting her largest number of listings makes her sales all but disappear, forcing her into deeper financial problems. In addition to her financial situation, she is scared that the murderer may be targeting her next.

Meanwhile, Rachel, who has no time for a life outside of her profession, meets Carlos Martinis, a twenty-three year old mortgage broker, and yields to the teasing of her friends in attempting to make this stud her boy toy.

As her world falls apart, she has to depend on a guy she wanted to make into a toy. Relying on love rather than her money is a hard lesson to learn, but one that she has to before it's too late and Carlos leaves her and the murderer makes his final move. Converting their passionate sex life to a true love will require admitting secrets that both Carlos and Rachel have to eventually reveal. But will these secrets bring them together or drive them apart forever?

Sometimes when you think your career has provided you with everything you would ever want, life has a way of opening your eyes to what little you actually have. While finding and accepting love can be the biggest challenge of a life time, revealing secrets can be dangerous. So, can it be possible to admit what is really important and toss away a life time of work to lock in on love?

STALKING LOVE
AN INTERNATIONAL ROMANTIC THRILLER
BY
Johnny Ray
Copyright © 2012
SIR JOHN PUBLISHING
ISBN # 978-1-940949-22-2

5

JOHNNY RAY is an award winning novelist who won the Royal Palm literary award for best thriller and is quickly making a name for himself as the master of the romantic thriller. He loves social interaction with his readers and can be found on

Twitter
www.twitter.com/sirjohn_writer

Facebook
www.facebook.com/authorjohnnyray.

He can also be reached by e-mailing at sirjohn@wwisp.com,

Or you can just follow him on his blog at www.sirjohn.us for updates and future releases.

Johnny Ray's other novels include:

DRONES
Published by Sir John Publishing in 2013

A WAR HERO RETURNS
Published by Sir John Publishing in 2013

JOHN RAIN – THE HAWAIIAN AFFAIR
Published by AMAZON DIGITAL in 2013

MODELS AND LOVERS
Published by Sir John Publishing in 2012

HER HONOR'S BODYGUARD
Published by Sir John Publishing in 2012

FOR LOVE AND VENGEANCE
Published by Sir John Publishing in 2012

SCANDAL – THE DEATH OF A LEGACY
Published by Sir John Publishing in 2012

THE SALSA CONNECTION
Published by Sir John Publishing in 2012

LITERARY AGENT – BEWARE
Published by Sir John Publishing in 2012

Chapter 1

After lifting Prince, her miniature toy poodle, from the floor and rubbing his head to keep him from barking, Rachel Contino used her intercom system to respond to a call coming from the ground floor of her condo. *Okay, now who else is stopping by to see us this morning?* She smiled at Prince, who obviously knew that he might have someone else to play with soon.

The response, however, shocked her. "This is Detective Lindstrom. I need to talk to you for a minute." The sound of his voice made her skin tingle immediately.

"I see." She swallowed hard. "I'll buzz you through." This investigation was supposed to be over. With her previous upbeat nature quickly disappearing, she lowered Prince to the floor. Her mind quickly flooded with questions he might have for her as she quickly reflected on her life. While she had always enjoyed spending money on her expensive clothes and jewelry designed by such names as Prada, Gucci, and Cartier to reflect her success, she knew they revealed the harsh reality of the sacrificed time and energy she had spent on acquiring them.

She was not nearly as vain as most people thought since she fully knew these cold, lifeless treasures did nothing to warm her bed at night. Her fabulous collection couldn't come close to filling the empty hole in her life which was threatening to swallow her. *Where has my youth and my very life gone? Where is love?* Inches from giving in to self pity, the thought of buzzing Detective Lindstrom in from below moments ago brought her back from the brink of despair.

Hurriedly, Rachel clicked on her e-mail account, looking for any last minute emergencies she needed to handle. As she was about to close out, an ad from yet another mortgage company opened. While feeling fully frustrated, her finger stretched for the delete key, but hovered as a photo of the mortgage originator, who was one very sexy man, materialized and filled the computer screen with his intoxicating smile.

"Oh . . . to be so young again." After glancing at the name below the photo which introduced him as Carlos Martini, she could only hope he looked as good in person as he photographed.

She glanced at her watch again before closing her e-mail to protect it from the detective's prying eyes. After she forced the brush through her hair one last time, she realized she had no time left to finish her makeup. With Prince yapping beside her, she hurried to answer the pounding on the door.

After picking Prince off the floor again and cradling him beside her, Rachel cracked the door and studied the city detective sweating outside in the latest of one of St. Petersburg's famous heat waves. She offered a smile as she hoped that after today she would never see this man's face again. Her stomach churned, and a chill traveled the length of her spine as she again realized that she would be forced to go over what she knew of the death of her friend and real estate client, developer Jonathan Harrell. What had transpired thus far had been one hell of a continuous nightmare, not to mention how it was slowly dragging her career to the brink of disaster with it.

"Detective—what is it?" She hesitated for a moment before she relented and opened the door wider.

"I'm sorry to bother you, but the case is being reopened.

This morning we received some new evidence suggesting Jonathan's death wasn't a suicide." With his short but stocky body firmly planted in the doorway, Lindstrom glanced around her. "Perhaps this conversation would be better handled if we continued it inside."

Rachel's muscles in her face tightened, erasing her desire to smile as she moved to one side to allow him to enter. "I thought you closed the investigation." Her mind flashed back to the endless problems caused by Jonathan's suicide, and how his death inside one of his condo units made her job of selling the remaining units next to impossible, especially during this current housing meltdown.

"Well . . . we thought so too, but as I said, we received some new information making us have some serious second thoughts." He strolled toward a chair at her dining room table. The sound of him dragging the chair legs over her stone floor made her skin shiver as she forced herself to remain calm.

While pulling her fluffy white robe tighter, Rachel hoped to avoid his staring eyes. "What did you discover?" Rachel studied Lindstrom's eyes, as he retrieved a pad from the inside of his basic blue suit which was probably purchased from a local discount department store–the cheap material certainly looked like he had anyway. With both the legs and arms of the suit several inches too long, he definitely needed a tailor. She knew her opinion was cruel and bit her lip, but from the first time she saw him, his clothes reminded her of seeing a scarecrow in a cornfield when she was ten.

"I need to ask you some more questions."

With feelings of anger boiling inside her, Rachel raised her voice so as to not waste any more time in getting to the point. "Am I being investigated?" She remembered the interrogations earlier–the accounting of her whereabouts–the frustrations of having to defend her answers. Thoughts of

Jonathan being murdered scared her. She didn't understand why her good friend and one of her best clients may have been killed. This investigation continued to frustrate her to no end, and especially if they thought she had anything to do with his death. Yes, Jonathan had threatened to give his listings to another agent, but she knew he had felt frustrated, much like many developers trying to survive in the market. She also knew that if Lindstrom had heard about his threat, he might consider her a suspect. While hoping that no one ever knew about this argument, the only disagreement they had ever had, she knew she had always worked hard for Jonathan and wanted to sell as much as she could for him.

Lindstrom smiled as he motioned toward another seat at the table. "If I was investigating you, this conversation would be at my office and not here. Please relax and have a seat. Please . . . I need your help." His normally rigid face turned soft and plaintive. Perhaps in his late fifties, Rachel wondered if Lindstrom had been in law enforcement all of his life. He had never strayed from his persistent investigation.

Breathing easier, but knowing to maintain her guard against saying anything she would regret later, she slipped into the white leather chair at the end of the table while scratching Prince behind one ear. "What do you need from me? You know I'll help anyway I can." She lowered her eyes to study the beveled glass tabletop which rested on a large white coral base. Maybe she over worked the snow-white color scheme in her condo, but she loved the resulting style. She knew she was refocusing her attention, but anything outside his stares would soothe her mind.

He leaned forward as his voice remained smooth and soothing. "I need to keep this as quiet as I can for a while and I need you to respect my request."

What is Lindstrom trying to hide? Jonathan had lots to

live for and many friends. Who would want to kill him? Obviously she wasn't going to hear what he discovered without agreeing. She studied his light-gray eyes, which contrasted with the gentleness of his face, and perhaps concealing an inner strength he controlled until when it was needed. His eyes reminded her of a wolf, ready to pounce on her at a moment's notice. "What makes you think he was murdered?"

She watched him scratch a note on his pad before returning her stare. "You had the listings on the condos he had developed. How much did he confide in you concerning his finances?"

She looked away, unable to withstand the intensity of his eyes any longer. "Some. We maintained a good working relationship, as well as being good friends. He understood the problems we're having in this market and knew I was doing my best to sell his condos for him. Of course I knew he was suffering with some financial problems. All developers are now." She selected her words carefully since she didn't want the detective to dig into their personal relationship to deeply. After crying many nights over his death, hiding their friendship behind this professional, but cold accounting would be best for everyone.

"We discussed the suicide note he left behind before –the one he supposedly typed on his computer for us to find." Lindstrom's slow diligent methods of operation irritated her the same way they had from the beginning of the investigation.

"And . . . as I told you before, I've no way of knowing for sure if he wrote that letter or not."

"That's understandable. However . . . this is what I need to know. Did he mention anything else about his current finances to you?"

Rachel considered her words before she answered. "He

remained anxious about the market, as he should have been, but I don't think he felt suicidal at all. If he did, he hid his condition from me very well." Memories of working with Jonathan resurfaced–the good times–the closings.

Lindstrom continued with his relentless questions. "Did he ever say anything about refinancing his loans with a bank out of Germany?"

No, now this is new. Why had Jonathan never said anything about this? "He never mentioned this to me, but I'm sure he was exploring all options."

Rachel studied Lindstrom as he continued to make notes. With the smell of cigarette smoke venting from his clothes, and no wedding ring on his finger, she imagined his life at local sports bars after work, that is, until he started to explain further. "I just learned that he had received approval on a new loan the day before he died. The bank contacted me this morning with questions concerning his death. They thought that he must have made other arrangements, and that was the reason why he hadn't followed through on the loan. The loan officer was surprised to hear he had committed suicide shortly after obtaining their loan approval."

"Ohmigod! He didn't say a word about the loan." While she had maintained some doubts about the suicide until now, this definitely changed her opinion. She quickly started replaying the list of suspects in her mind. Jonathan had a business partner, Donnie Moore, but the two worked close together and needed each other. Jonathan, who had been a developer for a long time, was divorced, but the marriage had ended a long time ago. Naturally, some of the owners weren't too happy about the falling real estate prices, but they had to understand that the collapse wasn't his fault. Perhaps one of them had maintained a secret grudge.

"I'm going to talk to everyone again that he had dealings

with. I know you provided me with a detailed list before, but I'd appreciate the help if you can add to the list anyone else you think might in anyway be connected to Jonathan Harrell."

Rachel leaned back in her chair. The list she had prepared for him before was long, and she knew that he would investigate anyone else she added to it. This wasn't going to win her any popularity awards. "I don't think he made any enemies, and I'm sure most people would consider him to be a great guy."

"So I've heard." He placed the pad back in his suit pocket. "I hope you'll consider one point that I need to make. If someone had a problem with him and his business, you might also have an enemy out there that you don't know about."

Was that possible? Could someone want me dead also? The tension escalated in Rachel's neck, stretching outward toward her shoulders. "Are you trying to scare me?"

Rachel studied his smile, a vain attempt to lighten the impact. "I think it would be negligent on my part if I didn't come here to warn you."

Rachel's heart fluttered as she realized how right he was, but forced her body not to reveal the fear overtaking her. "Thank you." She continued to breathe deeply, attempting to stay in control. "What do you suggest I do?"

"There are two things I recommend. First, don't take any unnecessary chances, and second . . . help me find out who is behind this murder. I promise to hold all information in confidence as best I can." He raked the legs of the chair along the granite floor again as he stood, making her wince with pain.

As she stood, her robe parted slightly. Seeing him focus on her bare skin scared her, and she quickly grasped the lapels. "Okay, I'll be in touch with any more names I can remember." She pulled Prince closer to her to ensure that he remained quiet.

"Thank you." He opened the door and closed it behind him as he left.

She breathed deeply before letting out a sigh of relief, only to have thoughts return of the new problems she faced in having Jonathan's will probated by the courts. This would delay clearing title further now, making the sales of his remaining properties not only difficult, but in this environment almost impossible. While feeling selfish in her needs, she knew Jonathan would approve. Business was always the center of their relationship. She knew he would want her to complete the project. She owed him that.

***

Thanks to the early morning meeting with Detective Lindstrom which caused her entire schedule to be off, Rachel drove as fast as she could without getting a ticket. Finally, she glided her luxurious BMW, her statement of wealth and success, into the corner of the estate in the Coffee Pot Area where Ruth Johnson, one of her friends and a fellow real estate agent, hosted an open house. As she studied most of the parking places quickly disappearing, she envied the fantastic turn out. Surprisingly, she didn't think other agents liked Ruth too much. As Rachel realized that Ruth must have really worked hard in promoting this open house, she whispered, "Good for you, girl."

Rachel created one of her award-winning smiles to highlight her face, just in case someone was watching her arrive. She liked her appearance, and one that was forced on her by her occupation. She loved remembering how many people had told her that she looked much younger than thirty-eight. She had always downplayed her extra weight around her hips, legs and butt by telling herself she was a jolly person, and one everyone loved. After glancing at her

Gucci outfit which she thought perfectly hid her big *cahootus*, as she referred to it, she reflected on the money she had spent on her teeth, skin care and haircuts, and how those decisions were the best investments she had ever made. While image meant everything in real estate sales, this shallow appraisal of herself reminded her of what the life in real estate had done to her. Status had become the central focus in her life. *Why does it have to be so hard to allow people to see the real me?* No, she had to maintain the image–the competition would jump all over any weakness.

As Rachel stepped out of her car, the heat from the sun high above baked her. She quickly rushed toward the front entrance, hoping to dash inside before the withering heat engulfed her. She didn't want her new designer clothes ruined by sweat, and while the wind slightly refreshed her, she didn't care to watch her professionally styled hair blown senseless either, making her look like some kind of punk queen.

While directing her steps along the cobblestones, where a scratch on the side of her new Prada shoes would be totally unthinkable, she studied an older Mercedes pulling into, perhaps, the last parking spot on the property.

When John Richardson sprang from his car, he was quickly followed by two of the other real estate agents from his firm. "Hello, Rachel. How's it going?" he asked, as his deep voice competed with the sounds of the sea gulls squawking above.

Rachel smiled at John, flashing all of the charm she could generate. "Busy, very busy, but as they say, it's better than the alternative." Rachel paused so John could walk with her before they entered the open house. "You're dressed nice today, and I love your tie."

John smiled in response to the cliché comment and compliment. "I can understand, and thanks." Rachel watched him staring at her eyes. She knew their green color, enhanced by contacts, provided another trick of the trade she enjoyed as she reflected on how many times others had told her they loved the way the color accentuated her hair. Additionally, she also enjoyed the way her hairdresser added the right tint of red to her dark-brown hair to produce what she considered to be a flair of excitement.

Rachel watched John turn and motion toward the two women with him. "You know Linda and Darlene, I'm sure."

Rachel flashed them a smile and studied the light cotton dresses they wore. They were so plain, but then again so cool in the summer heat. "Yes, I think we've met several times before. How are you?" She directed her question to both, acting as friendly as possible. Yes, she remembered seeing them before, but they didn't sell many properties in the price range she did often; in fact, she couldn't remember ever closing a property with either one of them.

Rachel waved at Linda who was walking beside her as she noticed the glowing personality of this new agent who obviously wanted to grab her attention by announcing cheerfully. "I'm doing great. In fact, I listed a house I wanted to talk to you about!"

This could be fascinating, Rachel thought. "Really–you go girl. Tell me. What did you list?"

"I listed Mr. Jackson's house on the corner of Ocean View." Linda's face beamed with excitement.

Rachel stopped to stare directly at Linda through her dark Cartier sunglasses. "Wow. That's great!" She knew Linda should indeed be happy since his listing would bring her all kinds of attention and perhaps many potential buyers. However, Rachel strained to maintain control since she had tried to obtain his listing for a long time, and had assumed it would belong to her soon. "So . . . how did you manage to talk Mr. Jackson into signing with you?"

Linda leaned closer to her so she could whisper. "It was a cold call. Can you believe it! I decided to go straight to his front door and knock." Linda's clean, fresh look radiated, as it should from a twenty-six year old with such a slim attractive body. Rachel even thought Linda looked a little skinny. Yes, she harbored a very jealous desire to own such a body.

With the shock registering slowly, Rachel remembered how she had worked on this nice, elderly old man for months. He had asked her to complete many different studies and comps to determine the price of the house he had owned for a long time. She really wanted to help him sell his house, which was much too large for him. With his children grown and his wife deceased from cancer several years ago, he needed something much smaller. "That's out of the ordinary."

"Yes. It goes to show that you never know." Linda laughed and looked upward at the royal palms in the front yard. "These are beautiful trees, aren't they?"

Rachel glanced at the royal palms and admitted they looked stunning, but her mind rehashed the listing she had lost to some skinny little girl in a cotton dress she knew possessed no ability in selling one in this price range, and especially the one listing she had hoped she had locked up. She forced herself to remain in control. "What price did you list his place for?" While Rachel attempted to hide her resentment, knowing her attitude created a bad trait in her personality, she also knew deep down that agents like Linda needed praise for their hard work.

"He wanted to start at one point eight. What do you think?"

"I see . . . that might be a little high. I told him the most he could hope for in this market is about one point five, and that he might need to settle for one point two. I wish you luck on selling his place. Please let me know what I can do to help you." Rachel glanced at the door that was left open by her friend hosting the open house. "I hope they have some good food today. I'm hungry." She knew it would only be a matter of time until Linda would lose the listing, and then she would receive another shot at obtaining it. There was no way Linda could sell this property for such an amount. Prices had come down, and were still going lower.

After walking through the front door, the grand entrance instantly captured Rachel's attention. While the handcrafted wood presented an incredible display of light and color, the marbled floor matched the tone set by a master homebuilder. Moreover, the large hanging light fixture accented the work to a degree that further enticed her to see what else this house had in store for her.

Ruth rushed over to greet her as she entered the house. "Rachel, it's so good to see you! I hoped you would be able to come and preview this one. I know you'll love this property, but then again, for as long as you've been selling here you might've seen this home before." She motioned to the interior of the house.

"No, this is the first time I've ever ventured into this one. So far . . . I'm impressed." Rachel analyzed Ruth's jewelry which looked expensive, but was clearly old and out of style. Rachel knew Ruth had the money since her husband, a doctor specializing in treating newborn babies with defects, had to be making a fortune. Why Ruth even put herself through the headaches of working as a realtor was beyond her.

Ruth handed Rachel a flyer. "These are very old friends of mine, and I do want to do a good job for them. If you notice anything at all needing to be corrected, or improved, I'm sure they'll be more than willing to look at suggestions. They're building a new home and they would hate to maintain both."

"Who does?" Rachel glanced at the flyer and the professional attention to detail the designer had put into the work. "These photos are fantastic. I love the deep colors and the angles he used to capture these rooms."

"Thanks! I hired someone that another agent had recommended to me. I'll give you his number later. It's at the office." As more guests arrived, Ruth turned to them, but shouted back over her shoulder. "Make yourself at home, and be sure to check out his office upstairs–you'll love it!"

Rachel's phone, attached to the side of her Gucci bag, started playing a Caribbean tune. "Hello, this is Rachel."

"Hi, we have a problem with the closing tomorrow." Cindi Arrondale, her personal assistant, sounded hoarse, and as if she had been yelling for a while, causing the tone in her voice to appear much more serious than normal.

Rachel moved away from anyone close enough to overhear her conversation before she asked, "What kind of problem?"

"The mortgage company is asking for another appraisal. They don't like the first one."

"Damn! They already approved the loan earlier. What happened?"

"Rachel, a senior reviewer kicked the appraisal out. I've been on the phone with them for over an hour."

"Have you talked to the mortgage rep?" She kept walking away from people, hoping to avoid anyone overhearing her conversation.

"Yes, he's working on the problem also, and he is as upset as we are. I thought you might want to make a call. The seller's not going to be happy."

"I've too many people around me to make a call now, but I'll be back in the office in a little while. I need to make an appearance here since we have our own open house next week, and I definitely want to make sure we obtain a good turnout for it.”

“Absolutely, but if you can, will you please bring me back something to eat so that I can skip lunch to keep working on this?”

“I’ll see what I can do. Thanks for staying on top of this for me.”

Rachel disconnected and headed for the stairs to check out the upstairs area. As two other agents made their way down, she recognized the first woman. “Hello, Carolyn, how’s it going?”

“I’m doing well. This is a great house. You need to see his office up here.” Since Carolyn had sold real estate in St. Petersburg for a long time, everyone respected her for her knowledge of the market.

“That’s what I’ve heard.” Rachel stepped far to one side to make room for them to pass by her. Yes, she knew she needed to lose some weight, but working all of the time left no openings at all to exercise. Her late night meals remained the only moments she could ever simply sit and relax.

The closing that was going bad dominated her thoughts as she worked her way up the stairs. Perhaps she needed to find another mortgage company. Her mortgage guy, Gary Baston, had worked some miracles in the past, but lately problems like this happened much too often.

As she wandered into the master bedroom, which was elaborately decorated and giving the impression that no one ever really lived there, she noticed a hard cold feeling emanating from the room. This was a sensation she knew well, as the emptiness reminded her of the condo she lived in. Still, she reflected on how her work as a realtor had earned her money to buy one of the best condos in St. Petersburg, as well as the many other investment properties that she owned.

After walking out of the master bedroom, Rachel moved toward the office she had heard about from the moment she had arrived at the open house. From having to spend so much time in her own small office, she looked forward to seeing this notorious one, where she was anticipating some remarkable designs and decorations. Perhaps she could pick up some ideas for redecorating her office.

Rachel bumped into another man coming out of the office as she entered. They quickly recognized each other as Michael Penske's smile flashed white teeth and sparkling eyes. "Hello, Michael. I didn't expect to find you here." She reflected on how Michael mainly worked commercial deals and rarely residential. If he did, they usually sold at very high prices. As she admired his dark-blue business suit, she remembered how he had always dressed nice. The designer tie with swirls of blue matched his suit perfectly, adding the ideal amount of color. The shade also complimented his deep-blue eyes. Michael looked to be in his sixties, but showed no signs of slowing down his active real estate practice.

"Hi there," Michael said as he moved backwards several steps to allow space for Rachel to enter.

I'm not that large she thought to herself as she watched him scramble before she responded with a hello.

"I heard about this office and wanted to check it out. Have you seen it yet?" Michael asked as he motioned to the inside.

"Not yet." She entered the office and stood still to take in the view. "Wow!" The room looked much larger than she was prepared for.

"That was my thought exactly." He paused. "This has to be at least twenty-five by forty. What do you think?"

"I'd think at least that much or more," she acknowledged as she sauntered around the office while glancing at the shiny bamboo floor. After arriving at one wall she froze, but finally asked, "What kind of wood do you think this is?"

Michael strolled over next to her and touched one of the intricately carved ornaments. "I'm not sure, but I think this is walnut."

"Wow. The cost had to be expensive, or should I say *very expensive* to make most of the office out of this kind of wood."

"Yes. I'd love to know how much he spent on this. He must have informed the builder that money was no object, and . . . it looks like the builder took him at his word." He moved over to the desk, examining the texture again, as if for the first time.

"I don't think I've ever seen one like this before–it's beautiful." She allowed her fingers to stroke the top of the desk. The hand rubbed wood with intricate designs in the textures dominated her attention. "I could enjoy sitting here and looking at this all day long."

"I know what you mean. I'm sure the desk was also specifically made for him," he added as he walked to the sitting area and studied one piece of wood after another.

Her phone rang again. "Hello, this is Rachel."

"Hi, this is Ann at the title company. I assumed you heard about the closing."

"Yes, Cindi called me. What have you heard?"

"Since this is a senior reviewer, we might not be able to do anything now but order another appraisal."

"Damn. This isn't right . . . not this late in the game." She walked to the far side of the office, trying hard to conceal her anger.

"I agree. Do you want to call the seller, or do you want me to call for you?"

Rachel considered allowing Ann to make the call since she knew the owner would be boiling mad. "I'm tempted, but I can't ask you to do my job. I'll call him when I return to the office. I'm at an open house right now, but I'll be back in my office soon."

"Okay, let me know what you want me to do."

Rachel glanced around and noticed Michael watching her. "Problems?"

"Yes. The mortgage company is asking for another appraisal right at the closing. Can you believe this?"

He uttered a small but controlled laugh, as if he appeared to understand. "I think this is why I'm so glad to be working in commercial rather than residential."

"But you work residential some, don't you?" She waited on his reaction.

"Yes . . . but only for my best commercial clients and since they usually pay cash, they don't worry too much about appraisals."

"That must be nice. I've a few cash deals, but most of the time they even want appraisals." She had wished she worked commercial for a long time, but making the change would result in a lot of risk she didn't want to take. She had made her name in upper scale condos, and it was the area she knew best.

He acted reassuring as he stopped admiring the room for a minute. "I'm sure you can work the details out. You have a great reputation."

"Thanks. I work hard at giving good service." She pointed toward the door. "I think I need to check out the food and head back to the office. It was good to see you again." She smiled as broadly as she could. Keep up the appearance, she thought. Make everyone think you're in control.

As he glanced around the room, he added, "I think I'll stay in here for a while. I need to update my office and this really gives me the inspiration I need." He pursed his lips like he was hooked on the design work.

"Okay. I'll leave you with it." She smiled again as she walked toward the door.

She stopped short, however, as he intercepted her. "I meant to say something to you earlier, but I never received a chance. I'm so sorry to hear about Jonathan Harrell's death, and I know how it must have affected you. Are you okay?"

Rachel allowed herself to breathe deeply as she considered her response. "It has been tough on everyone." She didn't know if she should say anything about the investigation being expanded or not. "I still have many of his units for sale."

"That's tough. I hate to watch this market deteriorate so bad that people start taking their lives."

Rachel snapped back as she lost control. "I don't believe his death was a suicide. I talked to the police again this morning. They also don't think the death was either. They believe he might have been murdered." Okay, she was supposed to keep this quiet–ooops.

Shock registered on Michael's face. "I didn't know. Do they have any suspects?"

"They're reviewing all of their information and conducting new interviews, hoping to find something. That's all I know."

"He had several partners . . . friends of mine. I hate to hear that he may have been murdered." He leaned forward so he could whisper, another indication he wanted to keep this private. "I also made an investment in his company . . . as a silent partner."

Rachel's eyes widened. *What kind of investment did he make in the development?* "I . . . I didn't know." She knew this information needed to be forwarded to Lindstrom.

"The remaining active partner in his development, Donnie Moore, is attempting to sell off the rest of the properties, many of which you have listed, and close the limited partnership. Hopefully, I'll receive my money back then." He glanced around to see if anyone else had moved into hearing distance.

"Yes, I'm dealing with Donnie now to sell the rest of the units that I have listed. I'll be so glad when I do." She allowed a strained face to replace her smile.

He straightened his back and moved away from her. "If you hear anything else, please let me know. I hope you keep this personal information confidential." He winked at her as he turned sideways.

"Yes, rumors are hard to deal with." With the conversation over, Rachel walked out of the office and headed downstairs, still wondering if she needed to tell the detective this new information.

After nearing the bottom of the stairs, she saw a young man dressed in tan-colored dress pants and a bright-blue, long-sleeved dress shirt rushing toward the kitchen. He looked neat and professional, even with the exception of not having a jacket on. She wasn't sure she had seen him before. Perhaps, she thought, another new agent attempting to break into the world of real estate.

The lingering fragrance of his cologne captured her attention. *Hmmm, very different–nice.* She guessed he might be twenty-two or so. At her age, she could only wish to be that young again.

As she walked into the kitchen she saw the large gathering of agents she had expected. She knew how the system worked: if you mentioned food, most agents come running. In fact, the extra pounds on most of them came from such gatherings. To attract the crowds, the mortgage companies and other professionals seeking referrals from the realtors hosted these open houses. Many times the cost could be expensive. However, without the agents sending them business they knew they would have a hard time making money in this market. To attract agents they always put on the spreads designed to be too hard to resist. Yes, they received competition from many other open houses, and they always had to stay one step ahead of them.

Again, Rachel noticed the man in front of her wearing the crisp, clean, blue shirt. With his back to her and his attention focused on Ruth, she studied his body. His broad shoulders filled the shirt, while his slim waist accentuated his fantastic shape. However, it was his butt, his damn nice butt, which completely mesmerized her as he shifted slightly from side to side while adjusting his stance. Yes, his *cahootus* looked much better than hers.

When Rachel caught herself staring, she quickly darted her focus to the side. *Oh God, I hope no one noticed me drooling like a silly little school girl in a trance. Who is he?* Still, he managed to dominate her attention again as she moved over to some of the other agents.

Ruth finally noticed her from across the room and interrupted this man long enough to motion for her to join them. "Rachel, this is Carlos and he's the one providing the food today." So that's the answer, he's a new mortgage contact with Bay Mortgage. Suddenly she remembered the e-mail she had received earlier in the morning from him. The photo depicted him well–just like she had hoped.

Rachel stretched out her hand. "Hi, it's good to meet you." She watched his eyes intensely penetrating her own, apparently allowing an internal pleasure she had noticed some men enjoying before. *Thank God for contacts.*

"I don't think we've ever met, but I know your name well. You have a great reputation." His voice vibrated in a slow deep drawl. She analyzed his eyes–a dark brown that reminded her of an adorable dog from a movie that she remembered loving. They looked so friendly, so trustworthy.

"Thanks, the reputation comes from lots of hard work." She concentrated on his eyes again, which were radiating more like dark coals now. She couldn't remember anyone with pupils so dark before. Of course he did have jet black hair and a medium olive skin tone perfecting his looks. She glanced at him again, trying to ascertain where he was from, but managed to shift her focus before she stared too long.

"I'm sure it does. Anything in life worth having usually does." He pointed to the food on the counter. "I hope you like this. I decided to work on a Tex-Mex theme today."

Rachel glanced at the food and the colorful array of dishes. "Wow, did you make this, or did you have the food catered?" She noticed the smell for the first time, a tantalizing mixture of spices, forcing her to realize just how hungry she was. She hated to eat too much at luncheons like this, but she knew that dieting was a losing battle. Okay, she knew she needed to get a handle on her weight.

He walked over to the food and waved his hands above it. "I was born in Houston, and this is the kind of food I grew up on. I tried to find someone who could cook like this here, but I finally gave up." He reached for a plate and handed it to her. "I hope you like it."

"It smells great." She finally decided to eat a good meal and worry about the extra calories later.

Several of the women waved at her, indicating they loved the food. Now finding a man, a special man, who can cook one day, would be fantastic, she thought. That is, if she ever had time to worry about a man in her life. She knew the endless hours of being a realtor allowed no such luxury, especially now.

Still, this young stud, Carlos, made her think of situations in her past, lost opportunities, *the what if* questions which haunted her at times. Rachel looked over at Carlos again and noticed his continued attention focusing on her. As she leaned over to take some of the food, her breasts caught his attention. While they usually managed to attract men around her, the attention today made her feel different. It was usually older men who drooled over her, not a young stud like this. While his attention did make her feel good, she rose to keep him from staring too much. She had received enough of a reputation of trying to seduce men, and one that she often tried to live down. Oh yes, she could see the other women watching her every move.

Rachel noticed Carlos's cards on the end of the table. "Who knows . . . perhaps we can do some business one day." She casually placed one of them in her coat pocket.

He flashed a wide thank you smile, filled with fantastic white teeth. "I would love to have a chance to show you what we can do for you." His interest wasn't unexpected. While many mortgage people hounded her for referrals, this time she might need to see what this tall, dark, but definitely young stud had to offer.

Chapter 2

Rachel gathered several folders on her desk, stacking them neatly to one side as she appreciated the work of Cindi who was always trying to keep her small, but professional looking office neat. While the paperwork never ended, over the years Rachel had learned how to hide the beast, her stacks of files, long enough to meet with a client or business associate. Carlos's great looks and super personality entered her mind as she glanced out a side window. She looked forward to this meeting as she sipped on some great smelling coffee. While she was still not sure if she was going to give him any referrals or not, she knew a slight detour from her relentless work schedule would do her good.

She heard a knock on the door as Cindi peeked around the edge. "Your appointment's here." Cindi glanced behind her before she stepped inside. "Hey, you didn't tell me this guy was like hot!"

Rachel laughed and rolled her eyes in a playful way. "I should've known you would've noticed." Since Cindi was twenty-two, she imagined Carlos probably noticed her also.

"Well . . . yeah!" Cindi glanced over her shoulder again. "Are you ready for him to come in?"

"Yes, but I want you to do some research for me while he's in here." Rachel handed Cindi a pad with an address on it. "I might have a chance to list this one and want to be ready. While I'm hearing what Carlos has to say, could you prepare me a competitive marketing analysis on this property? I need to call the owner later today."

"I'll work on it in a minute, but I still need to finish the marketing letters you gave me earlier." Cindi closed the door behind her as she stepped back outside.

Rachel pulled her compact out of her purse to check her makeup. All looked good except the eyes. Perhaps she should've worked on them more this morning and added some more green shadow. She quickly reapplied her lipstick as she heard another knock on the door. After she stood and straightened her jacket, she walked over to the door. The ever so slight flutter in her heart reminded her of how much she had daydreamed about him the last two days.

Rachel opened the door and saw Carlos flash her a large smile. "How are you?" He wore a gray pair of dress pants and a white shirt. The tie left much to be desired, but he made up for the discrepancy with his fantastic smile and gorgeous black hair. His light beige jacket had seen better days and one of those favorite types some men tend to never get rid of. She tried not to stare, but his belt buckle, the super large sized ones associated with a cowboy or westerner captured her attention when his jacket parted to one side. She shifted her eyes back to his eyes before she responded. "It's good to see you. Please come on in."

After he stepped inside and walked over to one of the large chairs in front of her desk, he waited on her to be seated first. Good. He possessed more manners than most of her normal clients which came to see her. As he glanced around the room he pointed to the walls which were covered with awards. "Wow, you've been busy."

"Yes, I work hard, and I've sold a lot of properties." She glanced at the wall also. The awards covering every spare inch helped her to portray herself as a top producer–the type most clients searched for.

"Well . . . I'm impressed." He continued to smile as he surveyed the room, obviously looking for something.

As he studied the room, she studied him. Just like she remembered, he must spend a lot of time in the gym. While all of his body radiated with muscles, the one part of his magnificent physique that she couldn't resist was his stomach, or . . . the almost lack of one. *How did he manage to stay so trim*? Yes, he looked young, but she was young once also.

She knew she needed to start speaking before she stared too much. "How long have you been in the mortgage business?"

He refocused his attention on her. "I've been doing this for about a year now." She watched him lean forward, increasing his attentive stare. "I went to school at the University of South Florida, and I entered the mortgage business right after graduation."

Like many realtors, she had been burned by mortgage people who didn't know what in the hell they were doing, and she had learned to be cautious. "How has it been going?"

"It was a struggle at first, but now I'm receiving many referrals and starting to make some money. That is . . . if the market doesn't totally fall apart on us." He spoke slowly, intently, but never shifted his focus off of her.

When it became too intense for her, she glanced away for a moment to regain her thoughts. "Hmm yes, the melt-down in the real estate market is causing some problems." She glanced back at him and saw the same passionate stare. His dark eyes, exactly as she remembered, were so different from any she had ever seen before. She made a mental note to herself to ask him about his heritage later. He must be a mixture of cultures.

"I know you have someone to send your loans to, and perhaps you even send your referrals to a friend who has worked hard for you in the past." He paused to study her face. "But . . . I would love a chance to earn your business, and I'm sure you've heard that before."

"Yes, you do have a lot of competition." While this was the truth, she knew to always keep her eyes open for new loan products evolving. This guy's good looks and natural charm could definitely satisfy some of her more demanding clients.

"The market is changing and giving us all a run for the money, so to speak. I know you handle properties in the upper echelons." He shifted his position in his seat to allow him to lean closer toward her. "I've many investors I use for that market also, but . . . let me ask you one question. Do you have any loans causing you problems?" He paused and smiled. "All I'm asking for is a chance to show what I can do. I promise you, I'll do whatever it takes to make the loans work."

She surveyed his bulky shoulders. "I'm sure you will."

"Like most mortgage companies, I can also offer pre-approvals." She noticed his stare checking out her breasts for the first time. While a tingle of interest crossed her mind, he was too young. Still, the attention made her feel good.

She closed her eyes for a moment, trying to think of words she could offer him in encouragement. "The main concern we're having right now, as you probably know, is the falling prices and obtaining property appraisals for what the contract price states."

A quick nod indicated that he knew all about this problem.

"Now if you can find a way out of this situation, you'll receive all of the business you can handle." She allowed her smile to fade into a serious frown for the first time.

"I understand fully, and in fact bad appraisals are one problem I've concentrated on much lately. Many of the investors are wary of appraisals, and I guess you can't blame them."

She hated to admit this fact and probably wouldn't publicly, but she decided to open up and tell him about the one she recently lost. "I can appreciate their problems, but they don't need to wait until the last minute to order new appraisals. I think if they have an appraisal, they should honor it."

The slight arch in his brow revealed some deep concentration, as he appeared to be thinking of an adequate response. The thick hairs in his brows made her envy his naturally good looks. She thought about how she worked on her brows for a long time and still they never looked as good as his. He probably never had to do anything with his at all–not fair.

"Is it okay if I ask you one question? Kind of . . . off the record?"

His mysterious mannerisms intrigued her as she smiled softly. "Of course that all depends. What question do you want to ask me?"

He continued to drift closer to her from across the top of the desk. "I think I picked up on the fact that you're having some appraisals being questioned."

She half grunted as the air erupted from her lungs. "Let me say I do know one mortgage company I'm thinking of not using anymore–ever. They recently cost me over thirty thousand dollars. I have a buyer wanting to buy and a seller wanting to sell. They're happy with the price, but the new appraisal is much lower than the property appraised for a few months ago. Because of a new appraisal they're all mad at each other and guess who everyone blames–me."

"Like I said, I've completed a lot of research lately, and I've discovered some intriguing facts that I think you might be interested in."

Okay, he had obtained her full attention now. "Really?"

He glanced at the door, as if he wanted to make sure no one could hear him. "Is it okay if I ask you who did the appraisal?"

She didn't order the appraisals, since that was the call of the mortgage company. Like many agents, however, she knew which appraisers were considered good and which ones everyone had a problem with. She also knew not to bad mouth any of them. "I don't think I need to name them, but they are well known."

He demonstrated an understanding of how it's not a good practice to discuss some appraisers, as such could come back to haunt everyone. "On most of my work, I order the appraisal."

She interrupted. "If you know the name of a great appraiser you can pass on, it would be fantastic. However, as you know, the problem is often the supervisors at the mortgage companies wanting a second opinion."

He waited for her to finish, as his rugged jaw revealed an inner strength she appreciated. "Exactly. This is what I'm learning. Now, think about this."

Well perhaps he did offer some information she needed to know. "Okay."

"Some appraisers are doing their best to help out realtors and providing as high an appraisal as they can justify. Everyone knows that realtors appreciate this help."

"Well–yes."

"However, some of them also obtain a reputation for inflating values, and the senior reviewers are on to them and almost always order new appraisals. To make problems worst, the next appraiser knows this also and wants to cover his butt. So . . . he always appraises lower."

"I guess that makes sense, but what do you suggest that we do about this problem?"

He removed some papers and a flyer from a file he

carried with him. "I constantly work with the underwriters to make sure there're no surprises. Most of my clients appreciate these extra services. In this particular case, it helps to know which appraisers they like and which ones they don't trust."

Rachel glanced at the flyers he handed her. The impressive quality indicated his home office spent top dollar producing the flyer. "Who picks the appraisers at your company?"

"I do." A large smile revealed his super white teeth. She suspected he professionally whitened them. If not, he was a very unusual guy. "And . . . I'm happy to say that only one of my deals has ever required a new reappraisal."

"Wow." Either he worked much better than she assumed, or he was absolutely full of shit. "Who do you use as an appraiser?"

"I've several available, but prefer Johnston Appraisal Service. Have you ever used them?"

Her face brightened at the name. "I have in the past, but not lately. I can't remember anything negative about them." She made a note to have her own mortgage guy check them out for her.

Carlos stood and moved around the desk to point to some of the features highlighted on the brochure. "My company has been around for about twenty years." He rose slightly as he pointed to photos of the manager of the local office.

"I think I've seen him around." She suddenly smelled his cologne floating across to her. Since she couldn't make out which one he wore, the smell intrigued her as she remembered the game she and many of her friends played in guessing the name of the cologne men they knew wore.

Carlos moved closer to her and turned the brochure over to the other side. "For our upper end clients, we offer many special accommodations which have helped us make a name for ourselves." She glanced over the list, but the smell now became much more powerful. As she continued to breathe in, analyzing each breath, she realized his smell contained a natural scent mixed with only a hint of cologne. It had to be; the scent smelled different and invoked such an intoxicating feeling. While most people would make her feel uncomfortable with them being so close, she surprised herself and leaned over closer to him to review the brochure.

Carlos stood straight and reached in his pocket to retrieve several business cards. "I would appreciate your help very much if you can recommend me to some of your clients. Also . . . if you have any cases not closing for any reason, I'd love to talk to them and see what I can do."

Rachel maintained eye contact with him as she accepted the cards. "I'll see what I can do for you." She still wasn't convinced he had obtained the maturity or experience to handle her clients who were generally wealthy and intelligent, not to mention demanding. A small test might be best.

"I appreciate your time very much." As Carlos turned to leave, she managed to sneak another look at his body. She quickly wondered how good he would look in more tailored clothes. He definitely had the body demanding the best.

"You're welcome, Carlos. Thanks for coming by." Rachel remembered when she had entered the real estate profession at about his age and the work she had to put into proving her ability to be a top producer. She knew what he must be going through, and knew how good the feeling would be to see him excel as a professional mortgage originator.

"Thanks for seeing me. I hope to see you again soon." After Carlos walked toward the door and opened it, she watched a new smile grow as he headed for the receptionist desk, and where Cindi was patiently waiting for him.

Chapter 3

Rachel turned off her office computer and rubbed her eyes. From having so much research to complete tonight, she had decided to remove her rings to give her fingers some rest. She smiled while she considered the spoils, so to speak, that came from a successful practice as she replaced them on her fingers. She remembered how people had asked her many times before as to why she wore such expensive jewelry, to which she had always responded, "Because I can."

It was now decision time. She could head home and enjoy some wine setting out on her balcony overlooking Tampa Bay–by herself, or she could head out to one of her favorite restaurants–by herself. It resulted in the same old story all of the time. She never knew exactly when she would be finished working the phone and this made it nearly impossible for her to plan her evenings.

She reached for her phone and quick dialed Aaron Bank, a guy who owned a boat that was much like her fifty-five foot Bay Liner. She wanted to make some changes onboard and knew he would be a great sounding board. The call went to voice mail. "Hello, Aaron, I was thinking about you and hoping to ask you some questions about some remodeling I wanted to do. Please give me a call." While Rachel knew Aaron was financially well off and highly educated, his silver hair reminded her of how much older he was than she was. While she assumed he was close to fifty, his features looked nice, even with the exception of him being slightly overweight. He did dress extremely well–something she suddenly wished Carlos would cultivate an interest in learning.

While the rings slipping onto her fingers added a hidden pleasure for her, she didn't own the one ring most girls loved. She stopped to study her wedding ring finger and tried to imagine what kind of ring she would like to wear one day. *Who am I kidding? At thirty-eight I might not ever get married.* She knew she worked all of the time and that her wealth had become more like a string of garlic around her neck than a magnet. Her success scared most men off, intimidating them.

She quickly called Jody Bright, another agent that worked much like she did, who answered immediately. "Hello, Jody, what are you up to?"

"Hi, I'm trying to finish sending out some thank you cards."

"Jody, good for you. Have you eaten yet?"

"Not yet. Are you going out to eat?"

"I think so. Can you join me?"

"Sure, where do you want to meet, Rachel?"

"How about meeting me at the restaurant on top of the Pier?" Rachel breathed easier, knowing that she would have someone to join her. Jody was only two years older than her. Rachel knew Jody acted crazy about guys on the outside, but she was also scared like her in allowing any of them to get too close.

"That sounds good to me. I'll be there in about thirty minutes."

When she reached over to the side of her desk to pile the rest of her papers in some kind of stack, she saw the brochure that Carlos had left. A smile crossed her lips. She wondered what he did on nights like this. A young guy like Carlos probably had girls crawling all over him–not that she blamed them at all.

She retrieved some of his cards he had left earlier and moved them to the side of her desk. Perhaps she could send him some business. While money came first, and these recommendations wouldn't be to her better clients, she did have some bones she might be able to throw his way. She studied his masculine and rugged photo on the card as she also slipped one of them into her wallet. Who knows, she might need the card one day.

***

Rachel heard the Caribbean music playing as she entered the restaurant. Many strategically placed lamps containing tungsten lights produced a warm glow enhancing the romantic settling of the penthouse type restaurant. A young but beautiful girl stood behind the hostess station, patiently waiting on Rachel to approach her. "Will you be dining by yourself tonight, or are you waiting on someone else?"

The words hurt as she remembered hearing them so many times before. It wasn't because she didn't have friends–she made lots of friends. Well, lots of people she knew. As far as close friends, perhaps not, and she knew it. She smiled at the young girl. "I've a friend who may already be here. Let me look around."

The hostess stepped to one side and revealed a trim body, something that Rachel knew she had concentrated on too much lately. However, she told herself, a great body wasn't the most important thing to her. She, after all, maintained a demanding real estate business. "Thanks." Rachel walked toward the lounge area, hoping to find her friend Jody.

The back part of the lounge contained several small tables with bar stools around them which allowed customers an easy way to stand or sit, while looking through the floor to ceiling windows. She knew that the view of the bay and the docks always fascinated their customers, both regulars and first timers.

As Rachel expected, Jody had already established residency at one of the tables where she sipped on a glass of red wine. Jody shared the excitement of jewelry and designer clothes Rachel loved. A new Gucci handbag hung from her shoulder. Wow! Rachel had remembered looking at this one, and she had hoped to add it to her collection.

Rachel waved toward Jody as she strolled over to her table. Since Jody had her phone against her ear, talking fast like she usually did, she simply motioned for Rachel to have a seat.

Rachel slid into a seat as a waiter walked over. "I think . . . I'll have some red wine also. Whatever she's drinking will be fine with me."

"Very good, I'll be right back." He turned and left them alone after glancing at Jody's legs. As usual, her short dress attracted attention since she was much slimmer than Rachel.

As Jody concentrated on her phone call, Rachel had time to glance around the room. After seeing Dr. Jim Robertson and his wife sitting a few tables over, she decided to walk over and say hello. They had purchased one of her properties a few years ago, and she had heard they might want to sell it again sometime soon. Unexpectedly, they offered a deep stare as if they didn't recognize her. She decided to ignore the slight rebuff and push forward. "Dr. Robertson, how are you? I was thinking about calling you."

While forced to respond, he still offered no smile. "I'm fine. Thank you for asking. You remember my wife . . . Ellen."

"Yes, I do. How are you doing?" She reached out her hand to shake Ellen's hand. The cold returned grip confirmed her intuition. Something was wrong.

Rachel decided to shift her attention back to Dr. Robertson and stood straight, making sure she revealed as little cleavage as possible. She sensed a problem, but couldn't tell exactly what. "How do you like the house you purchased from me? I assume you still love it."

His face turned stern. "Yes, it's still a great house to live in, and especially to entertain with. However, we're thinking about moving to something on the beach now and wondering how bad this downturn in the market will hurt us. Unfortunately, this may become one of the worst investments I ever remember making."

Not again, she thought. People loved her when the prices jumped through the roof, but now, when the market adjusts, it's as if the market collapse was her fault. "While the housing market is correcting, the important thing to remember is that you'll also be able to buy the next house at a bargain price right now."

"That may be true, but if I receive a loss on this one, I'll have no money to invest in the next one. I think we're going to be stuck. It would have been much better for us if we hadn't purchased such a large home." He shook his head. "If we only knew what was going to happen."

"I agree. Let me take a look at some numbers for you and I'll see what I can do."

He glanced over at his wife who spoke impatiently, "I don't think this would be a good time."

Apparently the wife maintained a much deeper resentment than he did. "I can e-mail the information to you, and especially since I'm sure it would be something you'll be interested in. Let me know of anything I can do for you."

Ellen maintained her frown.

Okay, time to change the subject. She pointed out of the window. "It's a great view from here, isn't it?"

"Yes, we like the view from here." Ellen lifted her head high, but turned to face Rachel. "I've heard the investigation into the death of Jonathan Harrell is still being pursued. It's going to be interesting to see just how all of this plays out."

She waited for Rachel to respond.

Rachel knew much better than to take the bait since Ellen could possibly spread her answers all over St. Pete by tomorrow morning. "That's what I've heard also. If you hear anything at all, I'd appreciate it if you would call me. Jonathan Harrell was a nice guy and a very good friend."

Ellen maintained her astute posture as she turned to the scenery of the town reflecting on the water. "Yes, we normally like watching the sunset from here."

"Good, I'm going to let you two enjoy the view since I've a friend waiting on me to join her."

"Good bye." The wife lifted her head higher and acted as if she was dismissing a servant.

Rachel wanted to say something else, but held her tongue. There would be another day. She walked back over to join Jody as her wine arrived. With Jody still on the phone, she looked over the menu. She knew she shouldn't be eating a large meal at this time of the night, but what the hell–she knew controlling her weight was a losing battle. She glanced at her body, analyzing all of the extra pounds accumulated around her hips, her upper legs, and of course, her butt. The expensive designer outfits she had purchased failed to hide the fact that she needed to whip her body into shape. Someday, yes someday she would, but tonight she needed something unique to eat–something that would settle her down.

Jody finally ended her call. "How are you?"

"Tired. There has to be a better way to make a living." Rachel lifted her glass and extended it toward Jody.

"When you find it, let me know. I've just been cussed out by one of my clients for the last hour." Jody offered a sour expression as a result of the call.

"Really!" Rachel offered her sympathy in a friendly nod. "I've been there before."

"Yes, he can't understand why we're showing his house to people who can't get approved for a loan. These damn pre-approvals the mortgage companies are giving out now aren't worth a shit."

Rachel laughed in full agreement with her friend. "Tell me about it."

"I'm going to invite some friends over Friday night for drinks. Do you think you can make the party? It's only going to be us girls."

"Yeah, I think I can make some time." Rachel reflected on how she never dated anymore and how these other girls were all in the same situation. While they all looked great in many respects, they all seemed to be doomed to their little old professional ladies club. "Perhaps we can go out somewhere later."

"We can talk about going out for sure." Jody laughed as she finished her glass of wine. "I'm game for anything these days."

Chapter 4

Rachel rushed through the Friday afternoon traffic, listening to her favorite CD and hoping to make the trip to Jody's place in time. While loving the feel of her new BMW, especially the new car smell, she knew that in times like these she must project a certain style, and she couldn't let the slowdown in the economy distract her clients and allow them to foster second thoughts. She needed to reassure everyone that the market was going to be fine; in fact, she needed to convince them that now, right now, was the best time to buy.

Jody lived in one of the Clearwater condos that Rachel handled. In fact, Rachel had handled the listings on the entire building of eighty units which presented a great view of the ocean. She owned one of the units below Jody and until recently considered her purchase a fantastic investment.

After parking her car, Rachel saw Gloria Sanchez, another one of the girls going to the party, walking in front of her. She hurried to catch her. "Hey, wait up!"

Gloria turned to yell back, "Come on, and hurry. This sun is still too hot for me."

When Rachel pushed the announcement button, Jody answered the call in seconds by yelling down to them. "Come on up, the rest of the girls are already here."

In seconds, the two reached the eighth floor where Jody was holding the door open, waiting on them. "Come on in—we have something to show you." She flashed a mischievous look as her eyes and face totally lit up.

They all immediately moved to the balcony where two other girls, Mary Jane and Margaret, stood as they laughed and drank martinis behind a telescope while pointing to the beach below them. "This you have to see." Mary Jane eagerly waving them over to have a look with one hand and pointed to the beach below with the other.

Rachel walked over to the edge of the balcony and glanced down toward the beach where Mary Jane was focusing her stare. She saw a group of guys playing volleyball on the beach. Big deal. People played on the beach all of the time.

Rachel watched Mary Jane training the telescope on the group of guys and heard her yell out loud again, "You should see the buns on this guy, and oh what muscles, ohmigod!"

Rachel rolled her eyes and walked over to Jody. "Perhaps I need to join her in whatever she's drinking." She gave a quick wink that was followed by a small laugh.

"Uh huh. You'll be over here soon, you'll see." She reached out into the air in front of her and acted like she was pinching one of the guy's butt.

Rachel turned to Jody. "I think you need to make my drink a double."

Jody laughed. "If the drinks will double the number of guys down on the beach, then hey, go for it."

Margaret, a woman in her mid-forties and the oldest one in the group, walked over to the small bar and retrieved the shaker. "I think we're going to need to make some more."

"Help yourself to whatever you want to make," Jody said as she walked over toward the telescope. "This is the first time I ever noticed this group playing here. I hope this becomes a regular gathering. I can get used to this."

Margaret started pouring vodka into the shaker as she brushed her long dark brown hair behind her back. "I promise . . . if my last husband owned anything like that kind of body, I'd found some way to make the damn marriage work."

Gloria added some ice to the shaker and smiled. "I thought you said he dumped you."

"Yeah, he did, but if he looked like him, I would have tried harder to make him happy. You must admit, there's a huge difference." Margaret stretched out her hands to suggest the size of her ex-husband's beer belly.

Rachel walked back out on the patio as Jody motioned for her to take a look. "Okay, let's see what all the excitement is about." She placed her eye against the telescope, allowing time to adjust her vision on several guys playing volleyball. Their movements happened too fast for her to stay focused on them. Yes, with their shirts off she saw a lot of muscles.

"What do you think?" Jody asked impatiently.

"I see several guys playing." She tried to focus in on one guy to obtain better details.

"Yes, there are several nice guys there, but we all have one guy we really like. Keep looking and you'll see what we mean."

Rachel scanned the area again. Their dark tans made them look like locals as the game continued in a fast and furious pace, indicating they had played many times before. Then, she saw the one they must have been talking about. One tall guy with jet-black hair and a well-toned body moved to the server position. Even while wearing baggy swimming trunks she managed to study his muscular legs and oh so firm butt. She concentrated on him until he pitched the ball in the air preparing to serve. As his rapid movements quickly evaded her focus, she struggled to find him.

"Do you see him yet?" Jody stood behind her, waiting for

a response.

"I think so." When Rachel saw him returning to serve again she recognized a face she had thought about a lot lately. "Ohmigod!" Oops, she didn't mean to say that out loud, but knew it was too late now.

"What is it?" Jody asked.

Rachel looked away from the telescope. "I think I know this guy." She turned to study all of the girls standing behind her open their mouths wide.

Gloria spoke first. "Tell girl, and I do mean tell all."

Rachel glanced first at Gloria and then at Jody. "This guy came by to see me a few days ago."

Gloria eyes stretched wide open as she leaned forward. "And . . . ."

Rachel glanced at each girl descending in on her like a pack of rats chasing a single piece of cheese. "Okay, okay, his name is Carlos and he's in the mortgage business. He came by to see if I could refer some of my clients to him."

Jody leaned over to the telescope again and focused in on him. "Let me say . . . if you don't send him some . . . well, you know, if you don't want him, let me know. I'm sure I can send him some . . . business."

Rachel laughed. "He acted professionally when he came to see me." She glanced over the edge of the condo at the guys on the beach. "I'll admit that he looks very nice up close."

Jody continued to study him through the telescope. "How old is he?"

Rachel studied the guys playing. She wasn't sure, but knew he looked young. She turned to raise her glass toward the other girls. "I'm not sure, but I'm willing to drink to young men and lustful nights." She followed up the proposed toast with a loud hearty laugh.

Everyone lifted their glasses together and joined in the

laughter. Several eyed the telescope, waiting on their turn. After pointing toward many of the empty or close to being empty glasses, Jody motioned toward the shaker. "I think we might need a full time bartender here tonight."

Gloria glanced over at the guys. "Now, if you can find us a *boy toy* like one of these, I'll even help cover the cost."

"I'm sure you would." Rachel loved the laughing and teasing of these friends, but stopped for a moment to watch the guys playing hard, and who had no idea they had become the topic of discussion among her friends. These guys were enjoying life and having a great time. She suddenly thought about how sad it was that the only thing the girls around her could do was simply enjoy the entertainment the guys put on for them rather than being a part of the fun.

Gloria nudged next to her. "Can't take your eyes off of him, huh?"

Rachel laughed. "I was thinking of how fascinating it would be to discover how he really lives his life, you know, from day to day."

"Uh huh. I think I see some wheels turning here."

Rachel decided to turn from the balcony before she really started some rumors; the one thing she definitely didn't need to start. Gossip wouldn't be good for business since she worked for many conservative clients. However, she knew the best way out of this situation required her to play along as if the idea was a joke. "Well, a girl can dream, can't she?"

Gloria saw through her laughter and pushed on. "I know you too well, you're not a dreamer. You didn't get where you are by being such. You're a doer."

Rachel kept thinking and laughing. She had really wanted to give this guy some business, but if this continued it would be impossible to do so. There was too much danger in feeding the rumor mill. "We both know a guy like him probably has all of the girls he could ever want, and at anytime he wanted them. And . . . if I did catch him, a stud like him would kill me."

Gloria raised her glass toward the center of the circle of girls as the effects of the martinis started playing its part. "And . . . what a way to go!"

The other girls quickly joined in, clicking their glasses together.

Margaret suddenly lifted her glass high for several seconds. "Okay girls, since Rachel saw him first, I think she should receive the right to go after him first–AGREED!"

"Do what? I think that would be a big mistake." She couldn't believe the way this was heading.

Margaret glanced at the beach. "I think all of us would like to own a *boy toy* at one time or the other. Let's face reality, younger men . . . they do possess a certain charm." She glanced at the beach again. "They certainly have the body. It's amazing, however, how looks don't last forever. My ex-husband was built like them when we first met. However, by the time we divorced he went from a six pack to a barrel, as he often referred to his stomach. He laughed–I didn't."

Gloria cocked her hip to one side. "I guess fair is fair, but if you don't nail him, I get the second shot." She slithered with a sexy move as she slowly moved her hands to her neck, where she tossed her head back while pretending to be living out a deep sexual fantasy.

Rachel lifted her hands. "I did meet him, and he appears to be a nice guy."

Jody placed a hand on Rachel's shoulder. "So, why are you not giving him some business?"

"He's still young. In this market, I can't take chances on a screw up. You know that."

"You know, this guy might surprise you." Jody glanced at the girls again. "Okay girls, this guy is off the market for now." She giggled. "Let's take a look at his friends."

"I didn't say I was going after him."

"You didn't say you weren't either." Several girls joined Jody in a quick wink.

Rachel glanced over at the volleyball game in progress and down at her body. She knew in her current shape she couldn't play at their level. Down deep, the embarrassment hurt as she hid her thoughts. "Okay, I'll see if I can send him some business."

"Good. I knew you couldn't resist the challenge. Let us know what we can do to help."

Rachel laughed. "Do you mean to help or to report to?"

"Honey, I want all the details on this one." Margaret nodded as the others joined in.

"You're all a bunch of nuts." While Rachel teased the group openly, she recognized the pressured on one hand, but then again, she felt relieved in knowing she had obtained a green light in proceeding without a lot of danger. After all, this game they played was all in fun. She hoped, however, not to hurt this innocent guy too badly in their games.

"Nuts. If there were a set of nuts here, this group of winches would . . . hmmm . . . I guess I better stop before I say too much." All of the girls laughed at Gloria losing control as she finished another drink.

Rachel knew while the kidding remained all in fun, she now had her work cut out for her. She needed to walk a thin line, so to speak, and be careful. She decided to shift the interest to another guy they had talked about for years. "I think you must be missing Ricky Yager."

The mention of the name stopped the conversation and especially the laughter for a minute. She knew Ricky hadn't been discussed for a while. While recognizing the result, she continued to tease them. "Okay, sorry, I was kidding."

Jody spoke first. "I was thinking of him earlier. I'll never forgive him for what he did, but he did give fantastic massages."

Rachel glanced around the room and continued, "I'll agree he was a good masseur, but I think I'll never obtain the truth out of any of you as to how good he performed." She followed up the comment with a wicked laugh before shoving her shoulder into Gloria who was standing next to her.

Rachel remembered the jokes and the teasing between the girls for the two years they had used Ricky's massage services. She had used him three or four times, and for the most part, he had remained strictly professional, but he had always left her with the feeling that if she had asked for complete service, he might have accommodated her by having intercourse with her. She reflected on the one time she had allowed him to massage her, giving her a fantastic orgasm. She had never seen him again after that, but she had thought of him from time to time.

She suddenly thought about the first time she had asked Ricky to come to her condo. She still remembered the apprehension in allowing a man into her condo to give her a massage. He had arrived with his own portable massage table and wraps to keep her covered as he worked on her body. His fingers which had worked the warm oils into her skin brought out sensations she had never felt before. No, she wasn't a virgin. But . . . from what she had experienced from prior guys, she might as well be. They had always left her wanting.

She remembered how his fingers had explored so close to forbidden zones, only to retreat. She wouldn't have stopped him several times, but she wasn't going to tell him to do more either. The situation became a standoff she fought with herself many times over. She daydreamed many times about the "what if" factor for so long until she finally yielded to his touch the last time she saw him. She remembered being so close to asking him to continue and have full intercourse with her. Even now she could only imagine what his dick would feel like inside her aching pussy.

She still didn't know if the others allowed more or did as she did. She also knew she would never know either. "Has anyone heard what ever happened to him since he went to jail?"

As the girls glanced at each other, an uneasy feeling circulated amongst them.

Jody spoke first. "I hope they keep him in jail forever for having sex with my little sister, Angela. She was only sixteen when this happened. I know that when he's released he'll not be allowed to come anywhere close to here." Rachel knew there remained much more to the story as Jody must have used Ricky many times herself. As far as how far she went with Ricky, Rachel knew she would never know.

After the other girls stopped laughing momentarily, they quickly turned their attention back to the beach and the guys as their laughter resumed. Rachel glanced around, thinking about how the martinis added to the strange giggles coming from some of the most professional women in St. Petersburg.

Jody turned to her again. "You know if this becomes a regular event, perhaps you need to kick your renters out of the unit you own below. We could even yell to them from there."

Rachel smiled. "I'm not sure how long I'll have good renters in the unit below. The ones now only have a short term lease and it will be expiring soon. If this market continues like it is, I may need to move into it and sell everything else."

Jody's face became serious. "You talked me into this one and told me the condos represented a great investment."

"Yes, I still think the condos here will be great over the long term. If I could sell the last fifteen units in here, it would help." Rachel knew to stay positive, even in times like this.

Jody's face reflected her concern for her friend Rachel. "I understand how Jonathan Harrell's suspected suicide or murder in this building isn't helping. I also know he was a good friend of yours."

"Yes, and having to tell everyone about what happened isn't good at all, especially since we worked together for a long time. I hope this is all over soon for both of us." Rachel knew it would be good to change the topic again, even if it meant back to the guys on the beach. "Okay, it's my time to take another look." She moved behind the telescope and focused on the guys.

Rachel heard the girls laughing as she saw Carlos turn and stare directly at her. *Ohmigod, is he psychic? Does he know I'm drooling over him?*

Luckily, a slap on her shoulder shattered her thoughts. She turned to see Gloria looking over her shoulder. "I can see the wheels turning in your head. He's going to be a very remarkable guy for you. If I were you, yes, I would go after him."

"We'll see, we'll see."

Gloria mocked back. "Uh huh."

Chapter 5

"We don't have much time left," Rachel said, as she surveyed the spread of food covering the island in the middle of the kitchen that Gary, her mortgage guy, had provided. "I hope we have a large turnout for our open house today. We need it."

While carrying several extra bags of ice, Cindi rushed toward the sink. "I think we're almost ready. Gary really did a good job in providing some great food. Those shrimp look great!" Her face flushed from carrying the heavy ice as she reached for a towel.

Rachel examined her outfit one more time. The suit tailored for her made her feel great, but the tight shoes designed by Gucci hurt a little. They were still new and needed to breathe a little. Perhaps she over did the jewelry, but she owned several new pieces from David Yurman that she wanted to wear today. She needed to convince everyone that the market remained strong and that she could still sell the record numbers which produced her well known reputation.

Gary soon entered the room carrying several more bags. "I think this is the last of the food." He glanced over at several boxes and laughed. "Thanks, I was planning on doing that."

Cindi moved closer to him. "Now you tell me." She smiled as they enjoyed watching him being teased.

Gary retrieved one of the fliers he had prepared to advertise the properties and handed it to Rachel. "Have you seen this yet?"

"Yes, they look good. Thank you very much." Rachel noted their quality, but they were still not nearly as nice as the one Ruth had used the previous week. She made herself another note to call Ruth for the number of the guy who had prepared the flyers for her. Apparently Ruth had forgotten to call her with the name, but Rachel knew Ruth generally stayed just as busy as she did.

Rachel thought about how she had used Gary as her *go to guy* in mortgages for a long time. In this market, however, she knew he was stuck in the same boat as everyone else. Sales had fallen way down and the prospects didn't look that good for a turnaround anytime soon. With fifteen units in this building still unsold, she now had them listed for much less than their original price. In fact, the cost of producing them was much more than what they currently sold for, a fact that hurt her most since she had also purchased one of the units on the second floor.

She reflected on the fifth floor unit that was still sealed off. That was where they discovered Jonathan Harrell's body. He had moved into the unit after selling his home situated directly on the beach since he also needed to raise any money he could. She knew the situation well. It was taking a long time to close out the project, and many of the pre-sales had never materialized. Yes, he could have sued and recovered over time, but time's the one commodity he didn't have any more of. As far as going for short sales— forget it. It would have ruined him.

"Is everything okay on the open house?" Gary asked, knocking her out of a nightmare-like trance.

"Yes, it's fine. Thank you for this." She quickly returned her focus to the task at hand.

Gary smiled and placed the fliers, along with a stack of business cards, on the island counter. "I sent out an e-mail this morning reminding everyone of the open house. Since the weather is nice outside, we should have a good turn out."

As she heard the laughter of women coming in the front door, Rachel glanced at her watch. While it was still a little before twelve, it wasn't unusual for some agents to arrive early. With the food ready, however, she smiled.

As they arrived, one agent after another told her how great the condo looked before they dug into the food, which is really why they came. She knew it, but hoped they would know someone, anyone, they might be able to show the condo unit to. The bank holding the construction notes had called that morning and she was happy to be able to tell them that she had this open house planned. She didn't know how much longer she could keep them happy.

Several more real estate agents smiled at her as they entered together. The first one in immediately jumped into why they must have come. "We heard about a party here about a week ago. Word is circulating that there're some really hot guys playing volleyball on the beach."

Rachel laughed. "I wonder who would start a rumor like that. However, if guys on the beach will help sell a few, I'll hire them to play during our next open house."

The first agent to head to the food replied. "You can definitely count me in. I also heard you know one of the guys. You know it's not fair for you to hide him away and keep him all to yourself, but . . . from what I've heard, I'd do the same." She piled on the food as if she was dining at an all you can eat buffet.

"Yes, I met one of the guys. He's very nice, but I think he has his pick of girls, and not one you can simply put a string in his nose and lead around."

"Well . . . I heard he looked extremely hot." She used her hand to fan her face, attempting to revive herself while she laughed.

In the world of real estate dominated mostly by woman,

Michael stood out as he suddenly walked into the kitchen. His distinguished looks and reputation for making large commercial deals had created a large following. Several of the women called his name out as they offered their hellos.

After he acknowledged their welcomes, Rachel saw him make his way over to her. "I hope you don't mind me coming to the open house."

"Sure, not at all." This surprised her, especially now knowing that he was a silent owner who wanted to remain anonymous. She had respected his wishes and had told no one, except the detective who admitted to already knowing about his involvement.

"Perhaps I can talk you into giving me a private tour." He smiled at Rachel before glanced around at the other women.

"Cindi, can you take care of everyone for a minute, I'll be right back." She motioned for him to follow her.

After walking into the back of the master bedroom, he leaned toward her and whispered, "Thank you for keeping my part in this a secret."

"I told you I would." She followed him into the master bath. "I'm sure you know these units well." She breathed in deep. "Have you heard anything from the investigations?"

"I heard that Detective Lindstrom is interviewing everyone who purchased any of his properties for the last five years. He came to see me and Harrell's main partner, Donnie Moore. I also know he has talked to the banks regarding their notes."

"It sounds like he's doing his job."

"I hope so. I hate to worry you, but if a killer in on the loose we all need to be careful." She watched him staring intently at her.

She swallowed before speaking. "I've been told this by everyone. This killer frightens me."

"Do you own a gun?"

No. She had never fired a gun before, much less owned one. "Do you think I need one?"

He smiled with a stern but pleasant expression. "This is something you'll need to decide for yourself. I carry one with me now all of the time. I'd rather be safe than sorry."

She realized he might be telling her the truth and that she might need to look into purchasing one. "Thanks for your concern. I'll think about it."

He placed a hand on her shoulder. "I didn't mean to scare you."

She moved out of the master bathroom before someone caught them lingering for too long of a period of time.

He followed her while glancing over his shoulder. "The reason I stopped by here was to invite you to a wine tasting charity I belong to. I'm sure you heard of the St. Pete Initiative for Shelter for All. If we don't do something to help people off the streets now, we'll continue to live with a major problem in our city."

Yes, she had heard of this charity for several years. The group consisted of many of the wealthiest people in the Tampa Bay area. They meet once a year to taste and buy expensive wines. A large percentage of the sales went directly to the foundation. In fact, many patrons were known to have donated vintage wines to the event so that all proceeds can be used by the charity. "I'd be honored to attend, but I don't know if I own any wine which will bring any large donations."

"Bring what you can, or if you need me to, I'll give you one of mine that'll bring a good price. There'll be some great people attending that you need to meet."

"Thanks, this is great."

"As you know, I'll be bringing my wife. You can bring a date with you. Perhaps you know someone who has some good wine to add to the auction." He turned to allow her to exit the master bedroom first, leaving her in her thoughts of who she could ask to go with her.

Since Rachel wasn't dating a steady boyfriend, she felt the panic quickly setting in. *Okay . . . like damn . . . now who can I invite to go with me?* Yes, she knew a lot of people, but this would be embarrassing if she had to go on her own.

Several agents approached them as they worked their way back toward the kitchen. As Rachel started to breathe hard, she forced herself to control her fears. She would work it out.

Michael walked over to the food. "This looks great, but I have a full day planned that I need to handle." He turned back to Rachel. "I'll send you the invitation tomorrow, so please mark your calendar. The event is in about two weeks."

"Thanks. I will."

He turned to the other woman and offered his goodbyes as he walked out.

Cindi walked over to Rachel as soon as he left. "What was all of that about?"

Rachel watched the other agents moving in close enough to overhear her reply. "He told me about the St. Pete Initiative for Shelter for All Charity. He wants me to attend their annual charity ball."

"Wow–sounds like fun." Cindi's eyes opened wide with excitement. "I heard the charity ball was a fantastic party last year." She should've known Cindi would know about the ball since her wealthy parents might also be attending.

Rachel knew being offered this prestigious invitation wasn't a bad piece of gossip to spread around to help her image, but her thoughts raced back to the thoughts of who would be available to go with her. "I'm sure the charity ball will be entertaining."

As Rachel turned around, she noticed her old friend Ruth standing behind her. "I'm glad to hear you're going." She smiled softly and asked the question Rachel hoped she could avoid until later. "Who are you going with?"

Rachel flashed a smile around to the other girls, hiding her fears. "I'm not sure yet. I still need to check my calendar to see if I can make it."

"I've been to this event for the last several years. My husband always drags me to this damn thing, but to tell the truth, I've always enjoyed this event after I sample some of the wines. I think you'll enjoy this ball. We'll be looking forward to seeing there." Ruth smiled as she glanced around.

Another wave of agents entered the room to her relief, allowing this pressing question to be deferred. She would work the details out, but had to make some fast decisions.
    ***

When the open houses finally ended, Rachel felt very happy with the turn out, and encouraged that maybe some of the agents might be selling one or more of them soon. As she hurried toward her car on the ground level under the condos, she had always thought about how it was such a waste to not build on this level. However, she knew people needed to park somewhere and the need for a safety valve for a possible hurricane landing. Of course, St. Petersburg had maintained a long time history of very few direct hits by a hurricane.

With her arms full and the heat still incessant, Rachel noticed a movement at the back of the lot. She saw someone quickly hiding behind one of the pillars. She waited for him or her to reemerge. It never happened. As alarms went off in her head, she quickly glanced around, but saw no one else. She quickened her pace toward her car while lifting her cell out of her pocket.

She tossed her bag over to the passenger seat and jumped in, locking the door behind her. While squeezing the phone in her hand, she cranked her car and headed for the back of the lot. The suspicious person she had noticed moments ago was nowhere to be seen. She didn't feel like she was imagining what she saw. No. She definitely saw someone walking around. Perhaps she did need to consider purchasing a gun.

Chapter 6

Rachel barely glanced at Cindi who was entering her office. "Did you lock everything tight when you left the open house?" She swallowed another sip of coffee, wishing she had added more sugar.

"Hey, you didn't tell me you saw Carlos on the beach playing volleyball." Cindi had talked about Carlos continuously since she first saw him.

Rachel smiled. "I didn't want your motor overheating."

"Hmm huh. What did he look like?"

"He looked like a guy playing volleyball." Rachel knew Carlos must have received this intense reaction from most girls in the past as a slight feeling of jealousy flowed over her.

"He called earlier this morning. All is set for the closing in a few days. This is one of the fastest we've consummated in a long time."

Rachel leaned back in her seat. "Yes, it's good to have one land in our lap occasionally."

"If you want me to cover for you at this closing, let me know."

Rachel knew Cindi could, and that she would do a great job. However, since Carlos sent this slam dunk to her, and she felt more appreciative of his generosity than she wanted to admit, she felt like she needed to attend this closing personally. While this was a lower priced house than she normally handled, it required little work on her part, and in this market any commission would be nice. The client he sent her became one of those dream clients she didn't receive too often. "I think I can handle this on my own." Rachel laughed as she handed Cindi a file she had worked on earlier. "But . . . thanks for offering."

Cindi walked toward the door and turned. "You also received an invitation to the Charity wine tasting. How lucky is that?"

"Well, I don't know. I'm sure they invited me to raise some money. I'm still not sure how much this is going to actually cost me."

Cindi crossed her arms and cocked her hip to one side. "Hey, we both know you'll make back many times what you spend, and the money you spend is all tax deductible."

"I'm sure you heard your parents talk about this charity function before. Tell me what you know about this ball."

"It's held at the St. Petersburg Yacht Club and is very formal. Which reminds me, you don't have long to find a good dress."

Rachel had already thought about this. She would need to start looking soon.

Cindi glanced at her sideways. "Who are you going to ask to go with you?"

Thinking she could trust Cindi, she rubbed her fingers across her chin. "I don't know. You know I seldom date."

"Who would you like to ask?"

Rachel still provided no answer, but had to tell Cindi something. "I'll need to think about it. I know a lot of people, but not sure which guy to ask. I'm not accustomed to asking guys out." While the awkward position made talking about this uncomfortable, she needed to face the truth.

"I'd set you up with one of my friends, but they're all too young for you." Yes, Cindi was younger, but she didn't needed to be so blunt, Rachel thought.

In an effort to regain balance, Rachel stared back at Cindi

and teased, "Perhaps, I should invite Carlos."

Cindi's mouth dropped open. "Do you think he would go with you?"

"I guess I'll never know unless I ask."

Cindi stepped back and laughed. "You know, he might go with you. He definitely wants your business." Cindi said, as she kept her eyes focused on Rachel.

"You know, it's not like I'm asking him to go on a romantic date. We both know this is a special event to see who's there and more importantly to be seen."

Cindi smiled broadly. "I think you may have discovered a way to entice one of the hottest guys in town to take you out. My hat's off to you, girl." Cindi's face radiated with a fresh new glow.

"Are you sure?" Rachel knew obtaining Cindi's approval would go a long way in building her self esteem. It was something she would need if she decided to ask him to go with her, but then again, she would be doing him a big favor in introducing him to some very important people in St. Pete.

"I'm sure he would appreciate the invitation very much. He should." Cindi's smile made her feel much better in confiding in her. "I've been thinking lately of the killer who may still be on the loose. You also need to find a guy to do things with; maybe not Carlos, but someone who can keep you from being so alone when you go out to eat late at night. I've been worried about you lately."

"I appreciate your concern, and the thought has crossed my mind lately." Rachel allowed her eyes to glance down at her desk. "I think this may be getting to me, but I promise I think I saw someone stalking me today."

"Where?"

"At the condos today. He disappeared before I could fully identify him."

"That's spooky. Did you call the police?"

"I've nothing to really report. It was simply a feeling." Rachel made herself a note to ask the detective about this mysterious person later. She also wanted to get his opinion on buying a gun.

Rachel lifted a file and opened it, scanning for all of the necessary documents. "I never expected this from Carlos." She smiled as she appreciated the small size of the file. She loved the little work required in handling this sale. When Carlos called to tell her he was working with someone completely approved and ready to buy, she remembered being highly suspicious. The doubt vanished when she met them, and especially when they wrote an offer on a house the first day out. They planned on moving to St. Petersburg and had little time to look before making a flight. Their previous deal had fallen apart and left them with little time to leisurely look.

Cindi pointed to the file. "I talked to the title company and they have everything ready for the closing. This should be a cake walk."

"I hope so." Rachel let her mind race forward to the closing. She needed to plan what she wanted to say to Carlos as a nervous feeling overtook her. Surely he wouldn't turn her down.

Chapter 7

Rachel smiled at the receptionist before scanning the reception area at the title company, hoping all of the parties had arrived. She had completed enough closings over her career to anticipate last minute problems and hopefully stay one step ahead of them.

After turning from a conversation with the seller, Rachel's purchasers smiled as they recognized her. While a friendly conversation between the two was always a good sign, neither the other agent nor Carlos appeared to be there yet.

"Hello." She reached out her hand toward her purchasers, flashing a smile. She had run slightly late due to last minute preparations, but she was glad she had put forth her best look. The purchaser's wife had selected a colorful outfit accenting her youthful radiance. Rachel remembered her style from the first time she met her.

With everyone returning their hellos immediately, the large smiles made her feel good. "Have you seen Carlos?"

The purchaser's wife, Nancy, answered first. "I think he's in the closing room with the other agent."

"That's good. I'll join them to make sure all is ready for us." She quickly headed for the conference room.

As Rachel walked along the short hallway, her hands felt sweaty. *Why am I so nervous? After all, I'm the one doing him a favor.* She had already decided that he would be receiving many referrals in the near future.

Upon entering the conference room, Carlos immediately stood and walked toward her. "Rachel, how are you? We have everything in order."

Diana Pettercoat, the other agent, smiled and leaned next to Carlos to examine the papers in front of them. Leaning too close, she thought. *Damn, why am I acting so jealous?* "I'm glad to hear the news. I saw the purchasers and the sellers out front, and they look excited. Is there anything else we're waiting on?"

Diana glanced at Carlos. "I think we're all ready. Have a seat and I'll bring everyone in here." She turned to walk toward the receptionist area.

Carlos flashed a large smile. "The purchasers are very happy with you."

"Thanks." They should be since this has been a smooth transaction so far. "I wanted to tell you how impressed I am with your work."

Carlos offered her a large smile. "Thank you." He wore a dark-grey dress pair of slacks and a white shirt, giving him a professional appearance. While she studied his simple tie coordinated with his sports coat, she also imagined his body bulging under his clothes. His muscular body appeared to be well toned like a professional dancer.

Following a brief moment of silence, they smiled and moved to the table. After he pulled out a chair for her, he slipped into the one next to her. "Carlos, I've something I want to ask you." With his questioning eyes glancing at her, and their dark-brown color penetrated her thoughts, she blinked her own to regain control. "Yes . . . I was wondering–."

"Hello, everyone." The closing agent, Mrs. Jefferson, walked into the room and lumbered to the head of the table. "Is everyone ready to close?"

Rachel turned toward her. "Yes, Diana's bringing them in here for us now. All of the parties are here." She refocused on Carlos. Damn. She had missed her chance to ask him in private. Luckily he didn't ask her to finish what she was saying. This was good as she breathed deeply. She definitely didn't want to be rejected in front of someone. In fact, she didn't want others to hear her asking him.

Adjusting the stack of papers in front of her, Mrs. Jefferson glanced over at Rachel. "You look good. How have you been?"

"Doing great, thanks."

"I hope these investigations into Jonathan Harrell's death end soon. They're running us ragged with one request after another for additional documentation." Her smile faded into a full frown. "I know you had a good working relationship with him. How are you holding up?"

"Yes, we did. He was a great guy, fun loving, but dedicated to his work. Have you heard anything on how the investigation is going?"

"I think they've ruled out a suicide, but they still have no suspects. While I also think Jonathan was a nice guy, apparently they think he must have produced at least one enemy somewhere in his past. Did you know anything about the pistol he had purchased that he was murdered with?"

Rachel blinked her eyes again. She hadn't allowed herself to think of the details of his death. "No, I haven't asked any questions concerning the pistol. I still have trouble thinking about his death."

Mrs. Jefferson paused before continuing, "From what I've heard, he purchased the gun for protection only a few weeks before his death. This may have been the only bullet ever fired from the gun."

"Ohmigod!" Rachel raised her hand to cover her mouth. "He must've known he was in danger." Memories of the last time she said goodbye to Harrell flashed in her head.

"I think his motives for buying a gun is what everyone is thinking about now." Mrs. Jefferson glanced over at Carlos.

"Did you know Jonathan?"

"I met him a few times, but never landed any of the loans on his properties. I heard he was a great developer, but that's all I know." Carlos glanced over at Rachel.

Mrs. Jefferson leaned back in her chair. "One thing's for sure, I'm keeping my pistol loaded until all of this is over."

Rachel eyes darted over to her. "You carry a pistol?"

"It never leaves my side." She patted her purse hanging on the side of her chair.

"That's interesting, but I cannot say I blame you." While Rachel knew she needed to follow up on questions about obtaining a pistol of her own, she knew to not let the fact out she didn't own one now.

As everyone involved in the closing soon walked through the doorway, the closing delayed any further conversation concerning the murder. Now, if it was only so easy to turn off the wheels turning in her mind. *Who was Jonathan so scared of that he had decided to purchase a gun?*

After the closing ended nearly an hour later, Rachel checked on her paperwork one last time before leaving, making sure that all was in order.

Carlos walked back into the conference room. "I thought I would find you here."

"Yes, I need to turn this closing into the office so I can get paid. Thank you again for the referral." She smiled, hoping to have a minute to talk to him.

"Perhaps we can close some more soon."

"I think we can. I'm impressed on how you work." She batted her eyes softly. "I do have one favor to ask you."

His dark eyes twinkled. "Sure, name it."

"I've a special charity event coming up in a few weeks and I was wondering if you would like to go with me?"

She watched him studying her face, allowing for several moments of silence. "Sure, I'd be glad to. When is it?"

"It's on the twenty seventh of the month, a Saturday night. I'll give you all of the details soon. It'll be a great way for you to meet many people here."

"This sounds great to me. Thanks for inviting me."

That was easy, she thought. She breathed easier, knowing her accepted request had eliminated a potentially embarrassing moment. With her heart still fluttering, she now needed to worry about finding the perfect dress since she had a date with a stud–a young stud. Wow!

Chapter 8

"You look fantastic!" Carlos smiled, as his deep, slow voice paid respect to Rachel for the work she had obviously put into her appearance. Rachel enjoyed having him study her. She had spent hours in the salon earlier today. She could only hope that the work of her hair stylist would be appreciated by her friends at the ball as much as he was showing now.

"You look good also, Carlos." While he looked as good as ever, he did wear a simple blue suit. A business one, for sure, but not of the quality or style she had hoped for. He also wore a large belt buckle. She needed to let him know, tactfully of course, that this wasn't Texas.

While standing in front of the door to the St. Petersburg Yacht Club, she stopped for a second to face him. "Thank you for coming with me." She reached over and straightened his tie.

"I should be the one thanking you." He leaned over and locked the focus of his eyes with hers. "This means a lot to me."

She studied the tie for several seconds, trying to decide if she should say something or not. It must be a ten dollar special from a department store. Whatever, it was too late to change the tie now.

"What is it?" He finally said as she studied him.

"I was wondering what colors would look best on you." She smiled, allowing herself to approach his style gently.

A genuine smile brushed across his face as he leaned forward. "The rose color you selected today looks great on you."

She thought briefly about how much time had gone into coordinating her outfit, the shoes, the accessories, the makeup and the jewelry. Nothing was left to chance. Carlos, on the other hand probably only needed to jump into his outfit to look great. It wasn't fair. "Thanks, I hope you like it."

After they entered the yacht club, they immediately followed the crowds drifting around, visiting the various tables where merchants were setting up to provide wine tastings. A large woman stepped toward them. "Good evening, it's good to see you tonight."

Rachel extended her hand toward her and allowed her to retrieve the tickets. "We're looking forward to this."

The woman glanced over at Carlos. "My name is Catherine, and I'm on the entertainment committee at the St. Petersburg Yacht Club. I hope you have a great time tonight since we've some great wines for the tastings that can also be purchased. This auction should be extremely interesting tonight."

Carlos looked at the tables before turning to Catherine. "I agree. I think this is going to be an exciting night."

Rachel watched Catherine glance back at her with a puzzled look on her face, knowing she was trying to ascertain the relationship between the two of them. Eat your heart out, she thought. "I brought a bottle to be auction off as well. Who do I give it to?"

Catherine turned and pointed to the far right corner. "A table is set up there for everyone to examine the wines for the auction later. Aaron Bank is coordinating it."

A smile crossed Rachel's face. "I know him. He's a good friend of mine."

Carlos nodded an appreciative *thank you* toward Catherine before reached for Rachel's left hand with his left hand. With a quick over the top movement with his right elbow, he wrapped her hand around his arm. For a young man, he possessed an uncommon natural ability to showcase his manners. However, he still had his moments when he allowed his western culture to creep in. The combination intrigued her.

With the floor crowded with people, Rachel knew it would take some time to reach the table. She soon saw Jody Bright rushing over to them, smiling broadly. As she flashed an inquisitive glance at Carlos, it was going to be interesting to see how he reacted to her friend's interest in him. "Rachel, I'm glad to see you made it." Jody said, as she shifted her smile to Rachel.

Rachel turned toward Carlos. "Carlos, this is another real estate agent that you need to know. She has been selling here for a long time."

Carlos smiled. "Okay."

"Her name is Jody Bright." After turning more toward Carlos, she continued, "And this is Carlos Martin. He's in the mortgage business."

Jody studied Carlos for several minutes. "Hello, Carlos. I've sold real estate for a long time, but Rachel is the top agent here now. I'm sure she'll keep you busy."

"I hope so. I can use some more business." Carlos smiled as he refocused on Rachel.

"I'm sure Rachel will introduce you to many people tonight, but come see me some time. I'd like to hear what you have to offer."

"Sure, I'd be glad to." Carlos glanced over at Rachel, sending a coded message of thankfulness.

As they moved on toward the table in the corner, Jody gave Rachel a wink behind Carlos's head. Rachel also saw her checking him out from behind as they left.

While several couples smiled at them as they crossed the

floor, they finally reached the far corner and stood in front of Aaron Bank. He immediately reached out a hand toward Rachel. "How are you?"

"Aaron, I'm fine, thanks. I want you to meet my friend, Carlos." She turned slightly in the direction of Carlos and waited for them to shake hands.

She watched Aaron studying Carlos intently. She knew Aaron would give her his honest opinion of Carlos later since they had been friends for a long time. Carlos stood tall and firm, presenting a gentleman-like presence. The pride inside her grew as he attracted the attention of her friends. She knew the gossip would start soon.

As Rachel handed Aaron the bottle she had brought for the auction, he glanced at the French Burgundy and whistled. "This should bring a good price tonight." He placed the wine on the table with the others.

Carlos moved to the end of the table and lifted the first one he saw, turning the bottle over to read the back. Rachel quickly realized he must have only recently reached the legal drinking age. While his knowledge of wines must be limited, she watched him lift one bottle after another, examining them in detail.

Aaron also watched Carlos's actions. "Do you see anything that interests you? I know wines very well."

Carlos smiled as he glanced at Aaron. "I see some intriguing names here. They're also many on this table with some age on them."

"Yes, many of these are collectable."

Carlos pointed to several bottles. "It would be nice to know when they peak. It would be a shame to hold them too long."

Aaron smiled at Rachel, indicating that Carlos may know more about wines than he thought. "What kind of wines do you like?"

"Since wine is much like life, I think one robust with flavor yet retaining its subtle uniqueness is worth the extra effort crafted by a master." Carlos handed Aaron a bottle of Pinot Noir. "This one could be interesting. What do you think?"

Aaron accepted the bottle. "It's six years old, and if you're looking for one to drink now it shouldn't disappoint you. However, I also think that it'll bring a nice premium tonight."

Over the next hour, Rachel introduced Carlos to many of the people she knew. As she looked for people to talk to, she watched the expressions on their face when she introduced Carlos. She could see the curiosity of the women. Man, if she could only be a fly on the wall listening to everything later.

However, she did watch many of the group studying his clothing. Most of the men wore expensive tailored suits, designer ties and jewelry like Rolex watches which further enhanced an impression of wealth. None of them wore a western belt buckle.

Cindi's parents finally managed to make their way over to them. Rachel remembered meeting them many times before when they came by the office to take Cindi out to lunch. She knew word would reach Cindi soon. Smiling as they reached out their hands, they glanced from one to the other. "How are you?" they both asked at the same time.

"I'm doing great. This is Carlos, I'm sure Cindi said something to you about him."

"Yes, she told us to keep an eye out for you tonight." Cindi's mother glanced at Carlos. "Our daughter told us you looked fantastic. I'll have to say that she has better taste than I thought." She beamed a look of approval toward Rachel.

Carlos looked confused and blushed slightly as he turned toward Rachel.

"Carlos, these are the parents of Cindi, my secretary that you met in my office." She waited for his response.

"I understand. Yes, I remember her in the office." His eyes darted back and forth. "She's a nice girl to talk to."

Cindi's mother studied Rachel, as if to analyze the match up with Carlos, but holding her cards close to her vest, so to speak. Rachel knew Cindi liked Carlos and would want to know all of the details as soon as her parents returned home later tonight. She moved closer to Carlos, as if to present them as more of a couple.

The mother finally looked over at her husband before returning her attention to Rachel. "Cindi really likes her job working with you. She keeps telling us of how well you're doing. She said you became the top agent in St Petersburg again last month."

"Yes, I had a good month." Rachel glanced around to see if anyone else heard the lavish praise. "If we can keep sales coming for the rest of the year, we might be able to break our record of fifty four million we set last year." She didn't need to say a word about how everyone else had a very bad month.

"Wow! That will be impressive, especially in a market like this." Cindi's father radiated a smile, as the mother restrained her emotions. Rachel could feel the concentration in her mind. Yes, he looked young, but he was still old enough to be a man. She thought how funny it was that when men dated younger woman all of the time they never have their motives questioned. She decided to break the silence. "Have you tried any of the wines yet?"

"We tried a few. I think we have some great wines to choose from." The mother's stare finally broke as she reached for her husband's arm. "Don't let us keep you."

"Not at all. We hope to find some good ones tonight." They turned and walked over to the first wine tasting table.

The wines poured freely as the host served large generous servings. They appeared to understand that the more they poured, the higher the bids would be later. While Rachel selected many bottles for later, she also saw Carlos making many choices. He definitely preferred reds.

Rachel pulled Carlos from one table to another until the auction started and the wine started playing with her head. They must have consumed more than a bottle during the hour of tasting. She continued to enjoy showing him off to the people circulating. Many of the attendees she knew slightly, but some of them were old acquaintances.

The first bottle went for over one thousand. This is ridiculous, she thought, but she allowed her awarding winning smile to radiate and cover her shock. She wasn't going to spend this kind of money on a bottle of wine. The next one went for only two hundred dollars. Perhaps, to save face, she should've bid on it, but it was too late now—someone obtained a bargain.

Carlos stretched high on his toes to glance above a person moving in front of him. "This is the one." He motioned toward the table.

She glanced at him, thinking he wasn't serious about bidding on this bottle until he raised his hand and made the first bid. "Five hundred." Wow!

The price quickly advanced. Carlos stood and raised the price to two thousand. She saw Aaron take a deep breath. Everyone knew he would receive no challenge. "Sold to a guy who apparently knows good wines and what he wants." He pointed to Carlos as the crowd clapped. Her choice in a date for the night ended up being much more than she had dreamed about. This would definitely increase her recognition. Everyone would want to know who he is and how she managed to snag such a hunk.

The bidding continued as the wine increasingly dulled

her senses. Jody remained next to her as the last of the wine was auctioned. "This has been a good night. We raised a lot of funds for the homeless."

"I'm glad to be part of this." She studied the suit Carlos wore again, before pointing toward Aaron. "Did you notice Aaron's suit?"

"A little, why?" He glanced back in Aaron's direction.

"I think that's a Capperelli he's wearing."

She saw Carlos smile. "Capperelli suits are hand-sewed; I think that one's machine sewed. If it is . . . it's a copy." He shifted his stare from Aaron as his words sunk in.

Hmmm–that's an astute observation, she thought. "I'm surprised you noticed so much detail."

Carlos moved his hand to the lower part of her back, massaging it. "I think he's a nice guy." He offered no excuses for his observation. "I think I'm glad I own a truck tonight since we purchased several cases of wine."

The truck–she had forgotten about his–truck. He drove a truck. While it was a late model, it was still . . . a truck. Perhaps no one would notice them leaving. If she guessed wrong, she knew she would hear about this later.

Chapter 9

"Park over there." Following Rachel's instructions, Carlos pulled under the cover at Rachel's condo. The world swirled around in her head. *How much wine did I actually consume tonight?* Apparently much more than she had realized as she waited for him to open her door. Rachel smiled as she reflected on the looks of those watching her being escorted by Carlos.

Rachel tried to focus as Carlos opened the door and extended his hand toward her. While reaching for his hand, she prepared herself for the high step which presented her with difficulties the last time she got out. This time the adventure would be more so as she twisted in the seat.

"Here, let me help you." He stepped in closer and reached an arm under her side. The strength in his arms encouraged her to trust them.

Rachel pushed forward, allowing her body to rub close to his. His powerful smell registered as she slid to the ground. "Thank you."

"It's really not bad when you get accustomed to it." After safely reaching the ground, he held her arm while directing her toward the entrance to the elevator. "I'll come back for the wine in a minute."

Rachel stopped. "No, I can walk on my own. I'm not too bad off." She motioned for him to carry the wine.

While waiting on him, she noticed a car, a dark sedan, pulling slowly out of the garage. She knew that such a feeling would be hard to explain, but she knew someone was checking her out. She quickly shifted her attention to Carlos who was lifting almost a full case of wine and apparently unaware of the car. The car sped off when Carlos stepped under a light.

The gun–she needed to take care of buying one soon. The thoughts of learning how to shoot flooded her mind as they walked. After walking into her condo, she hurried to the kitchen and pointed toward a small room. "I've a small wine cooler in the dining room. See if you can place the wine in it. If not, I'll make space for them tomorrow somewhere."

She saw Carlos glancing around the condo as a yapping Prince ran over to him and sniffed his leg. Carlos immediately lifted him and scratched his head. "Hello there."

After she locked the door and retrieved Prince, she carried him to his cot where he always slept. "Thank you for carrying the wine in for me. I'm sure the bottles were heavy. You'll have to excuse Prince; he's getting old and needs lots of attention lately. "

He smiled. "It was nothing. I assume you have had Prince for a long time."

She rubbed prince's head. "Yes, a very long time and I worry about him." She glanced at Carlos and his muscles again. Perhaps he was right. For him, the wine was nothing to lift. She felt the same emotions she had received the first time she had seen him. The reality quickly settled in that she was alone with him. Now what?

He turned and lifted one bottle from the case, the one special bottle he had paid dearly for. "What do you think? This baby has to be good."

She fought the uncontrollable urge to laugh. "I hope so. It should make you a good investment."

"Where is a corkscrew?"

"What? You're not planning on opening it, are you?"

"That's why I purchased it." He walked to the kitchen.

This is crazy. She knew she needed to stop him, but the thoughts of enjoying some great wine crossed her mind. She felt good–too good.

He returned from the kitchen, screwing in the cork screw. "Is it okay if we use these glasses?" He pointed toward the cabinet built in above the wine cooler.

"Sure, those will be fine."

He lifted them and moved in next to her on the sofa where she slid over toward him, allowing her head to rest on his shoulder. He kissed the top of her head as he placed the bottle on the cocktail table in front of them. She suddenly realized that her hand lay on his leg. While she didn't remember placing it on his leg, her hand rested on his thigh as if it possessed a mind of its own.

While slightly angry at having so much wine, and her perception of reality becoming dulled, she also welcomed the thoughts of allowing herself to be so uninhabited. Her eyes scanned the muscles in his legs from his knee to his crotch. She knew he had to know she was staring.

While this wasn't the first time a man had turned her on like this, it had been a while. Rachel breathed harder as a rush of warmth overtook her. This is crazy, she thought, knowing he hasn't even touched her yet.

Rachel watched him lean forward to retrieve the bottle and a glass. He poured the wine slowly and handed a glass to her. She needed to remove her hand from his leg, a movement she wished she didn't have to make. She wished she knew his thoughts. While he stayed in control too much, his strength frustrated her and made her yearn more to control him, to possess him.

"Here, I think we'll enjoy this." Carlos handed her the glass and poured one for himself.

Rachel sat high enough to face him. "I can't believe you opened this bottle. You should've saved this wine for a special occasion."

"There'll always be other bottles, but this time will never come again." He raised his glass toward her glass.

"That sounds like a good toast. You're an interesting guy."

"Thank you. I wanted to thank you for a good night, and for introducing me to so many people at the wine tasting."

Rachel reflected on her thoughts of having him hauled around as a *boy toy* and parading him in front of her friends. Yes, she was older than him, but he was appearing to be anything but a boy toy. "You're welcome. I'll let you make it up to me some time." She couldn't believe she said that.

They both drank the entire glass before continuing their conversation. The warmth continued to fill her body as she slid in closer to him again. She handed him the glass and laid her hand on his leg. She saw him place the glass on the table as well as his own. His pants stretched tight enough for her see a bulge beneath the fabric. She tried to resist the urge to touch his manhood. Grabbing him would be too forward she told herself. *Why doesn't he make a move?*

She tilted her head back and closed her eyes. The welcome mat was out, she thought. Her plan worked as he leaned over and kissed her neck. The warmth of his skin next to her own excited her as she allowed a moan to escape. He must know that she wanted him. He had to know.

His hand rested on her neck, slowly caressing the skin, allowing his fingers to gently roam. She breathed in again and sensed his great all-natural smell. His hands moved over her shoulder and edged toward her breast. She knew the size of them always excited men in her life before. She hoped her breasts would create the same effect on him.

She heard him breathe harder as he slipped his hand under her bra. His fingers worked magic on her as the nipples became rigid instantly. Perhaps she was moving too fast, but she reached out and worked her hand up his leg until she was able to massage the bulge under his pants. Oh god, she wanted him now.

He reached for her hand. What? He pushed her hand away from his crotch. "Are you sure about this?" he asked, as he turned to face her.

She opened her eyes, attempting to focus. "I don't mind at all. I promise." *What does he want me to do, beg for it?*

"Sorry, just checking. I know you drank a lot tonight."

She didn't want this minute to slip away. She raised her hand to his crotch again, massaging him with her fingers. "I can make you feel good, if you want me to."

A silence grew into minutes as she continued to massage him. This time he didn't resist her as he leaned over and kissed the top of her head. Good. She wondered why he doesn't try to kiss her lips. She wouldn't resist.

She increased the rhythm on his penis as he started growing from her constant work. She, at the same time, became wetter by the minute. She reached for his zipper. He reached for her hand. "What are you doing?" he asked.

"I want to make you happy." She lied; she wanted to make herself happy.

"Once you start something, I need to know you'll finish what you start."

As she tried to focus, she thought he would know that. "I understand."

She watched him lean forward to pour another glass of wine for them. As he leaned back with the two glasses, she unzipped his pants and also managed to unfasten his belt and hook. With his hands full with the two glasses, he offered no resistance. She glanced over to see him closing his eyes and smiling. After she slipped her hand under his boxers and fully around his cock, his manhood swelled immediately.

Glancing at him again, she watched him take a sip. She lowered his boxers to see him. He looked large, and exactly like what she had hoped he would. She massaged her hand up and down the shaft, bring soft groans from him.

"Do you want your glass?" He spoke slowly but deliberately, as the wine slowed his movements.

"No, I'll drink some more in a minute."

Carlos's only response came slowly. "Okay."

He reached behind her head and pulled her down toward him. She didn't resist. He laid the glasses down and shifted his weight. She slid lower. *What is he doing?* He pulled her further. Now, she understood as her face rested inches from his cock. She studied his cock rapidly pulsating in front of her. *Should I go down on it? Suck on his dick*? Her mind kept switching back and forth. She heard him groan. She knew if she did this for him, he would owe her big time and that generated a feeling she liked. Surely, he would return the favor later when they were more fully aware of their senses.

She leaned forward to kiss the tip, sending it into a rapid pulsation. She licked her lips, and then kissed the tip again. Now that she had started, she wanted to make him happy, hoping future rewards would be great. She licked him in a small circular motion. He groaned much louder now. She leaned forward and slid her mouth over his shaft, taking in all she could. His pelvis thrust in and out as she allowed him to slide in and out of her mouth. The taste of his juices wasn't bad. She remembered some bad experiences before. Maybe the wine had dulled her inhibitions, but she enjoyed feeling him excited.

When he finally came, she quickly swallowed and licked his dick for any spills. He actually tasted good. After she glanced over again to see him peacefully resting, she nestled in his lap to rest and dream. Tomorrow he would make her happy. Tomorrow she would use him as a boy toy. Yes, she had plans for him–her new boy toy.

Chapter 10

A rustling sound startled Rachel as she forced her eyes to open, to focus. Her head hurt, her body ached, and her mind was totally confused. *Where am I?* She stretched, pushing her legs along the couch.

Suddenly she saw him, standing silently above her, as the memories of the night vaguely registered. "Carlos . . . ."

A warm hand touched her forehead. "Good morning, sleepy head. I wondered if you were planning to wake up before I had to leave." His hand slipped to her cheek, rubbing the skin softly. "Are you okay? I think you drank way too much wine last night."

"Ohhhhh . . . ." She knew she had. "What time is it?"

"It's almost eight. I've a closing in a few hours, and I need to stop by my office first."

"Eight–wow! I've some work to do this morning also." She forced herself to rise on one elbow. Luckily, he leaned over to help her as her eyes flickered open wide for the first time to see him standing in front of her, looking as fresh as ever. She knew her hair had to be a wreck. With a quick glance down, she saw her dress pulled up close to her waist. *That's one view he should've enjoyed.*

He reached over and pulled her dress down to gently cover her legs. She glanced at his face, and his calm, gentle eyes softly paying her attention. *Ohmigod, what did I do last night?*

"Can I get you anything before I leave?" His smooth voice seemed to be treating her like a little girl.

"No, I think I can manage. I really need to get moving."

"Okay, I'll call you later to check on you." As she heard him walking toward the door, she forced herself to glance at him leaving. She started to tell him thank you for the night, but he was the one taken care of the night before. He should be thanking her.

***

Rachel quickly glanced at the clock on the wall of the reception area at her office. *How could it already be ten?* She didn't stop to chat with Mary, the receptionist, trying to appear normal. Yes, many times she often saw clients early in the morning. No one would guess that a guy had spent the night with her, that is, unless she revealed her secret on her own.

Cindi's smile beamed at her as soon as she entered her private office. "How did your date go last night?"

"It was a good night. I didn't know so many people would be attending." Rachel walked toward her desk, hoping to not draw too much attention.

"My parents told me they saw you last night with Carlos." She bounced in her chair with excitement, apparently eager to hear all of the details.

The chipper attitude would've been pleasant and fun any other day but now. Rachel's head and neck hurt from lying in such an awkward position the night before. She still couldn't believe it. She went to sleep sucking on his dick! She could just imagine the look on his face when he woke. Surely he wouldn't tell anyone about what happened.

Rachel collapsed into her seat. "Your parents had a good time last night." She knew she was acting unstable, but she forced herself to hide the fact as best she could.

A knock at the door interrupted their discussion. As Detective Lindstrom stepped forward, his stern face indicated that he wasn't on a casual stop-by. Thoughts of interrogational questions he might be asking this morning quickly eroded her last bit of reserve as she waited for him to state his reason for being there. "How are you this morning? I was hoping to catch you here."

Cindi walked over to him first. "What brings you here today?"

He slowly moved to close the door behind him. "I hope this is okay. I've some bad news to give you."

Rachel indicated with a hand motion that it would be fine to close the door. "You look serious. What is it?"

"I hope you don't mind if I ask you a question first. I need to know where you were last night." His rough, low voice scared her.

Cindi spoke first. "She went to a charity event last night with Carlos."

He looked over at Cindi, allowing his glaze to indicate that he would rather hear the answer from Rachel. "What time did you go home last night?"

Rachel leaned back in her chair. "I'm not sure exactly. I think about eleven or so."

"I need to know about after you returned home. Did you go anywhere later?"

Rachel's curiosity peaked. *Why was he here?* "Why are you asking me these questions?"

His eyes glanced back and forth between the two girls. "We just discovered another person dead in the condos you're selling. The same one Jonathan Harrell died in."

"Ohmigod!" Rachel moved her hands to cover her mouth.

Cindi stood her ground, wrinkling her brow. "Who was it?"

Rachel watched his intent stare. "His name was Donnie Moore, one of Jonathan's business partners."

With the air escaping from Rachel's lungs she fought to inhale. She forced herself to focus. "Yes, I know him. He operated as a silent partner and not many people know of his involvement with Jonathan. What happened?"

"He left a suicide note, much like Jonathan had, but as you can imagine, we have some serious doubts. I'm sorry to ask this, but I need to know what time your date left you last night."

"Why is this important?"

"The time of death is estimated to be somewhere around midnight to as late as four in the morning."

Rachel could see Cindi studying her for a response, but she had no intentions of sharing her past night with her. "Cindi . . . let me talk to the detective alone for a minute, please." Cindi looked startled as she slowly complied. Rachel knew she would need to explain to her more fully later.

With the door closed, Rachel continued, "I hope this can remain quiet. Can I trust you on this?"

Detective Lindstrom's light-gray eyes quickly let her know he would, if possible, but no promises. "I need honesty and nothing more or less."

"Carlos, my date, stayed with me all night." She watched his reaction. While she had a hard time knowing exactly what went on inside of his mind, she could imagine many possibilities. Did he consider her a slut, nothing more than a cheap bitch, or did he think she was having a secret affair with a young boy?

He made a note on his pad he always carried with him while showing little emotions. "I assume . . . he would corroborate your statement."

"If need be, I'm sure he would."

"And you stayed with him the entire night." He kept his eyes focused on her, making her wish she said nothing now.

Her stare rebuked his, as she leaned forward to insure she wasn't misunderstood. "He left my place at eight this morning."

He grinned slightly as he continued, "My guess is that whoever killed Jonathan also killed Donnie. Why someone is using the ridiculous disguise of a suicide is beyond me."

"I met Donnie several times, but I mostly dealt with Jonathan." The news sank in of another murder. *Who could the killer be? Am I next?* "I liked Jonathan. He was great to work with."

Detective Lindstrom placed the pad in his pocket. "We need to find any other common links between the two men. While I've some other people I need to contact as quickly as I can, I hope I can talk you into coming to the station later today. Your help in this will be extremely important."

Rachel's headache dulled her thoughts, but she knew she needed time to gather her story together. "I think I scheduled a full day, but I'll do what I need to do. Do you think I'm in danger?"

"If I were you, I would remain extremely cautious. It's good, however, to hear that you have a new boyfriend for now. You said his name was Carlos."

She didn't think she would call him a boyfriend, but didn't want to give any further explanations for now. "I don't think he would like to know there's a killer out there. You did say you'd try to keep this quiet." She accentuated her smile to ask for his discretion.

"I understand." He walked toward the door wearing the same suit she saw him wearing many times before. "You have my number, so call me when you get free. I need your help."

Rachel followed him, closing the door behind him. She knew it would only be minutes before Cindi would come in asking questions. With her muscles trembling, she needed to go home and to her bed, but she knew there was no way.

Cindi's expected knock forced Rachel to reaffix her

placid smile. With Cindi's face expressing concerns mixed with questions, Rachel knew that she needed to confide in her to some extent, but would allow herself to only go so far.

Rachel motioned for Cindi to have a seat. "I need you to cover for me this morning. I got very little sleep last night."

"I hate to say it, but your eyes do look red." Cindi leaned forward attempting to be a friend more than a secretary. "Carlos must've stayed late last night." Rachel's stare froze as she was unable to come back with a swift enough response. After Cindi noticed the hesitation, she appeared to quickly understand. "Oh my God, are you telling me that Carlos spent the night with you?" Her face beamed.

Rachel massaged her forehead as she attempted to relieve her pounding headache. "We drank a lot of wine last night. I don't think he was in any shape to drive." She confessed to all that she wanted to for now.

Rachel's carefully planned words appeared to work in deflating Cindi's overactive mind as her smile faded. "I understand. I think my parents returned home last night in much the same shape." Cindi's concern looked genuine. "So . . . it looks like you and Carlos hit it off well last night."

Rachel smiled, thinking about the night. "I think he enjoyed himself. I introduced him to many people which should really be good for his business."

"That's great. Are you planning on seeing him some more?" Cindi's eyes twinkled.

Rachel breathed deeply, thinking of the possibilities. "I wish I had time to spend with him, but you know how I work."

"You do work too much. Maybe this is what you need."

Thinking about what the detective told her, Rachel stared back at Cindi. "With a killer on the loose, it might be a good idea to have someone with me when I go out. He's nice."

"Nice? He's a hunk."

Rachel rolled her eyes. "I think he made a big impression on you."

"Well like yeah, but you're the one who has him on a leash so far."

A leash–she only wished. "It was great to have him take me to the charity event last night. He's young, and he needs someone to teach him how to dress, but I think he could be groomed into one great guy." Rachel smiled as she thought she'd handled the situation correctly, hiding her true feelings of being treated as his party girl instead.

"I'm sure once he attends several of these functions he'll adjust. I assume you're talking about his western flair for dressing."

"Yes, and he does need to do some updating. Perhaps it would be great to help him out. We'll see."

"So . . . what's he doing this morning?"

Rachel leaned back in her chair. "He said he had a closing today."

Cindi stood to leave, but glanced back over her shoulder first. "That must be the large one he's working on at Treasure Island."

"He told you about the loan?"

"Yes, the other day when he was here. He was excited about it. You cannot blame him, since it's slightly over a three million dollar deal."

"Wow! He never said anything to me about it." He was definitely a man full of surprises. Perhaps his commission from this loan is where he made the extra money to buy the wine the night before.

"I hope everything works out for you with Carlos. I need to work on my mail outs and since we don't have any appointments today it'll give me a chance to catch up." This made Rachel remember lying to the detective about her schedule. She simply didn't want to go see him anytime soon.

"Thanks. I told the detective I would come by later to talk to him. If you need me you can call me, but I think I'll go home and rest a little first." She glanced at the phone. "Perhaps I do need to check on Carlos before I leave."

"I thought so." Cindi winked before she closed the door.

In the quietness of her office, Rachel closed her eyes as she analyzed the latest murder in her building. She knew she needed to go by the condos and talk to some of the owners as she could only imagine how much they hated this market. While selling the remaining units would now be the ultimate challenge, she needed, however, to first talk to the attorney handling the properties and the title company before going to the condos.

Her mind drifted back to Carlos and the night before. *What does he think of me now? What time did he wake up?* He looked so fresh and clean. *Did he shower before he left?* She had so many questions–too many–for a head hurting this much to think about. She hadn't been with a man for a long time and she still couldn't believe what happened the night before. This was totally not like her. Oh yes, she needed to call him and get things straight.

She reached for the phone and dialed the number on one of his cards which were still sitting on the side of her desk. He answered immediately in a low voice, "This is Carlos."

"Carlos, this is Rachel. How are you this morning?" She tried her best to sound cheerful.

"Hi, I'm fine. You're the one I was wondering about." He said as his voice continued in a strong, but smooth whisper.

"No, I'm fine. Are you in your closing?"

"Yes. I need to call you back when it's over, if that's okay."

"Sure, I understand. Perhaps we need to celebrate your closing later."

"Sounds good, I'm thinking of going to Tarpon Springs for some Greek food tonight. What time will you be home?"

Rachel shifted in her seat. "I . . . hmmm . . . usually work late."

She waited during a long silence. "That's okay, perhaps later."

"No–wait. How does . . . around seven tonight sound to you?"

"It sounds like a date to me. I need to attend to my clients now, but I'll see you later."

"Okay, bye." She heard the line die.
***

The traffic along the Sponge Docks sidewalks in Tarpon Springs moved steadily along. She remembered going there many times before, but the shops looked different this time. She would love to do a little shopping, but knew Carlos had food on his mind. "Have you eaten at this place before?"

Carlos glanced around the street. "I've tried several restaurants here, but not this one." He answered as he pulled into a parking lot.

Rachel studied his clothes. His dark blue jeans looked both rugged and masculine. However, his large belt buckle–a different one–overpowered the look. She needed to approach this subject soon. Carlos also wore a blue pullover which reinforced his casual look, making him look so natural in his clothes. His flat stomach and the bulging muscles in his shoulders and arms filled out the shirt. "I like Greek food, and especially Greek wine."

He smiled at her. "Just remind me to keep an eye on you tonight." He flashed a flirty smile.

"I can generally hold my own, but last night was an exception." She studied his face as he turned off the engine.

"For a wine tasting, they poured rather large samples, but I think they knew what they were doing." Carlos said as he smiled and rolled his eyes before he laughed loudly.

"Have you been to many wine tastings?" She saw him leaving his seat and knew he would answer her when he opened her door. As expected, she soon heard the door opening and saw a large smile on his face as he extended her his hand. She glanced down. *Why do they need to make trucks so high off of the ground?* She reached for his hand to steady her as she now wish she had worn a pair of jeans as well. Yes, the short dress she wore must be giving him a show as she envisioned him studying her panties. "Thanks, exiting from a truck this high off of the ground is something I'm not used to."

"I'm sorry about this, but I've always wanted a truck like this. I guess this is the toy I always wanted." He studied the truck as his face beamed.

Rachel stepped on the ground, feeling safer. With the smell of the docks filling her nostrils, she actually liked this Greek village atmosphere. "Thank you for bringing me here. I should come here more often."

"You're welcome. I think the food here will be great, and I've wanted to try it for long time." He pointed to the restaurant which was apparently on his mind for the night. "I understand they stock some great wines also."

They entered the restaurant and glanced around. The colorful painting on the walls, the smell of Greek seasoning, and the low lights set the mood for a fascinating evening. Rachel pointed to a table in the back of the restaurant as an older waitress approached them.

Rachel soon stopped at the table, waiting on Carlos to pull out her chair for her. "Thank you," she said as she glanced around to see if anyone she knew had entered the restaurant. She never knew when she would be recognized.

She watched Carlos move around to his seat. The pride in being with him grew as she studied his body. She was actually on a date with a great looking guy. Young yes, but still a stud, she thought, as she remembered the words of Cindi from the office earlier.

She reached for the wine list out of habit as she watched Carlos smile and reach for a menu. "I think you must be the one who's a wine fanatic."

She smiled. "I'm not sure I would call myself a wine fanatic, but I've had several years to study wines." She flinched slightly. That wasn't exactly what she wanted to say. Yes, she was older, and perhaps more experienced, but she didn't need to make him think about it. She needed to be careful.

She located several that she thought would be good and narrowed her choice to two which she pointed to. "Which of these do you think would be better?"

Carlos studied the selection and pursed his lips before glancing at her. "They're both Cabernets. The first one is a blend of merlot and the second one has more cabernet franc in it. Since I know I'll be having a rack of lamb tonight, both would be great. However, knowing the wines you liked the most last night, I think you'll like the cab franc the most."

Rachel wasn't sure she believed what she heard, but the words sounded impressive, knowing his age. "Okay, let's go with the cab franc." She turned to the waitress and pointed to the selection. The waitress glanced over toward Carlos for his approval which he quickly gave.

Carlos studied the menu, allowing her more time to study him. She needed to ask him about how he stayed in such great shape. He must be going to the gym often. A quick glance down at her middle section embarrassed her. She needed to do something about her weight.

After he glanced up and caught her staring, she spoke

quickly to cover her intense obsession. "Have you ever eaten saganaki?"

"Sananaki! You mean the flaming cheese?"

Hmmm, he knew more than she thought. "Yes, I thought you might like it."

"Sure, why not." He leaned forward. "I came here to enjoy Greek food and to relax. This place is incredible. How much do you know about the history of this place?"

"I've been here several times. It's a great change of pace."

He continued, as if giving a lecture. "The Greeks are well known for their abilities to dive. When word circulated that some of the best sponges in the world laid on the ocean floor west of Tarpon Springs, over five hundred men quickly made their way here back around the beginning of the nineteenth century. Many made a fortune and returned back to Greece. Obviously, many stayed and opened great restaurants as well as continuing the sponge business."

"Yes, this is a very unique place."

After the wine arrived, the waitress uncorked the bottle and poured a small amount in Carlos's glass for him to taste. She watched him lift the glass to examine the clarity of the wine, swirl the wine with precision and smile before he lowered his nose deep inside the glass. She studied his eyes which quickly refocused on her as he slowly raised the glass to take a sip. She realized he knew much more about wine than she thought, but at his age–how?

He looked over at the waitress. "This isn't bad; however, the wine does need to breath for a minute."

"I understand. Would you like something else while you wait?"

Carlos smiled. "I closed a good sale today. Do you happen to have a split of champagne for such an occasion?"

The waitress eyes danced between the two. "I think I've

just the thing for you." She turned and left without waiting for a response.

Carlos watched her walk away and lowered his head to talk softly. "I hate to bring this up, but tell me more about this murder you started telling me about on the way over here."

Rachel attitude dropped all day. The more the day advanced, the more she worried about the possibilities of a murderer on the loose. She glanced nervously around the room. "The two guys who were killed owned the condo complex where I've sold many condos, and where I still have many left to sell. This market is hard enough, and now I need to contend with more problems."

"Do they have any idea who the murderer is?"

"I know they're investigating many people, but I don't think they have a prime suspect yet." She leaned forward. "I told you that Detective Lindstrom came to visit me this morning."

"Yes, I remember. You said you were going by later to see him again."

"I did. He's trying to find someone with a motive in killing both of them. They built many projects together. It'll take some time to track down all of the people they did business with. In the mean time, he has scared me to death with all of this." She shifted in her seat. "He thinks I should think about buying a hand gun. What do you think?"

"Have you ever used one before?"

"Never! I've had no need for one until now." Her hands shook at the thoughts of holding a pistol in her hands.

"A pistol might be more dangerous to you than to someone else. However . . . just knowing you own one can deter some attackers. If you need help in picking one out, please let me help you. I know guns very well."

Rachel glanced down and swallowed before she

continued, "I've one other item I need to tell you. When the detective asked me about my whereabouts last night I told him about us. I hope you don't mind." She flashed an awkward smile.

"Us? Oh, you mean our spending the night together." His eyes quickly penetrated her thoughts.

"Yes. I told him you would corroborate the story if he needed you to do it. I think he believed me, however," She watched his face for his reaction.

"I think that night will be one we'll always remember."

"Or wish we could forget." She caught herself laughing. "I can't believe I passed out like I did."

"Yes . . . you totally surprised me. I wasn't expecting . . . ."

"Don't say a word. I can't believe what happen either. And I'm not blaming you. I know you drank as much as I did."

"Perhaps more, you drank only one glass of the good wine while I finished the bottle at your place. I should've stopped you."

"That would've been nice, but you acted as if you were enjoying what I was doing for you."

"Of course, what guy wouldn't enjoy it?" He smiled and winked. "I never dreamed you would keep at it all night."

"All night?"

"Well for most of it. I was in too bad a shape to move."

"Ohmigod. You must think I'm terrible."

"Not at all. Don't worry since this'll always be our secret. I'll see if I can return the favor later."

Rachel leaned back in her seat. "Well for now, you can simply be my bodyguard until this killer is located. That will be payment enough for now."

"It'll be my pleasure." He reached for the wine to pour the first glass for the evening.

"I'm serious. This killer is starting to scare me." As her voice cracked, she knew she sounded frightened.

He smiled. "I can understand. Anytime you need someone to look out for you, call me." He extended his glass toward her.

"Thanks. I appreciate the offer." She allowed her eyes to graze over his body again as the thoughts in her mind raced. While he remained much too young for her in many ways, he also brought out an intense inner feeling she couldn't deny.

"Are you hungry?" He glanced at the menu.

"Yes, I think so. However, I'm trying hard to watch what I eat. I may order a Greek salad."

He cocked his head to one side. "I think what I want is a rack of lamb."

Not fair, she thought. I eat almost nothing, and he eats like a horse. He has all muscles and no fat, and I'm stuck with this big cahootus. "How do you stay in such great shape and eat like you do?"

"I stay active and work out every morning. I don't always eat like this, but tonight I wanted to celebrate." He lifted his glass again. "To a great night."

Chapter 11

Rachel handed her condo keys to Carlos, allowing him to open the door for her. The wine made her feel good, but she hoped she would remain in much more control than she had the night before. She surveyed his body again as he turned his back. The effect of her unrestrained assessment sent another wave of heat over her since they were entering her place again.

After he opened the door, he stood to one side to allow her to walk ahead. "Thank you. I hope you don't mind doing me a favor by checking the condo for me. The recent murders are making me be cautious, perhaps too much, but then again, you never know." She smiled, waiting on him to agree.

He smiled and closed the door behind them before venturing through the condo. The entrance into the condo which was across from the dining room slightly opened to the kitchen. While she only owned a two bedrooms condo, the square footage measured large for a condo in St. Petersburg. As she watched him walk in front of her, she wished she could read his mind. How did he really like her place?

After having cleared most of the condo, he stopped in the kitchen. "I remember this room. I would love to cook some meals here."

Rachel laughed. "I'm not sure the oven has ever been used. I never cook." She glanced around the kitchen and noticed how new most of the appliances looked.

"What a shame. I love to cook."

Rachel walked over toward the refrigerator. "I'm not sure there's anything here to cook."

"I remember you talking about how much you work. Working all of the time has to get old." He kept studying the kitchen.

"Well, if you really want to use the kitchen and cook me a meal, you're welcome to it anytime. I'll not stop you."

Carlos walked around the kitchen, admiring the design. "I think that would be great."

He glanced at the living room, as Rachel walked into the room behind him. She studied the couch where she slept the night before. "Most of the time this is comfortable, but I still have a headache from last night."

He smiled and walked over to the couch, straightening one of the pillows. "Perhaps, I can give you a massage later." Rather than walking behind her and giving her one right now as she would've hoped, he pointed toward the sliding door leading toward the balcony. "I think I need to check out the balcony as well." He walked on without waiting for a response.

As he opened the door and stepped outside, a gentle breeze came in from the bay. She watched him survey the sparkling lights which were scattered in all directions. "It's beautiful from up here."

"Funny, I used to come out here all of the time, but I seldom use the balcony anymore." She glanced around and couldn't really understand why. Somehow with Carlos standing beside her, the view generated new feelings in her.

As she walked over to him and pushed closer beside him, she pretended to shiver. He turned toward her slightly and placed an arm around her before he again returned his attention to the scenery around him. "I think this would be a great place to drink a glass of wine after work."

She smiled, thinking about the night before. "We drank

plenty of wine last night. We can open another one if you want, but you'll need to keep me warm."

She saw him glance at the wine cooler in the living room. "Wine might help to keep us warm." He backed from her slightly. "I might need to watch you closer tonight however, you know, just to make sure you don't drink too much."

"Don't remind me, but remember, I'm a big girl, and I don't think you can out-drink me two nights in a row." *Is that a challenge I just offered him?*

After smiling, he moved back into the living room and started to study the wines in the cooler. Like a small puppy dog, she followed him. "If you don't mind, I think I'll change these clothes and put on something more comfortable."

"Not a problem." He positioned one bottle where she could read the label. "Do you remember this one?"

"I think so." She smiled and glanced at her bedroom. "I'll be back in a moment."

After closing the door behind her, she moved fast. While she was practically throwing herself at him, he walked around so casually. She needed to find something nice, something sexy, but yet conservative. She started stripping the Dolce and Gabbana dress off as soon she stepped out of her Prada shoes. She slowly walked to her closet and hung them carefully, wondering if he had noticed the quality of her clothes. While he dressed so casually, he still looked like a million dollars.

She stepped in front of the mirror to study her shape. Not too bad . . . okay, who was she kidding? She had to lose some weight. She knew that her large breasts might be the only assets she could light his fire with. She decided to leave her panties on, but she hesitatingly removed the bra. After thinking that a fluffy white robe hanging in front of her would be perfect, she pulled it on and tightened the belt.

Carlos opened the wine and poured her a glass as she entered the room. He nodded his head at her before he reached for his glass. "That does look comfortable."

She knew the belt fasten low enough to allow him to see her cleavage, and a little leg never hurt anything either. She hoped she didn't act as if she was begging for sex again. His pleasant smile confused her, especially since he didn't attempt to look down her robe. Was he not interested, or was she that bad?

"Shall we go back out onto the balcony?" He pointed toward the sliding door they had left open.

"Sure, why not?" She followed him to the railing at the end of the balcony and snuggled in closer to him, allowing him to place an arm around her. "How did you decide on this wine?"

"I knew you wanted something to warm up with, and this wine is a Pinot Noir which should do nicely." He lifted his glass and touched hers.

She slowly tasted the wine as a smooth robust flavor exploded in her mouth. With the wine adding the perfect mood, she allowed her arm to reach around his waist. The texture of his muscles quickly registered as she tried to control a sudden tremble in her hand. "You feel good," she whispered before she thought about what she was saying.

He smiled, but didn't say a word. However, he did pull her closer to him, for which she felt happy. She began to massage his back, almost with an uncontrollable urge. "I think someone promised me a massage."

He made it clear he wanted to study the view, but he slid his hand toward her side anyway. "Yes I did." He reached for her hand and led her back inside after he closed the outside door. When he started to stop at the couch, she walked in front of him, leading the way toward her bedroom. He didn't object. This was a good sign as she breathed deeply.

After stopping in front of the bed, he turned to face her, allowing her to make the first move by wrapping her arms around his neck. His massive shoulders and height excited her more than she had remembered from before. She pressed her breasts in close to him, hoping he would notice them.

She backed from him slightly as he pointed to the bed. "Lay down and I'll see if I can make you happy."

She liked the words he used as she flashed him a large smile before glancing down at her robe. "Do I need to take this off?"

"That's totally up to you." For the first time, she saw him glance down to study her breasts.

She reached for her tie and pulled, allowing the robe to come lose and expose her skin. She wanted him to lift it off her shoulders so it would fall to the ground, but he waited for her. What the hell, she slid it off on her own.

He studied her breasts as he raised his hands to hold them. "They're very nice."

She groaned softly as his soft but warm hand massaged her shoulder. She leaned her head backwards to his face and watched his eyes focusing on her tits. She closed her eyes, hoping he might kiss her, but nothing happened.

"Would you like another glass of wine before I give you a massage?" he asked.

She stared at him. "Are you trying to get me drunk again?"

"No . . . not really. I simply think it's a great wine."

"Sure, please pour me another one."

He quickly returned from the kitchen with another glass. She accepted the glass and studied him in front of her. She could tell he had already worked up an erection underneath his pants, a fact which further excited her. "You're not going to go to sleep on me again, are you?"

She laughed and finished the glass in one gulp. "I hope not." She saw him standing so close in front of her. She wanted to touch his cock. *Should I?*

He reached over and placed a hand on her bare shoulder and gently massaged her skin. As he moved closer to her, his cock throbbed right in front of her. Yes . . . she knew he must be thinking of the night before as she reached over and placed her hand directly on it. He didn't move. "I assume you loved what I did for you last night."

"Yes, you were great." He paused. "Perhaps we shouldn't be doing this."

What? Is he trying to back out on me? She increased her pressure on his manhood. "I see no reason to stop, unless you don't like me." She leaned back to allow him to see her fully exposed breasts again.

"No, it's not that. I don't want you to do anything you don't want to do."

"That's crazy. I never do things I don't want to do." She continued to study him.

"Are you sure?"

What is it with this guy? "I'm sure." She looked back at the bulge in his pants since he hadn't backed away from her. She placed her hand on it again. Here goes nothing, she thought, as she reached with her other hand and unzipped his pants while he remained perfectly still. The snap and the belt, the one with the large buckle came next. The pants fell easily. She pulled on the shorts and saw him pulsating in front of her. It looked the same as the night before. "You're going to take care of me too tonight, right?"

"Sure."

She leaned over and kissed the tip of his cock as the pulsating increased. She liked the way he became excited. She slipped her mouth over the end and sucked as he groaned. When she pulled the full length into her mouth, he jerked violently one time after another. She knew he wanted to come, but no, not this time. She leaned back and let his cock throb in front of her. "I think someone offered me a massage."

Seconds later, he pushed her backwards on the bed. "Here, let me help you turn over."

Lying on her stomach, he rubbed the top of her shoulders. His hands massaged her so damn good. Indeed, his hands worked like magic, moving up and down her back, working one muscle after another. She noticed him stand for a second before hearing him kicking off his pants. In seconds, he re-directed his massage up and down her legs as well as her back, making the relaxation incredible.

As Rachel started drifting off in a fantastic sleep, she noticed him pulling down her panties, something she didn't object to at all. After the panties slipped pass her feet, he slid on top of her again, continuing his magic. She couldn't talk, only groan. He reached for her butt and squeezed tightly.

Rachel hoped he would turn her over and massage the front side, but instead, he quickly slid on top of her with his entire body. She groaned as a low shudder rolled over her body and her nipples tightened. She wanted him to touch her pussy, to prepare her for him. Her mouth stayed dry, and her breathing became harder.

Carlos pushed her legs apart. *What did he have on his mind?* When he slid higher, she understood. His dick slid along her legs, quickly moving toward her crotch. She should say something. She wasn't sure she was ready. He throbbed against her outer lips, gently exploring. The tip slid in easily. Good, she felt wetter than she thought. He apparently knew it as well as he thrust inside without hesitation. This wasn't the way she wanted to have sex, but this position wasn't bad. She lay still, allowing him to do all of the work. His thrusting increased steadily. She knew he penetrated deeper and deeper into her with each shove. She couldn't remember ever screwing like this before. This position was new to her, and not bad.

He stopped for a minute. "I need some protection, but I don't think I have any with me."

What? She had never thought about the possibility of pregnancy. With the last boyfriend she had been on a pill. Surely, he carried some rubbers or something with him. "You don't have anything with you?"

"No. Do you have any here?"

"I haven't had a boyfriend in a long time." Reality set in. She wanted him, but what to do?

He leaned over and kissed her cheek. "I'm sorry."

"Can you play with me?" She turned over on her back and spread her legs. She looked at his dick still fully erected. "Please, I'll help you also."

Carlos leaned over to her and allowed his finger to find its place. She immediately groaned loudly as his fingers massaged her briefly before entered her, spreading her wetness around. It felt so damn good as the convulsion kept building. It had been so long. She grabbed the back of his head, letting her fingers work through his hair. Ohmigod! The relief exploded through her body.

The sensation returned over and over for what seemed forever. This had to be the best ever. She went limp as her breathing slowly returned to normal. After she finally opened her eyes, she saw Carlos leaning over her with a pleasant smile, pleasantly studying her.

Rachel rubbed his skin, exploring the smooth but muscled body. She lowered her hand and massaged up and down his torso. On one trip down he reached for her hand and moved it to his dick. She suddenly remembered her promise. She had no way out of it.

After he turned on his side and pulled her toward him, she kissed his chest and worked her way downward. She stopped briefly at his navel and sucked on it. He pushed his hips toward her, eagerly waiting for her as she slid down further and saw his pulsating pride. She opened her mouth and allowed him to enter her. Since she felt exhausted from him massaging her and bringing her to a great climax, she hoped this would be over quickly.

For while she felt like she owed him this, she actually wanted him to be happy and in return, hopefully want her as much as she wanted him. She slid over the shaft and increased her sucking force. He pushed forward over and over until she knew this was it. She could feel the buildup of energy inside him. As she swallowed and swallowed, she knew he must be happy. Surely this would be only the beginning of many great times with him–surely.

Chapter 12

Rachel hung up the phone from another previous buyer calling her office to complain about the falling market. *When would it end?* The market needed to come back soon. She rubbed her forehead, attempting to massage away her growing headache.

A knock at the door startled Rachel enough to force her to adjust the look of doom on her face. When she recognized Jody, her fellow real estate friend, a candid smile quickly replaced the false one she had forced. "Hi there, remember me?" Jody walked in and sat across from Rachel's desk.

"I think so," Rachel said with a sarcastic return.

"Since you've been with your boy toy, we don't ever see you anymore." She winked.

Rachel enjoyed the last few weeks with Carlos, where she had walked a delicate line between treating him as a boy toy, and in reality, become more like a baby doll for him. However, since she knew her image meant everything, she needed to keep it up. "Hmm, we've been busy."

"It must be nice." She glanced around the room. "So . . . how's your business going?"

"It could be better. How about yours?" Rachel straightened some papers on her desk.

"It sucks, but I think the market will be better soon." Jody played with her jewelry, a nervous habit she slipped into often, and one that always amused Rachel.

"Has the detective been by to ask you any more questions on the deaths in your complex?" Jody intensified her focus.

"Not lately, but I know he has seen several of the other

owners." Rachel leaned back in her seat.

"The pressure is getting to me. I'm thinking of selling my condo. What do you think?"

The shock registered on Rachel's face. "You want to sell in this market?"

"I think trade would be a better term." Jody kept swinging her necklace in a small loop.

"You know the problem. The units have a history of deaths in them. That's what's bringing the prices down so low, and why I'm having such a hard time selling the rest of them." Rachel leaned back in her chair. "Under the law we have to disclose this information."

"I understand the law," Jody said, "I also know I feel uneasy in the condo most of the time. It's hard to describe, but I think things in my condo are being moved. It's kind of like someone is moving them slightly to let me know they've been inside. I know my curtains are being pulled open a little. I would never leave them like that."

Rachel could feel the apprehension in her friend's voice. "Have you discussed this with the detective?"

The intensity of Jody's jewelry being swung increased. "I don't want him to think I'm a babbling insecure female."

"Don't you own a security system?"

"Well, yeah, but I don't trust the system anymore." Jody stopped swinging the chain for a minute.

"Then change it."

She started swinging the chain again with new vigor. "I've thought about it. In fact, I plan to call the security company and request some changes be made." After breathing in deeply, Jody smiled and regained some of her color that had been draining from her.

Rachel leaned forward, attempting to add to the comfort. "Don't worry, everything will be fine."

"Anyway . . . back to your boy toy. The girls are meeting

again at my place tonight, and I know they'd all love to see you. Do you think you can break away from him for a while?"

Rachel's kneejerk reaction was to glance at her watch. "I don't know. I still have some clients coming in later today. I don't know if they want to see some properties today or tomorrow, but I can call you in a few hours."

Jody's eyes flashed a question that Rachel picked up on quickly. "You still didn't say anything about Carlos."

"I haven't talked to him today, but I'm sure he can take care of himself for a night. He's really a nice guy."

"Hmmm Huh. I bet he is. I know the girls will want to hear all about him."

Rachel's stomach contracted, leaving her nauseous. She tried to hide it. "I bet they would."

Jody laughed as she stood. "I think you'll tell all after we pump some drinks into you tonight. Most of the girls will arrive by seven."

"I'll see . . . you know how it goes."

"Unfortunately yes." She turned to one side, as if to make sure that Rachel saw her new Chanel purse. Yes, it looked beautiful. "I know we'll see you later."

Rachel smiled as Jody left, while wondered how she planned to handle these friends of hers. How was she going to hide the fact that Carlos wasn't, as they would imply, a boy toy? The last thing she wanted them to know was that he was turning her into a toy for his use instead.

***

The German couple took forever to view the last house in Clearwater. Rachel knew the party would be in full swing by the time she arrived, but knowing that she would be the talk of the hour, she rushed to make a showing. At least she was close by.

The entire party was standing in the entrance as she

entered. Their unstable moves indicated just how much the booze had flowed. "Hello everyone." She smiled broadly and scanned the room. Mary Jane, Margaret, and Gloria were crowded behind Jody. Rachel slowly pulled the door close behind her.

"We've opened several bottles of wine, take your pick." Mary Jane pointed to the kitchen behind her.

"Wine does sound good." Rachel moved past the crowd, feeling the pressure of their attention on her.

She located a red, a cabernet, and started to pour. She loved her new outfit, and was now glad that she had stopped by her condo to change before she met the German couple. She glanced around to discover the group following her like a group of dogs in heat. She knew what they had on their minds.

Margaret lifted her glass first. "TO FRIENDS." While all of the girls lifted their glasses to the center, their focus quickly shifted toward Rachel. "I know you've a story to tell, and we want all of the juicy details."

Rachel allowed her stare to flow from one to the next in a slow controlled manner. "I bet you would." She smiled broadly, as if she hid a secret she wasn't going to let go of easily.

Gloria, with a devilish smile, reached for the bottle and poured more wine for Rachel. She poured to the point that the glass would be hard to hold and Rachel would have to start drinking. "You know we want to know. We can keep a secret. You know we can be trusted."

Sure, Rachel thought. The stares became intent and she knew she could only resist so long. "Okay, you guys. What do you want to know?" Rachel slid into one of the bar stools by the kitchen island.

All of the girls' echoed one word, "Everything."

"Okay . . . I've been spending a lot of time with Carlos."

"And . . . how is he?" It was like Margaret to strike straight at the heart of things.

A larger than ever type smile flowed across Rachel's face. "Fantastic, or perhaps that's not a good enough word." She batted her eyes.

"I never thought you could pull it off." Margaret raised her glass, as if to salute her.

"So . . . what have you been doing together?" Gloria leaned forward, flashing her eyes lids that she had painted a dark blue to accent her naturally colored eyes.

Rachel nodded her head forward enough to indicate she should know the answer to her question.

"I mean besides the obvious." Gloria faked a blush before returning her focus on Rachel.

"He enjoys doing many things. I'm afraid he may be more active than this girl's used to. He does have a lot of . . . endurance." She laughed low and deep.

"Yes, I could tell from here he looked very athletic." Mary Jane held a hand above one arm muscle to emphasize the size of his biceps.

While they all wanted details, Rachel hoped to not have to give any more than she needed to. She knew Carlos wouldn't appreciate the humor. Since she had a position to maintain, and the attention and envy coming from these women made her feel great.

"I can tell she wants to keep this hunk all to herself. I guess this won't be another guy, like our masseur we played with earlier. However, I don't say I blame her. Let me know when you get tired of him." Mary Jane smiled, as she patted Rachel on the shoulder.

"By the way, where is *boy toy* tonight?" Jody asked, joining in on the fun.

"I talked to him a few hours ago, and I told him I was coming by here. He said he had some friends he hasn't seen

much of lately, and would grab some beers with them."
Rachel lifted her glass and drank a long sip of the wine.

"Hmmm huh. Perhaps we can meet his friends one night.
Perhaps he could even bring them by here." Margaret
glanced over at Jody.

"Hmm yourself. I don't think this is the place to have an
orgy. These condos already have enough of a history to live
down." Jody glanced around the room as the girl's mood
around her turned seriously attentive.

Gloria spoke quickly, obviously not wanting to end the
fun. "I'm sure a little party wouldn't hurt the image here.
Have they learned anything new on the murders?"

"As far as I can tell they have no leads, but are still
digging. I told Rachel earlier I'm thinking of selling my unit
and moving to another one on the beach somewhere." Jody
glanced over at Rachel.

Gloria apparently didn't want the conversation to end her
good time, so she quickly changed the subject. "You know,
we haven't been out together for a long time. I heard about a
new place that opened a few days ago that's suppose to have
a great band and dancing. We can all go there later tonight if
you want to."

The girls glanced around with heads nodding yes. The
wine flowed quickly, and most of them knew by having
several of them together it would be less awkward than
going on their own. "Good, I'll call for a van that can take
us. This way we can all go together." Mary Jane moved
quickly to open her cell phone.

Rachel glanced at her watch and hoped the group
wouldn't stay out too late.

Chapter 13

Rachel watched Mary Jane rush to a vacant table before another group at the nightclub could claim it. Jody quickly walked over to another table and asked for a fifth stool which wasn't being used. An older guy with long, gray hair nodded, indicating the chair was unoccupied and she could have it.

With all five firmly in place, a waitress walked over, ready to take orders. The music played so loud each girl had to yell their order to her. The low lights also made focusing hard, especially with the flashing overhead lights above the dance floor.

Rachel glanced around the bar, which was decorated to excite the crowd of party revilers that frequented the bar. The neon lights of many well known types of liquor were scattered around the room.

Mary Jane yelled over the music. "This is an interesting place, but kind of loud."

With the drinks ordered, the group tried to focus on the dance floor. A small army of want-to-be dancers packed the entrance to the crowded dance floor. Many of the couples had dressed to dance. "Wow, I never thought this place would be so crowded. Perhaps we should've waited until the newness dies off. We've some serious competition in finding any free men here," Gloria shouted above the music.

After a song ended, and much of the crowd left the floor, one guy moved across the floor and ushered his partner under the spotlight. His flamboyant steps made Rachel think of a professional model's walk. With the remaining crowd quickly moving to the side of the floor, making a larger area available to him and his partner, he dominated the attention of everyone. Eventually, the band began to tune their guitars for the next song, but gave no indication of the song they had selected.

With the hush falling over the crowd, the lead singer approached his mic. "And by special request, we'll play a song no one will ever forget." The crowd waited patiently as the band soon started the Bee Gee's classic *Staying Alive.*

Rachel suddenly recognized Carlos, as he went into a perfect rendition of John Travolta's famous dance from the movie Saturday Night Fever. His movements and style electrified the crowd which urged him on. Rachel's quick glances around the table confirmed that all of her friends knew the guy dancing was Carlos. Their mouths all opened with astonishment, or was it shock?

Rachel refocused on Carlos, as he executed one sexy move after another. Wow, he danced well. Her mind flashed back to the times she had made love to him.

Jody nudged Rachel in a teasing display of fun. "You go girl. This guy has missed his calling. He should've been a professional model. I'd buy anything he's selling."

The pride swelled in her until she saw his partner. In her early twenties, slim and built like a ballet dancer, her long blonde hair flowed as she matched Carlos moves. After following a few more moves, the rest of the crowd quickly moved in on them to hunt for their own dance space. Carlos and his partner quickly vanished in the crowd.

"Wow, he's one hell of a dancer." Gloria stood, trying to relocate him. "Are you going to dance with him tonight?"

The knot in Rachel's throat caused her problems swallowing the sangria she had ordered. "I don't think so. I'm not a dancer."

"Come on, it'll be fun." Gloria eyes flashed in a frenzy of

excitement.

"No. There's no way. I think it's good for him to have a night out like this. I never knew he danced so damn well. I'll need to make him take me out later." She lied. She could ever learn to dance like them. *How am I ever going to compete with a dance partner like this?* She slowly slid lower in her seat and hoped he wouldn't spot her tonight.

Rachel's friends didn't press her on the subject, to which she whispered a private *thank you* under her breath. Perhaps they knew the truth, perhaps not. In any case they were true friends down deep.

After several more drinks, and especially since no guy had asked any of them to dance, the girls decided that it was time to call for the taxi van and go home and back to their private lives. Reality was so sad, but so true. While the girls excelled so much in their professional lives, they all failed miserably in their personal lives.

As they stood to leave, Rachel made one last glance at the floor. Carlos was still dancing on the floor, moving eloquently around a new partner; one as beautiful and talented as the previous one. She smiled, as she knew they couldn't resist him any more than she could. *Will the girls ever believe I control him on a leash anymore? Could I even convince myself that I do either?* She definitely had work to do and plans to make. This competition wasn't over yet, and not by a long shot.

***

Rachel remotely unlocked her BMW and opened the door fast, hoping to slide inside and to presumed safety. While it wasn't that the garage under Jody's condo was unsafe, the stories she had told earlier did keep her mind working over time. With the murderer still on the loose, she was glad to have Carlos with her most of the time. Now, if she could only hold on to him.

She turned onto the road running in front of the gulf and accelerated. With visions of Carlos still dancing in her head, she replayed his moves on the floor as she quickly daydreamed about dancing with him. While these thoughts of dancing with Carlos excited her for a moment, they soon turned to depression when she realized she knew nothing about dancing.

Rachel glanced in the rear view mirror at a car that was following about fifty yards behind her. She didn't remember one pulling in from the side driveways or overtaking her. As her mind raced, she kept her eyes focused on the car.

When she saw a couple standing at an intersection in front of her, she slowed down to see if they planned to cross or not. They remained, however, on the side of the road, apparently waiting on someone. Rachel glanced in the rear mirror again to see how close the strange car was staying behind her. It had vanished–no lights were anywhere.

As she approached her turn to pass over the intercostals waterway, she breathed easier, knowing she would be home soon. She glanced in her mirror again. With a new set of lights following her, she floored the accelerator. Seconds later, she glanced back; the car had made no attempt to keep up with her. She breathed slower, but increased her speed anyway.

Why couldn't Carlos be with me tonight when I need him? Okay, the night may have been her fault. She's the one who allowed her friends into talk her into seeing them tonight, leaving the door wide open for Carlos to go out dancing on his own. Another thought entered her mind. What if Carlos discovered someone new and found her irresistible? And by the way, who were these girls? She only hoped that they were strangers he had picked up as dance partners, and not someone he knew or liked. Surely he wouldn't take one of them home and to his bed. As the sudden thought raged out of control, she forgot all about the car behind her.

Rachel eventually glanced behind her again, and when she saw no one following her, her thoughts returned to Carlos. *And just where were the friends Carlos was going to drink beers with tonight?* She had assumed his friends were guys and not girls. While they had made no commitment to *not see* other people, and this was something she thought she wanted, she now had second thoughts.

Her mind went back to only a night before where she had dinner with him and had him follow her back to her place. She knew she had seduced him again, but the money she spent on an expensive bottle of wine was well spent. She also worried that if she pushed too hard, he might leave. Nevertheless, she knew that she must find a way to control him, to make him her *boy toy*. She suddenly began to hate the use of this term, especially as used by her friends.

She knew she was losing control, and she really had no one close to confide in. Like Carlos, her parents had died when she was young and this dangerous ground she was walking on scared her. She would call him tomorrow and try to strengthen her grip on him. He wanted referrals, and access to her client base. She would help Carlos, yes, but her assistance would cost him.

After Rachel pulled into her condo complex, she watched a car slow as it passed by. She blinked her eyes and turned her head to attempt to identify the car. She glanced too late as she quickly bit her lip; someone knew where she lived now.

Chapter 14

Rachel glanced at the clock on the wall at her office. She had left Carlos a message two hours ago. *Is he still sleeping?* It was almost ten. *Where is he, and more importantly–who is he with?* Her head hurt from the lack of sleep. *Why didn't he call me last night to check on me? He should have. It would've been nice.*

She checked her schedule for the day. It wasn't nearly as busy as it should be. She had spent a lot of time with Carlos lately, and the lower number of sales calls had resulted in less clients. She knew that the distraction was costing her.

Rachel walked to her door and opened it to find Cindi on the phone, but in the process of saying goodbye. The fresh, clean look of Cindi's new outfit made her smile. Cindi always dressed well. Her parents were wealthy and all of the money she earned working for Rachel probably went straight to buying clothes she wanted. Cindi still lived with her parents and openly bragged about how it was stupid to pay for living expenses when she had great parents to pay for everything.

"Cindi, I need to work late tonight and make some calls. See if you can pull up some numbers for me out of the beachfront database."

"Sure. I assume you're not going to be with Carlos tonight?"

"It would be good to, but I'm falling behind on my sales." She wanted to see him, but she would need to arrange to meet him after she finished her calls.

Rachel studied Cindi's intense stares before she spoke.

"Can I bring you some coffee? You look like you could use it."

"I look bad, huh?"

"You look tired." Cindi flashed a large smile, as if she more of a trusted friend, rather than her assistant.

"Perhaps you're right. Coffee sounds good." While Rachel needed a friend, she wondered just how much she could trust Cindi. She wasn't sure, but decided to push anyway. "Have you ever taken any dance lessons?"

A wave of intrigue passed across Cindi's face. "Why, are you thinking of learning to dance?"

Rachel tried to look normal and not to raise too many questions as to why she asked. "I thought lessons might be a fun way to learn some new steps, and I've been to several places lately where knowing how to dance would have come in handy."

"I see. So . . . what kind of dancing do you want to learn?"

Rachel breathed in deep. "I think I need to learn something modern, you know, something you would use dancing around town."

"Interesting, I thought you were asking about ballroom dancing." Cindi leaned forward and continued, "I'm not sure anyone teaches the kind of dancing you see in bars. Most of the time, you just learn from the guys who ask you out."

Rachel tried to keep her face straight, knowing Cindi was probably right. "It was just a thought."

"Let me makes some calls, and I'll let you know what I find out."

Rachel smiled and walked back into her office. After glancing at her body, she wondered who she was kidding. She needed to lose some weight to be any good at dancing. Perhaps a gym is what she really needed.

Two hours later, Cindi walked in with another cup of

coffee. "Are you going out for lunch today, or are you working straight through?"

Rachel glanced at her watch. "I didn't know the time was so late already."

"I'm going to the café around the corner, and I can bring you something back." Cindi placed the coffee on the table. "By the way, I located a place offering dancing classes you might like."

"Really, where is it?"

"It's in Tampa. They offer group lessons three nights a week and each night they learn new dances. You know, dancing might also be a great way for you to meet new people who could be buying or selling."

"Maybe, and I need to do something to relax for a little while anyway. Since I need to go to Tampa for some shopping, I might stop by and see what they have to offer." Rachel knew this was unusual for her, and she really had no time for such, but she still wanted to see what they could do for her. She didn't want to be embarrassed about not knowing how to dance. If she planned on holding onto Carlos, she needed to at least try to learn. After she learned the basic steps, maybe Carlos could help her learn more.

***

The dance studio situated on a street off Dale Mabry looked to be almost vacant. The signs advertising the group and private lessons appeared to have been around forever. She started having second thoughts until she saw a guy walking in the door. Well at least someone was inside. She opened her car door and headed toward the entrance.

As she entered, she saw a large dance floor in front of her that had a string of chairs lining the walls. On one side of the studio she saw a small setting area filled with small tables surrounded with chairs. The wooden dance floor glistened with polish as she contemplated the dance lessons offered at the studio. "Hello," she yelled out, hoping to find someone working inside.

A young woman suddenly emerged from a small office and smiled at her. The guy Rachel had seen entering the door in front of her was now following behind this woman. "Hi, can we help you?"

Rachel smiled broadly before extending her hand toward this guy. "I'm thinking about taking some lessons, and I thought I would find out what you offered here."

"That's great. We would love to see you join us." The guy quickly lifted a brochure from a side table and handed it to her. "My name is Lester, and this is my wife, Nancy."

"Hi, my name is Rachel Contino." She didn't know if they would recognize her name or not. If they did, they acted as if they didn't.

"What kind of dancing do you want to learn?" Lester asked.

"I'm not sure. I think I want to learn what I need to know when I get asked to go out dancing in the clubs."

"I think I understand. We offer many kinds of private lessons, and I think you would also enjoy the group lessons. We've many people coming here to learn to dance and make new friends. They often go out dancing together on the weekends." Lester leaned forward.

"Making new friends could be good for business." Rachel glanced around the studio. "The problem is . . . I never know when I need to work late."

"It's not a problem. You only pay for the lessons you take. If you want to, of course, we offer private lessons and we can be flexible on those times to some extent." Rachel watched Lester studying her before he continued, "How much dancing do you do now?"

She knew she might as well admit the truth. "I do none. This is all new to me."

"Don't worry since we start with simple steps. You'll learn to dance in no time. In fact, we offer a group class tonight to get you started. You can come for free, if you're interested."

"I don't know. I'm still thinking about it." Rachel fought internally over her decision. Perhaps she had moved too fast.

"Here, let me show you something." Lester reached for her hand and pulled her out on the dance floor.

As if on cue, Nancy started some music–a slow waltz type tune. Rachel watched Lester line her up in position before him, as he straightened his back, and flowed even with her. "The first thing we'll learn is the frame. This is the foundation for all dances." He worked with her several moments in adjusting her to the proper position. "Now we move together. Simply take a step backwards as I step forward." As she followed his directions, the steps felt easy enough.

He smiled at her. "Believe it or not, we're dancing. This is really all there is to it."

For some reason Rachel doubted that, but she enjoyed the slow even movements and the reassurance of his touch as she followed his lead. He demonstrated exactly the feel of confidence that she needed as she made her mind up. "Okay, if you think I can learn, I'm willing to give dancing a try."

"Very good. Can you make it tonight?"

"I think so, but I can make no promises." Rachel glanced at her watch.

"Please come tonight since the lesson will be free. This will give you a chance to check us out. What do you think?" Rachel saw Nancy smiling as she waited for an answer.

"I'll try for sure."

"Okay, good. I hope to see you tonight." Lester stood, walked next to his wife and winked. "You'll love it."

Rachel turned to leave as the thoughts of not hearing

from Carlos all morning worried her. She knew she needed to learn to dance, and she definitely didn't want Carlos to know until she had learned how.

***

"I'm glad your back, Detective Lindstrom's waiting for you." Cindi pointed toward Rachel's private office.

A frown crossed Rachel's face. "How long has he been here?"

Cindi leaned forward and whispered, "He's been here for only about five or ten minutes. I started to call you, but I knew you'd be here soon. He appears to be in a serious mood."

"Hmm. I guess you better hold my calls." *What news or questions does he have for me now?*

Rachel walked into her office and saw him studying a file. "How are you, Detective Lindstrom?"

"Hi, your secretary told me you would be back soon. I hope you don't mind me waiting in your office." He made no effort to stand.

Rachel walked to her seat and tossed her business bag on the floor beside her. "What can I do for you today?"

"I received some interesting news today and wanted to see if you can help me." He leaned forward. "I need to know what you know about the loan Jonathan Harrell and Donnie Moore were working on."

"Like I said before, I knew they were trying to line up some new financing, but that's about it." She maintained her glaze on his eyes.

With his face remaining emotionless, he continued to stare back at her. "I also need to know more about your relationship with Carlos Martin."

Rachel wrinkled her eyebrows, but forced her smile to cover the shock she knew had registered. "Why do you need to know about him?"

The detective ignored her question as he increased his stare to the extent she now had to glance away from him. "Have you talked to Carlos today?"

"No . . . why, should I have?"

"He has been in my office for most of the morning answering questions."

What is going on? She breathed deeply, trying to clear her head and think. "What did you want to find out from him?"

"I learned Carlos was attempting to broker a deal with them on refinancing their loan on the condo complex."

Rachel's mouth opened. "What are you talking about? He has no experience in working this kind of deal."

"His input was minimal. He simply extended a referral to another broker, but he still retained an interest."

"He never said anything to me about the loan, and no, I haven't talked to him today. I've tried, but he hasn't returned any of my calls."

He opened his files and glanced at them. "I understand, since we only let him out a few minutes ago. I came straight here after I dismissed him."

Rachel began to shake. "Are you saying he's a suspect in the murders?"

"No. I'm not saying he's a suspect at all. I just need to know what he knows. With an approved loan, I see no reason for Jonathan to commit suicide, or even to suggest that he was suicidal."

"Now, I'm curious. What did he say about this?" The muscles in Rachel's face tightened.

"Carlos said he made a referral for Jonathan when he met him at a business after-hours meeting. He had no idea the loan had been approved. At least that's his story." He glanced at the file again. "On the night when Donnie Moore died, you said Carlos spent the night with you." He allowed the words to trail off, indicating he wanted some feedback.

She steadied her hand, hoping he wouldn't notice the shaking. "Yes, he did."

"And what time did he leave?"

She knew exactly what time it was. Those moments when she woke and realized she had fallen asleep lying in his lap all night giving him pleasure would be permanently pressed in her mind forever. "Like I said, it was eight. I remember being mad at myself for running late getting to my office. We both drank a lot of wine the night before."

She saw a small smile being repressed. "One last question: Are you sure that he did stay with you all night?"

"YESSSSS." She raised her voice, indicating that was the last of her patience in answering these questions.

He acted as if he understood as he lifted his hands. "Sorry, it's something I needed to ask."

Rachel knew her face was turning red, but she now had questions she also wanted answered. "Other than the referral he supplied, what other contact did Carlos have with Jonathan?"

"He said he made a few calls, but that he never met him again after the one time. From talking to him all morning, I think he's telling the truth. We only have a few leads, and we need to follow up on all of them." He glanced around the room before he closed his file.

"I need to ask you something while you're here." She leaned forward to whisper. "I have this feeling that I'm being stalked, and I have several others friends that I know who are having this same sensation."

She heard him lightly whistle under his breath before his facial expressions turned serious. "If you have any doubts at all, don't hesitate to call 911. Also, if you have anyone in particular causing you concerns, I'd be glad to check them out for you."

"That's good to know. I think someone followed me home last night."

"Are you sure?"

"How can you ever be sure? I realize that I might just be paranoid, but I think you understand." Rachel wanted to direct her attention toward him, but his cold, grey eyes haunted her too much. She glanced away, avoiding his stare. His slow, methodical mannerism was driving her crazy.

He stood to leave. "I know in your business you work in the field with many people. As such, I think you need to exercise some extra precautions right now."

"Trust me . . . I do." She pointed out to her secretary. "She knows my schedule and who I'm working with. We also maintain a coded expression to let her know when I think I'm in trouble. This message is sent to the broker so he can intercept for me. She also knows to maintain contact with me until the authorities arrive, if need be."

"I know many realtors have these systems in place, and I'm glad to hear that you're using it." He moved toward the door. "Let me know if you think of anything else that you think I need to know. We'll stay on top of this." He smiled and walked out of the door.

Rachel leaned forward and buried her face in her hands. This pressure was building and quickly becoming too much for her to handle. However, she needed to maintain control, especially in this market. She knew she would make it through this real estate correction, but the sooner the better. Her mind raced to access the information she received. *What is Carlos involvement in all of this? And more importantly, why has he never said anything to her about this loan?*

As she reached for her phone to call him again, she stopped to think about the night she had spent with him. She consumed a lot of wine that night and had fallen into a deep sleep. When she woke the next morning, he was fully dressed and looked all clean and fresh. She really didn't know what time he had gotten up. In fact, she really didn't know that much about him.

Cindi interrupted Rachel's thoughts as she slowly walked in. "I'm sorry to have overheard. What do you think?"

Rachel wondered if Cindi had been listening and just how much she may have heard. "I think I need to talk to Carlos."

"I understand. I still think he had no knowledge of this loan being approved."

"Why do you think that?"

"Call it intuition." Rachel smiled as Cindi moved into the seat in front of Rachel. "Tell me about the dance studio."

A wave of relieve flowing over Rachel's body. Good. While she wasn't going to ask her about sleeping with Carlos, Rachel knew that Cindi must be wondering about it. "The dance studio looked interesting. They offer a group dance lesson tonight that they invited me to."

"That's good since you don't have any appointments tonight. Are you going to take Carlos with you?"

Rachel glanced to one side since she hadn't told Cindi about watching Carlos dance the night before. "I've the feeling Carlos is already a great dancer, and I think this might not be very interesting for him."

"So . . . you're going to surprise him with your new talent later?" Cindi's perky attitude made Rachel feel good.

"Well, this is for Carlos, but not just him. I need to learn anyway, and just maybe dancing will help me to lose a little weight. What do you think?"

Cindi smiled before she stood. "I think dancing would be good for you." As she turned to leave, Rachel glanced at Cindi's slender waist, thinking about how she would love to be so slim. Okay, she would take the lessons.

Chapter 15

As Carlos stood in the doorway to her condo, Rachel studied his blue jeans and a camp shirt that he had pulled over a dark blue tee shirt. With his sandals completing his casual style, he still retained an interesting flair of sophistication. "Hi, I'm sorry I'm late."

Rachel smiled and moved to one side to allow him to enter her condo. "It's okay, I haven't been home long." She closed the door and followed him toward the kitchen.

"How was your appointment?"

Rachel resisted the temptation to tell him that her appointment wasn't business, but a dancing lesson. "Everything went fine." She placed an arm around him after he stopped in front of the island.

Carlos turned to face her. "I know we didn't have much time to talk on the phone today. I would've told you about the referral I gave Jonathan if I thought the loan amounted to anything, but I never heard anything and thought the application had been turned down. In fact, I did try to call Jonathan several times, but he never returned any of my calls."

She studied his deep stare. His dark-brown eyes remained, as usual, so overpowering to her. "I think I believe you." She leaned in closer to him and his muscular body immediate affected her as it always did. While he didn't return the hug, he didn't move away from her either.

"It's my job to find new clients and to take care of them as best as I can." He leaned into the side of the island.

"I understand. Relaxing is exactly what you should be

doing." She moved in closer to him, further enjoying the feel of his muscular body next to her. "I'm so glad you're here with me tonight."

He smiled as she massaged his chest. "Me too–it's been a long day, and one I really wish I could forget."

"Perhaps tonight I can make you forget everything. So . . . if it's a deal, we'll leave business behind tonight." Rachel concentrated on his eyes.

His returned smile indicated that he was tired, but willing to follow her lead. "Yes, tomorrow will be another day." He raised his arm to allow her to move in closer to his chest. Without hesitation he pulled on her robe, and it fell open, revealing her totally naked body underneath.

She quickly blushed, but allowed him to view her naked. As she really wished she could lose some weight, she hoped his attention would be on her breasts and not her extra pounds in her midsection. While she waited, hoping he would touch her on his own, she finally becoming impatient and reached for his hand to direct it to one of her breasts. "Do you like them?"

"Of course, they're very nice." While he gently massaged the one he held, but he never raised his other hand.

"Let's go to the bedroom." She reached for his free hand and pulled him behind her after giving him a devilish smile. When she reached the front of the bed, she started to allow the robe to fall to the floor, but stopped as she thought of her extra pounds. "Perhaps we need to turn out the lights first."

"Why?"

"You know I'm a little *self-conscious* about my weight."

She watched him smile. "I guess we need to work on getting you in shape one day."

This was not exactly what she wanted to hear, and he didn't really need to agree with her. However, after she nodded her head toward the light switch, she felt happy to have him obey her request. "Thank you." With only a slight amount of light filtered in from the windows, this was much better.

She allowed the robe to fall to the floor, as she imagined his eyes were still studying her. She felt his hand move to her breasts again and slightly massage them. "Your hands feel so good." She raised her hands to his face and caressed his smooth and tender skin. Apparently he had shaved before he came over. "Here, let me help you remove your shirt for you."

He released her breast and directed her to the bed, pushing her backward until she sat on the bed in front of him. In the dim light she watched him strip, revealing his muscular body that shimmered in the filtered light. She reached for his stomach and examined the tightness of his incredible six-pack. "You look so good," she gasped, as she studied every inch, and each individual muscle.

After his pants fell, he leaned over to remove his shorts. Even in the dim light, she could see his manhood in front of her. He had moved her in this position many times before, and she knew exactly what he wanted. Ever since the first night, she had never refused him. Not that she liked doing it for him; she simply didn't know how to tell him she didn't. He stood still, waiting.

As she reached toward his throbbing cock, he closed her hand around it. In seconds, he placed his other hand on the top of her head, massaging her scalp, as she, in turn, worked her hand up and down his shaft. She heard a deep groan as he increased the pressure on her head. She leaned forward and kissed the tip, as the pressure on her head increased again. Unable to resist, she opened her mouth and let his dick slid inside. He entered her so deep that she knew he must be touching her tonsils. His hips immediately began to rock forward as she knew he was losing control. She allowed all she could take of his huge dick into her mouth.

Damn! She wanted to make him happy, but she wanted to be satisfied also. She tried to slow down his intensity by removing his cock from her mouth and kissing it, but he thrust again toward her and re-entered her mouth. She forced her head back. "Please make love to me tonight. I need it. I promise I'll make you happy again later, I know you love this."

He stood still for a minute. "Okay, I understand." He pushed her backward on the bed. She slid higher upon the bed as he climbed on top of her. Multiple kisses soon slithered around her neck as his hands moved to her breasts, and his fingers pinched her nipples.

She pulled his head lower as she needed to feel his mouth, his lips on her tits. The warm moist feeling of their touch sent her into new waves of spasms. His tongue circled her, driving her further over the edge. She ran her fingers through his hair, pulling him to her. "Ohmigod!"

He straddled her and worked his way upward. Soon, his dick positioned between her tits. He pulled them together and started fucking her tits. She loved the sensation.

She now had flashes of heat shooting through her body. "I want you. I want you now."

He slid down and adjusted his weight on her while his manhood rubbed her stomach as he worked his way lower. She knew she felt wet, but she would've loved for him to play with her first. Apparently he understood what she needed as well since he didn't hesitate. After having made love to her many times now, he pushed directly toward her with his full length slipping in without any hesitation. She arched her back and lifted her legs slightly, as his thrust increased in strength and pace.

Rachel thought about the lack of a condom, but she knew he would want oral if she said anything. Yes, she knew this was dangerous, but she couldn't stop now. While she wanted to tell him how much she loved it, she knew to remain silent. She might say the wrong word. Oh God! If this was love, why couldn't she tell him?

He raised on his knees enough to where he could touch her. With his fingers massaging her, she could no longer hold back. The climax built and built, robbing her of all control until she let out a scream as she came. Then another and another followed the first. *Ohmigod! I hope the walls are good enough to hold in these screams.* But then again, she really didn't care. She screamed again.

As she drifted back into reality, he gently moved in and out of her. Wow, sex could never become any better than this. "Thank you." He said nothing, but maintained his slow rhythm. "What can I do for you now?" Being happy and satisfied, she wanted to make him happy.

"Turn over." He moved from her enough to allow her to flip over. "Now get up on your knees."

She obeyed him since she knew what he wanted. He soon entered her as he stretched her open and explored deeper. The angle of penetration excited her immediately. His rhythm increased constantly as she heard him moan. While she had collapsed, he never slowed as he kept going on and on. She knew the problem. She wasn't tight enough for him. Even as large as he was, she wasn't tight enough. She could only imagine what her body would be like after she delivered children. This was something else she needed to talk to her doctor about. Oh God, she hoped he wouldn't become too frustrated.

Finally he came to a stop, breathing hard. He turned over to his back and lay beside her. She moved to her back and rested on his shoulder. "Are you okay?"

"Yes, I'm fine." He didn't move.

She knew better. She reached over and wrapped her

fingers around him. While still large, it no longer throbbed. She massaged it, stroking the full length of his shaft. "I guess I owe you."

He remained silent, but she knew. She leaned forward and tightened her fingers around it. "Do you want it?" She wanted to force him to talk to her.

"Yes." He breathed deeply. "I need it."

One thrust is all she needed for encouragement. She just hoped he wouldn't tell anyone about how she did this for him all of the time. However, he did make her happy tonight. "Just lay back and relax."

She leaned forward further until she saw his penis in front of her again. The strokes kept him hard, and she soon noticed the throbbing she had learned to love. She loved knowing she had created such a desire in him. Rachel kissed the tip and opened her mouth again. She wanted to finish this as quickly as possible so she started to suck him hard. Without mercy, she slid up and down on him as fast as she could. The sound of slurping filled the room as it mixed with his loud groans.

"That feels great. I'm going to come." He talked slow as his voice thickened.

Her lips and tongue joined in on the action, ruthlessly working him. His hand moved to the back of her head, pushing her face into him as close as he could. She knew he wanted to make this final moments last as long as he could, but she wouldn't let him rest as she sucked harder.

"Oh shit, oh shit," he finally screamed, as he could no longer contain himself. He came hard as he convulsed every muscle in his body. The hot cum came spurting out of his dick like a geyser. She swallowed fast. She had to, as he came over and over. Finally, she felt his body relax. Apparently he felt too exhausted to move or talk. She kept licking and swallowing. She wanted him happy. She wanted him to remember how good she treated him. She wanted to tell him three little words. *Why can't I tell him? Why not?*

Instead, she watched him drift off to sleep. As she massaged his scalp and snuggled in next to his shoulder, she knew he wouldn't sleep long–he never did.

***

"Are you sure you don't want to spend the rest of the night here?" Rachel watched him stand and reach for his shorts. The sight of his naked body dominated her thoughts, even after making love for hours. She watched him slip the shorts up, covering his massive manhood.

"Yes. I think I need a good night sleep since I've a lot of catching up to do tomorrow. The guys kept me out late last night also."

Guys? Hmm huh. She saw the *guys* last night, but she decided not to press the point for now. It would be better if he never knew she saw him dancing last night. "I do have something for you before you leave."

He smiled broadly as he pulled his dark tee over his head. "What is it?"

"Well, I couldn't help myself when I stopped by the mall this afternoon. I had to do something while I waited for my client, so I did a little shopping." She studied his face since a little shopping was an understatement.

She stood and walked over to her closet to retrieve a large fluffy robe to cover her naked body with. Next, she reached into the back of the closet and retrieved several packages. "I hope you like this."

He sat on the side of the bed as she handed him the gifts which had been professionally wrapped by the department store. "Wow, you shouldn't have done this!" He flashed a smile.

"Well, if you remember, we have several dinners coming up with some of my friends, and I want you to look great."

He slowly opened the packages which contained several Gucci shirts, a sports coat, shoes, and a belt. His smile faded as he studied the gifts. "You shouldn't have. These are expensive."

Yes, his comment was an understatement. She had spent several thousand dollars. "Don't worry about it. I want you to look good."

He studied the belt first. "You don't like my belt buckle, do you?"

"Not . . . that it's not nice, but I think this looks much more sophisticated, don't you?"

A shock registered when he tossed it beside her. "Don't think that I'm not grateful, but I like to buy my own clothes."

The hurt had to register on her face. "If you don't like them, we can go back and exchange them."

"This is too much of a gift. Thank you . . . but . . . ." He glanced at the other gifts next to the belt.

She couldn't believe what she heard; he was rejecting her gifts–her gifts! She forced herself to think before she spoke. *You ungrateful kid*! "Well . . . we can talk about it later."

"Perhaps." His smile showed every indications of being forced.

"Okay, okay, we'll talk about it soon. Where would you like to go out to eat tomorrow?"

"I'm not sure. I've a lot of work to catch up on. I'll call you." He stood and slipped into his camp shirt. "I'm sorry about the clothes, and I hope you understand." He didn't wait for a response as he turned to go.

A sinking sensation overtook her as she thought he might be walking out on her. "Wait." She moved toward him and hugged him from behind. "I'll take the clothes back."

"Thanks." He turned and kissed her forehead. "I'll call you."

Chapter 16

Rachel twirled and adjusted her balance before completing a double spin on the dance floor at the studio. The dance instructor controlling her movements gave her the confidence she needed to stretch her abilities. She loved the nights of dancing and the great feelings of accomplishment that came with it. She still couldn't believe she was doing this.

After the music stopped, the instructor stood in front of her and held both of her hands. "I think you're really getting the hang of this."

Rachel beamed a large smile. "It feels good, but I know I'm still a long way from being as good as the other girls here."

He squeezed her hands harder. "They've been dancing for a long time, and you've only been at it for two months. I think you're doing great."

"Uh Hmm–right. I know you tell that to all of the girls." She glanced around at the group of other woman being taught by other instructors. The private lessons weren't cheap and Rachel knew many of the women came here only because they had no one special to teach them. Most of them were much older than Rachel.

"Really, I think you'll be ready to enter some competitions soon."

"Competition–me? I don't think so." She blushed at the thought of dancing in a competition, but it would be fun. *Who am I kidding? I'm not ready to let anyone know I'm taking lessons, especially Carlos.*

"Don't be so modest. You'll do great. I can help you prepare for it." He remained so firmly placed in front of her that she knew it was useless to resist.

"We'll see." The thoughts kept running in her head since if she was to do well, it would give her the confidence she needed to go out dancing with Carlos. Things weren't going great with him for the last few weeks. Ever since she had presented him with the gift of clothes he had acted differently, strangely ignoring her except for the sex they enjoyed several times each week.

"I'm not going to take no for an answer. In fact, I've a surprise for you today when we talk about your next set of lessons." Rachel knew what that meant; they wanted her to sign up for more lessons and to spend more money. Her sales had fallen dramatically recently, and several of her rental condos remained unoccupied. For the time being she knew she needed to start watching her money.

"I'll take a look at what you have to offer, but remember the real estate market is terrible right now, and I really need to be working harder." While she knew the time spent with Carlos and these dance lessons cut into her work time, she was too scared to not make time for Carlos. If she worked late, he went out on his own and all she needed right now was for him to find someone new.

"Here, let me give you my surprise." The instructor pointed to one of the small tables off to the side of the dance floor. "I know you want to learn to dance good enough to turn some heads when you go out dancing. Am I right?" He pulled out a chair for her.

"That would be great if it happened, but I doubt it will." Rachel adjusted into the chair as she crossed her arms.

"We've a dance cruise coming up in about a month, and we'll be holding a dance contest onboard." He smiled and handed her a flyer.

Rachel glanced at the information, and the price of three hundred dollars for the entrance fee. "I'll just be throwing away money trying to do this."

"I did say that I had a surprise for you." He glanced around him and waited for Rachel to unfold her arms. "For those signing up for a new set of lessons, this dance contest will be free. The studio will pay all costs!"

"Wow, that'll be good." She crossed her arms again. "And just exactly how much is these next set of lessons?"

He turned the flyer over. "The cost is seven hundred dollars. This includes everything you'll need to prepare for the competition."

Rachel pursed her lips. "In a competition you need a partner."

"Yes. Don't you have someone you've been dating? You mentioned Carlos's name several times."

"Yes, I know one guy I'm actually trying to learn to dance for. He's very good."

"Then it shouldn't be a problem." He turned the flyer over where she could see a photo of the boat. "I'll tell you what. I'll let you bring him with you several times to the lessons, and in this way I can help you both work together."

Rachel smiled. "Thanks for the offer. I'll think about it."

The instructor smiled, indicating he knew she would do her best to talk him into dancing with her.

***

Where is he? Rachel walked back out to the balcony while she finished her glass of wine. The twinkling lights of the city skyline could only hold her interest for so long. She slid into the lounger and thought of the times Carlos liked to be out here with her. A rush of heat consumed her as she thought of the time he talked her into having sex on the balcony. He stretched out on the lounger and lowered his pants. Like a sex slave she dropped her panties and with her robe as cover from anyone looking their way, she backed into him, straddling him. She closed her eyes, relieving the moment.

When she heard the doorbell ring, startling her out of her fantasy, she rushed to the door to let Carlos in. It would be nice to see why he ran so late.

"Hi, I stopped to buy some wine and cheese. I didn't have time to eat tonight." He walked in and gave her a hug.

After closing the door, she followed him to the kitchen. "I think I might have a few things here you might be able to survive on." She allowed her robe to flow freely, showing off her legs at the bottom and her breasts above. She had removed her bra earlier, allowing her breasts to dance for him, and to hopefully entice him into making a move.

"That's good. You said you had some news for me." He smiled as he glanced into her eyes.

"Carlos, I've heard you're a great dancer." She waited for his response.

"Yes, I love to dance–why?"

"I've been taking some dance lessons for the last month and I was hoping to surprise you one day with it." Rachel fluttered her eyelashes.

A smile spread across his face. "Really!"

"Yes, really. I'm still not sure how good I am, but I'm working hard on it." She loved to see his interest in her lessons. "In fact, the studio where I'm taking the lessons is having a contest in about a month, and I was hoping to talk you into entering the competition with me."

His smile vanished. "What kind of dance contest?"

"It's for students of the studio and their guest. They have rented a boat for a dance cruise, and the contest will be on board. It should be a lot of fun."

"It's going to be hard to dance in a competition if we've never danced before." This wasn't exactly what she hoped he would say.

"Here's the good news. As part of my package, the dance instructor will work with both of us." She smiled and waited for him, hoping he would accept. Surely all of the hard work in learning to dance wasn't for nothing.

"I'll think about it, but I generally don't like dance contest." He reached for the bottle. "I hope you like this one."

She knew he could hold his alcohol much better than she could, and she had already drank one glass of wine. She needed to seduce him not only with sex tonight, but with something stronger. She wondered how he liked brandy. "It looks great, but I recently opened a bottle also. I think I'll stay with the white. Do you like chardonnays?"

He glanced at her bottle on the counter. "I do at times, but usually with dinner." He opened the bottle of Pinot and poured himself a large glassful. "I didn't know you were taking dancing lessons."

She still couldn't tell if he approved or not. She had that hoped he would be impressed. "It's been great exercise and I do need to drop a few pounds." She forced a smile, looking for some support.

"I'm sure it helps. I go to the gym every morning around five to work out."

Five in the morning! There's no way she was going pop her cahootus out of bed so early in the morning. "You've got to be kidding me."

She heard one of the loudest laughs coming from him she had ever heard. "Not at all; I have some buddies that I meet at the gym every morning."

She made a quick note to share this with her girl friends. Perhaps this is where they needed to go to meet guys, especially if they all looked like Carlos. "You go every morning?"

"Almost, since I teach a class on Yoga there three days a week." He raised his glass toward her glass in a small salute.

"So, do you think you can teach me *Yoga*?" She looked at him again for some encouragement.

He smiled and leaned closer to her. "Everyone can learn yoga. It's not a sport you compete in. You do yoga for yourself and set your own goals." He lifted his glass and tossed down a large drink before he motioned for her to follow him to the balcony.

She allowed herself to laugh loud enough for him to hear. "Don't you offer classes anytime later than five in the morning?"

He returned her laugh. "The gym offers other classes, but they cut too much into my work time. I need to be available when my clients can meet with me."

Yes, she knew exactly what he was talking about. This fact Cindi had reminded herself about several times lately. The dance lessons and nights spent with Carlos were cutting deeply into her schedule. Even today she had put off showing a house tonight to be with him. Every time she did this, she knew that there was a chance that another realtor could take over her client. "I understand. How is it going with your clients now?"

"With the prices of real estate declining, the refinancing market has dried up. Thanks to a few short sales, I still make some money. However, I think we should call them long sales since they take so long to close." He laughed and poured another drink. "I say that because the loans, as you know, take a long time to complete."

She joined in on his laughter. "I don't do a lot of short sales, perhaps I should."

"It might be something you should consider. I can get you some numbers of people in the mortgage companies who might be able to help you."

"If this market keeps going like it is, I might take you up on the offer." She stood next to him and surveyed the night lights. She still couldn't believe she hadn't come out here much until she met Carlos. She noticed his glass empty. "Here, let me pour you some more wine."

She walked into the kitchen and poured the glass full. Before she left, she stopped by her liquor cabinet and pulled out the brandy, sitting the bottle on the counter. She studied a little wine in the bottom of her glass and fought the urge to top it off. No, tonight she would stay in control. Tonight, she wouldn't be his toy. Tonight, he would agree to go to the dance contest with her.

They watched the twinkling of the city lights as she made several trips to the kitchen to refill his glass. When he finished the last of the wine, she poured a full glass of brandy for him and walked outside. "Here, I think you'll like this."

He glanced at the glass. "What is it?"

"Since your last glass finished the bottle of wine, I thought you might like some brandy."

He smiled and glanced back at her. "I think I've already drank enough wine." However, he lifted the glass and sniffed the brandy. "It does smell good." After he raised his glass to take a small taste, his eyes quickly opened wide as the strong alcohol registered in his mouth.

"You need to take it slow. It's meant to be enjoyed." She smiled as he moved an arm around her shoulders. She allowed her hand to drop beside her and massage his hips. He didn't move, but she knew he liked it. "You never did say anything else about going to the dance contest with me."

He turned to kiss the top of her forehead. "I'm thinking about it. Who's going to be on this boat?"

"They have many clients taking lessons that I'm sure they'll talk into entering. This dance could be a good way to meet some people. From the prices of these lessons, I'm sure most of those attending will be influential people here in the Tampa area." She could feel the information turning over in his mind. He needed to meet people as much as she did. She had, in fact, introduced him to many of the people she knew. While these connections could be the main reason he kept seeing her, she would like to think the sex was good for him, but she wasn't sure. She also hated to admit her fears, but she had no way of knowing if he wasn't screwing anyone else either. While she forced her mind to avoid the question for now, she knew she needed to talk to him more about this subject and soon.

"Okay, I'll let you know." He turned to watch the flashing lights of a plane above. "When is the dance?"

That was a good sign. "We've about a month to prepare." She rubbed his stomach with her fingers, allowing her fingernails to tease him.

He turned to her and pulled her slightly closer to him. She knew the brandy was lowering his resistance. She lowered her hand to his crotch. While not up to its full strength, she knew it possessed potential. "I think you must be tired tonight."

He raised his glass. "This isn't bad. Give me a minute and I'll pour us another one." She smiled as she watched him walk toward the kitchen.

When he returned with two glasses, she accepted her glass and smiled. She knew this would be her undoing, but the wine earlier had also relaxed her. She moved in closer to him again. He pulled her head toward his shoulder. "I cannot believe the weather is still this warm late at night."

She motioned for him to move to the recliner on the far side of the balcony. She remembered him enjoying her give him a blow job there before. With a slight stagger, he followed her lead and made himself comfortable. She kneeled beside him and whispered. "How does that feel?"

"I think I could go to sleep here and be perfectly happy."

She leaned over and kissed him on the lips. He responded by sucking in on the top portion of her lip. She felt the fire beneath. Perhaps the booze was too strong for him. He wouldn't be fun as a boy toy if he went to sleep on her. She needed to excite him quickly. She lowered her hand on his crotch. It still wasn't too excited, but she knew what to do to correct the situation.

She saw him look around and smile. That's all she needed as she went to work on unzipping his pants. The snap and belt, with the usual large buckle, relinquished their treasure as she pulled his shorts low enough to work her hand around his throbbing manhood. It throbbed on contact as she knew it would. Now that she had him where she wanted him, she suddenly thought about how she wanted to be satisfied also. However, could he make it to the bedroom?

She heard him groan as she massaged him. "I thought you might want something."

"Sure." The words slipped out of his mouth as she knew he was struggling. She opened her robe and leaned over to him, allowing him to kiss her breasts. His tongue worked like light sandpaper, gently rasping her nipples.

"Why don't we go to the bedroom where we can be more comfortable?" She rose slightly above him, but never released her grip on his manhood.

"I don't know. I think I like it right here." He looked at her hand playing with him.

She stopped with a thought. "I know you like the way I suck on it. If I do it for you again, right now, you'll take me to the dance cruise, I mean, we've a deal, right?"

He said nothing for a few moments. She increased the rhythm on his shaft, moving up and down the full length. He opened his eyes briefly as she knew what he was thinking. She stopped stroking and slid her hand up toward his stomach where she stopped, waiting on him to respond.

"Okay, okay . . . you win." As he reached for her hand and pushed it lower, she smiled, knowing he would be spending time dancing with her. She would work on this sex issue later since she needed to be satisfied more often also. While her mounting desires needed attention, this would be one more night of being his party girl.

"Good, we have a deal." She lowered her head to see it pulsating. She would've never believed he had turned her into such a sex slave for him. It was suppose to be the other way around. However, she knew, or at least she hoped, no one else would ever know the truth.

His body remained relaxed as he allowed her to do all of the work. After he came quickly, just as she had hoped, she rested for a moment. When she later rose to kiss his lips, he didn't kiss back. She knew he had already fallen asleep. She rushed inside to find a blanket for him. While she had worn him out and gotten him drunk, she now wondered if the effort was worth it. However, as she studied his face, she realized, of course, it was damn well worth it.

Chapter 17

Rachel rushed out to Cindi's desk, throwing the list of houses she had selected in front of her. "I need to set these up for showing this afternoon. They'll be here around three this afternoon. It should take about four hours to view all of these, but the good thing is that they need to make a decision today or tomorrow. I'm not sure what time they're leaving tomorrow, but I know it's early. I want this nailed before they leave."

"I understand. I'll work on it now." Cindi smiled and reached for the phone. "By the way, Carlos called and said he was on his way over."

"Really!" Rachel smiled as she thought about the night before. This impending sale made her feel great also, since she knew she had this one in the bag. "Tell him to come on in, and just maybe he has some good news on the Johnson's loan I gave him last week."

Cindi looked at the list. "This is going to take a few minutes to set up."

Rachel didn't respond, but hurried back to her office to retrieve her makeup kit, and quickly review her face in a mirror. All looked great except the lipstick. She rushed to freshen it as she glanced at the clock. Damn, she didn't have long to prepare for her appointment. Perhaps, she should make some of the calls for Cindi. Torn between taking time to see Carlos and preparing for her appointment, she inhaled deeply, hoping for a solution.

Minutes later, she heard a knock on her door and glanced up to see Carlos smiling, patiently waiting on her. "Hi, it looks like you have Cindi jumping through hoops today."

"Hi, oh yes, we've only a short time to get ready for my appointment today."

"I didn't know you made this appointment today. I was hoping to talk you into going canoeing this afternoon."

She glanced at him as if to say *are you stupid,* but quickly changed her expression. "I'm sorry, I can't today."

"Not a problem. I can find someone else to go with me." He moved around the desk to give her a hug. "Is there anything I can do for you?"

"No, we have it all under control." She allowed her eyes to glance around her room, hoping he would understand that she needed to concentrate on her job right now. "I was going to call you later. Have you heard anything about the Johnson's loan?"

"I called on the loan package this morning, and it looks great. I know of nothing else I can do on it until they send the appraisal in, and I did call him again this morning also. He promised me that the appraisal will be completed by tomorrow morning."

Rachel studied his clothes, as if for the first time. The casual clothing indicated that he was, in fact, planning to take the day off, apparently to go canoeing. Canoeing . . . hmmm, that's something else she had never tried before. With her big cahootus, yes this adventure would be comical. "How long will you be out canoeing? I was hoping to go shopping tonight when I finish showing these houses."

"Shopping?" He cocked his eyebrows into a distorted expression.

"Yes, I thought it would be great to buy some clothes to dance in. Dancing is a new life for me, and I need to buy some outfits. I would love to get your opinion on them. I also hoped to find something for you that would make us look like a team when we perform on the dance floor." She hoped this would make him happy.

The look on his face wasn't what she had hoped for. "I'm not sure. I'm not too big into going shopping. I think you understand. I own all of the clothes I need, but I do appreciate the offer."

Rachel leaned over and ran her hand up his arm, massaging his muscles as she went. When she reached his neck, she studied his eyes. "We're going to be dancing together soon, and I know nothing about dancing clothes– please." She batted her eyes softly, hoping for the best.

She watched Carlos breath in deeply. "I'm not sure what time I'll be back, but I'll call you as soon as I do . . . okay?"

"Okay. I also am not sure exactly when I'll be through with these showings. Call me when you finish and have a good time."

He leaned over and kissed her forehead. She had hoped for more, but knew her lipstick may have scared him. It was kiss proof, but she knew he probably didn't know that. "I'll call you." He turned and headed for the door.

"Bye." Rachel started to say more. In fact, she caught herself wanting to tell him much more. The words, *I love you,* briefly floated across her mind, but he left before she could speak. Well not totally gone, she could hear him talking to Cindi. The loud laughs of her secretary indicated how much Cindi loved to chat with him. She knew Cindi liked him, as a jealous mood overtook her feelings of ecstasy that she had experienced only minutes ago.

"Ohmigod." she whispered to herself. She suddenly wondered who Carlos was going canoeing with now. She knew she didn't own him, but they were dating. She was afraid to really approach the subject. While Carlos never volunteered much information about himself, and she never really pushed, it was in moments like this that she often questioned why she resisted asking him. She knew she needed to talk to him about this and soon.

She heard Cindi laugh again. *Damn it, I need her to concentrate on working and not my guy.* She started to stand when she heard him leaving and the conversation that was full of laughter ended. Good.

***

Upon returning to her office from a full day of reviewing houses, Rachel handed her client a stack of papers with information on those they had visited. "I know you want to talk and compare notes tonight. How early can we start tomorrow morning?"

The couple glanced at each other. "We would like to start as early as possible, since we might want to see some other ones as well as go back to see one or two of these. How does eight tomorrow morning sound to you?"

"That sounds good to me since I know you only have a limited amount of time." She had really hoped they would've fallen in love with one today and not require another full day of her time. She did have other clients that she needed to be working with.

"Okay, we'll see you later."

Rachel knew it would be great to take them out to eat, but she needed to see Carlos. She only hoped they would stay loyal to her for one more day, and not go off and do something stupid on their own. She knew the market was flooded with for sale by owners and short sales. "Good, I look forward to it."

As quickly as they left the door, she reached for her phone. Carlos had not called her all day. *Where is he? How long does it take to go canoeing anyway? What am I supposed to do now?* It was already seven.

Rachel decided to do some more research on possible matches for her client. Twenty minutes later her phone rang. "Hi, this is Carlos. I just received your message."

She forced her voice to relax. "How was your canoeing?"

"It felt great, and I made some new friends today."

"That's good." She quickly wondered just who these new friends were. "I had hoped to shop at the stores tonight. How long will it take you to drive to the International Mall in Tampa?"

"I've already showered and could be at the mall in about thirty minutes, how about you?"

Perfect, she thought. "That sounds good. I'm hungry and we can eat also, if you want."

"Okay, I'll see you soon."

***

Rachel scurried to complete the files, stuffing them into her working bag along with her laptop. She would work more on completing the paperwork tonight when she returned home. She turned out her lights and walked around the office before yelling to see if anyone else remained in the building. It felt strange with no one else working late.

The office often gave her an eerie feeling when she worked by herself, and especially tonight. "Hello." Still, she heard no reply.

She hurried to the front door, set the alarm, and locked the door behind her. As she scanned the parking lot, she saw three cars in the lot. She knew this wasn't too unusual as many agents could still be out with clients. However, she slowly studied one car, a dark sedan with windows too dark to see in, parked in the far back side of the lot. *Could someone be inside, sitting there, watching me leave?* She felt the muscles tighten in her chest.

Rachel hesitated, trying to decide if she should run to her car or go back inside. This is ridiculous, she thought. She headed for her car. While her face pointed toward her car, her focus kept studying the strange car. Her fingers wrapped around her keys tightened as she quickened her pace. She unlocked her car and jumped inside.

Rachel pulled out of the parking lot and glanced back. Perhaps it was a Lincoln, but an older model. She tried to look through the windows as she left, but to no avail. She thought about turning around and getting the tag number. No . . . she reversed her thoughts and hit the gas.

***

Rachel watched Carlos walking toward her car as she opened her door. Maybe she acted crazy, but she had called him back on his cell before she arrived at the International Mall to ask him to meet her at her car. She didn't know if someone had followed her or not, but she had this scary deep down gut feeling.

Rachel flashed Carlos a smile as he closed the door for her. "I'm so glad to see you."

He apparently noticed the look of concern on her face. "What's going on?"

"Don't laugh at me, but I've this feeling that I'm being followed."

She watched Carlos quickly survey the parking lot. "Do you mean here?"

"I don't know. I saw a car in the parking lot at work that I think I've seen many times lately. I know these murders are making me nervous." She reached for his hand and stared into his eyes. "This isn't a good feeling."

"I understand. Until they catch the guy responsible for this, you need to be careful." He tightened his grip on her hand as he walked with her to the entrance of the mall, and passing all of the eating and drinking establishments.

The aroma smelled too good to be ignored for long. Damn, she wanted to eat and eat, but several slim girls coming out of the Blue Martin made her have second thoughts. Yes . . . they looked young and beautiful, and– SLIM. Rachel glanced over at Carlos. His eyes gave away the fact that he had noticed them also. She increased her tension on his hand and kept moving.

After strolling into the mall, one of her favorite places, she relaxed as she pulled him along and rushed forward. She knew that containing her excitement would be impossible. When she glanced at him, however, it was obvious that he didn't share her excitement and acted more like a little boy in tow. Too bad–she was walking on her turf tonight.

***

While the stores had closed too fast, Rachel had made the most out of the short amount of time available. She really appreciated Carlos carrying the bags of clothes she had purchased, and most importantly she learned his sizes, and to some extent his taste. She would bend slightly, as long as he fit into her lifestyle. *How can anyone turn down such a gift?* She would be back here soon to do much more shopping.

Right now, she needed food. Damn the skinny girls. She could tell he was wearing out, but a good glass of wine would make the night all worthwhile. Walking inside one spot where the music played a great fast beat song, she saw him look around and smile. She hoped the sound of music and seeing people dancing would make him happy.

They walked to the back of the bar and toward the dance floor. She could tell he wanted to dance, but she wanted a table and a glass of wine first. She spotted a table and pointed toward it.

Carlos pursed his lips, but headed for it. "This table is in a good place."

Yes, Rachel saw him checking out the place and particularly–the girls. All dressed to kill. Wine, she needed wine.

After a waitress quickly moved over to them, he ordered some wine for them. However, his attention focused on the floor for a while before he turned toward her. "I guess we need to see what you've learned."

Rachel's heart started skipping beats. She had trouble swallowing, as the place suddenly became hot. *Yes, I want to dance with you, but what if you see just how bad I dance?* "Okay, but let me have a drink first."

As he smiled and turned his attention back to the floor, she studied his features again, especially his high cheek bones and rugged chin, almost as if for the first time. His eyes were so dark and brown that they seemed to radiate in the dim light, while his shining black hair reflected every spot light in the bar. With a proud sense of ownership, Rachel studied the stares coming from the *skinny* girls walking around, admiring her prize.

After the wine arrived, she raised her glass to his, but since the music played too loud to hear well, she simply smiled. She knew she would need to dance soon, and she had to calm her nerves. She gulped the wine.

Then it happened. One of the skinny girls walked over and stopped in front of Carlos, calling him by name. He stood and walked around to offer her a hug. Carlos slowly turned toward Rachel and leaned over where she could hear. "This is a friend of mine I dance with sometimes. Her name is Rita."

The girl moved in closer to Rachel, smiling. "Hi, it's great to meet you." However, she quickly turned her attention back to Carlos. "Where have you been lately? I don't see you out dancing much."

"I've had to work a lot lately. This is one of the realtors I work with. Her name is Rachel Contino."

Rachel smiled, but wished he had told *miss skinny* that she was his date, not a business associate. His words hurt, but she let the moment pass. She worked on something witty to say, but was beat by Rita's quick response. "Well, you know what they say, all work and no play makes Jack . . . ."

"Yeah, yeah." Rachel heard Carlos respond, as his eyes became much more brilliant and penetrating in the flashing lights of the bar.

Rita pointed to the floor. "I know you have business to discuss, but can I talk you into dancing one time with me? I love this song."

Carlos glanced over at Rachel. *What can I say? No . . . and forever be known as a bitch.* "Okay, but don't forget where to bring him back." She smiled at Carlos, hoping he appreciated this act of kindness.

That one dance lasted through two glasses of wine. She could see where Carlos loved to dance with her–Rita was a fantastic dancer. The music changed as a slow romantic tune started. Rachel's heart started to beat fast. Surely, he wouldn't dance a slow dance with her. She saw the two turn face each other, as she stopped breathing.

***

"Thanks for carrying these packages inside for me." Rachel held the door open for Carlos. She could've managed on her own, but wanted an excuse to get him inside her condo. The thoughts of watching him dance with someone else ate at her all the way home, but it was all the encouragement she needed to get off her big cahootus, and on the dance floor. Three glasses of wine didn't hurt either.

"Since I want to look good on the dance floor, I hope you like the clothes I purchased tonight." She closed the door behind him.

"I think you'll look fine, but we do need to see about buying you some dancing shoes."

Shoes–she loved shoes. "I think that would be great."

He smiled. "I'm not sure you understand. Dancing shoes need to be comfortable and sturdy if you're going to be able to make the turns." He pointed to the shoes she wore.

"These aren't good for dancing."

"Why not?"

Carlos smiled as her pointed to them. "First, the toes are exposed, which can hurt when I step on them. Don't laugh–it happens. Secondly, the hill needs to be secure, or it'll slip and come off, which could twist your ankle and quickly end your dancing fun."

"Hmmm, you seem to know what you're talking about." She wondered how many girls he had helped dance before. "When are we going out dancing again? I enjoyed it."

"Everything depends on you and your schedule. I like to go out every chance I can."

Thoughts of him going out and dancing with others quickly returned. "I think I can work out sometimes late at night."

He smiled. "That's good. I know you want to win this contest you hooked me into going to."

"I don't think you complained too much about our deal." She flashed him an evil smile and watched him blush.

"Okay, okay. A deal is a deal." He glanced around the kitchen. "I know you have an early morning appointment, and I need to do a few things also. So call me tomorrow when you can."

"I will." She walked over closer to him and kissed him. She wanted him, but knew he was right; she needed to be fresh tomorrow. In fact, she knew she needed to do more research tonight. She really needed this sale. "I'll call you as soon as I write this deal up."

He hugged her tightly one more time before he turned to leave. She walked over to the refrigerator and retrieved another bottle of wine before heading for her extra bedroom that she had converted to an office. She had work to do before she went to sleep, and very little time to do it.

***

The alarm startled Rachel minutes after she had finally entered into a deep sleep. Oh God! While her tired body was begging for more time to sleep, she was too scared to turn over and miss her early morning appointment. As she rolled out of bed and headed for the kitchen, she stripped off her nightshirt along the way. She definitely needed a glass of water and maybe an aspirin this morning.

The kitchen looked a mess with the bags of clothes she had purchased lying around. She quickly glanced at them as her senses sharpened. Something was missing. She went through her purchases in her mind and knew she had purchased more. Rachel eventually realized that she couldn't find two of the outfits she had remembered purchasing.

She rushed to the door and checked the alarm system. It wasn't on. *Did I forget to set it? Was someone inside my place last night?* Panic set in as she reached for her phone and called Carlos. He never answered.

Chapter 18

Rachel rushed into her office, carrying her work bag and an emergency package from Starbucks–she needed to have her coffee and donut. She knew she only had a few minutes before her appointment would arrive. After rounding the corner of the agency office, she saw Cindi talking to Detective Lindstrom. Cindi had tears falling down her face.

The detective moved toward Rachel as she rushed toward Cindi. "What's going on?"

Cindi spoke first. "Jody's in the hospital with a gunshot wound."

The shock caused Rachel's head to spin. *Ohmigod–no, don't tell me this.*

The Detective moved fast and grabbed Rachel, helping her into one of the guest chairs. "Careful. You don't need to fall."

Cindi rushed behind him, squatting beside Rachel. She felt the support from both, holding her straight. "Oh God, Jody, nooooo." The world quickly faded away.

***

With a blurry light waking her slightly, Rachel could hear voices, and the feel of a gentle squeeze of someone holding her hand. With someone placing a cool cloth on her head, she forced herself to focus, knowing she must have passed out–how embarrassing. *Jody*! The detective's words returned. What happened? She had to know. She reached for the cloth, attempting to remove it.

"Careful, you need to remain still for a minute. You passed out, but you're going to be okay." The Detective's voice expressed a deep concern.

Rachel's eyes focused enough to see maybe ten people in her office, staring at her. It had to be the others in the office. "I need to stand."

Rachel struggled to raise her head as someone helped her and she slowly focused on the detective kneeling in front of her. "You need to take it slow. We'll help you to your chair again. I wouldn't try to stand too much."

She knew he was probably right, and accepted the help from several people ushering her to her seat. A glass of water came into focus as she heard Cindi whispering to her, "Here, try to drink this." She accepted the cold water.

Rachel saw the detective glancing around. "I think Rachel is going to be okay now. Please give us a few minutes." Another officer, a woman, knelt beside her.

Rachel studied the patiently waiting detective, as she asked, "What happened?"

"Jody is alive, but in critical condition at Bay General Hospital. She's in a coma." Rachel knew he was stalling, waiting to see how she would receive the information. "It looks like she may have tried to commit suicide, but like several other recent cases, we have doubts. This situation follows the other deaths too closely."

Rachel sobbed.

"It happened in her apartment about three hours ago. Several neighbors heard the shot, but couldn't tell exactly where the gunshot came from in the building. We had to go one unit at a time until we located her. When I arrived I thought she was dead, but I found a pulse. We rushed her to the hospital."

"Ohmigod, what are the doctors saying, will she make it?" Rachel's deep stare pushed the detective further.

The detective glanced at the woman officer, as if looking for permission to continue. "I don't know. It's still too early to tell. The doctors are working on her now."

"I need to go see her."

She tried to rise to her feet, but he reached out a hand to her shoulder, stopping her. "I don't think anyone will be able to visit her anytime soon." He glanced at the other officer again. "The gun was inside of her mouth when it fired. The bullet ricocheted off her skull and . . . ."

"AND WHAT?"

"It removed a large part of the front of her face."

Rachel's stomach convulsed. An image of Jody, one of her best friends, with her face blown off, made her grasp for air. Her head became light again. She fought back only to become numb. She froze. *Who could do such a thing to another human?*

A paramedic-looking guy quickly arrived into the room. "How is she?"

"Not good. I think she needs something." Those were the last words Rachel remembered as she passed out again.

***

With the soft texture of Rachel's favorite pillow and the warmth of her comforter covering her, she fought the druggy effects of a sedative. She knew she was in her bed, but couldn't remember how she had gotten home. She groaned slightly as a gentle hand touched her forehead. She opened her eyes to find Carlos sitting beside her.

On the other side of the bed, Rachel saw Cindi and her broker standing behind Carlos. "What time is it?"

"It's almost noon. You've been sleeping for a while." Carlos's voice whispered smooth and slow.

"I can't believe this. I've work I need to do today."

Her broker, Mr. London, spoke softly. "Rachel, don't worry about anything. Everything has been taking care of."

"What do you mean?"

"I met with your client this morning myself. They wrote

an offer, and everything looks good. You need to rest today."

The news sounded great, but she wondered how she would ever catch up. "I've got to work."

Carlos touched her shoulder. "Doctors orders, you're to stay in bed today. I've cancelled the rest of my appointments today, and I'll be here with you." She smiled at the thoughts of having him with her the rest of the day and taking care of her.

She glanced around the room. "Thanks, everyone. Thanks for everything." However, her thoughts returned to Jody–oh God no. Jody–why?

Chapter 19

"How is she today?" Rachel heard Carlos asking Cindi in the outer office. She knew she needed to concentrate, since she had clients to take care of. In this market she needed to work three times as hard just to keep her head above water. She forced a smile, waiting on him to enter.

She saw him glance around the corner. "Come on in. I thought I heard you outside."

"I just came from the hospital. They're keeping Jody protected from all outsiders. The last two weeks have turned up no suspects. It's amazing that no one saw anyone fleeing the building."

"You don't think she really did try to commit suicide, do you?" She allowed a serious look of doubt to cross her face.

Carlos cleared his throat, apparently realizing his wording sounded improper. "That's not what I meant. The detective came to my office again yesterday and asked me questions for hours. I can tell they have no clues at all."

With the emotions coming back over her, she hoped the sedatives in her body would help. She didn't have many left, but she knew that she could get more if she needed to. "I'm trying hard not to concentrate on it. I must."

"I understand. I talked to the detective about this yesterday." He pulled a box from behind his back. "I hope you don't mind, but I got the size of your shoes from Cindi." He handed Rachel the present as Cindi walked in the door.

Rachel smiled as she accepted the present, looking like a shoe box. She owned lots of shoes. *Why would he buy me shoes?* She opened the box. "OHMIGOD" She yelled as she saw the dancing shoes inside.

"I talked to the place where you signed up for dance lessons, and I have it all arranged for us to come tonight."

"Tonight, I don't know. I need to be working."

Cindi walked closer. "It's my fault. I told him you have no appointments tonight."

"Yeah, but I need to make some calls to set up some appointments." Both Carlos and Cindi's stare hardened as they outnumbered her. "Okay, this might be the best night for me to go, but remember . . . if I go broke you have to take care of me." She made it sound like a joke, but down deep she knew how bad her cash flow had become.

***

The strength in Carlos's frame comforted her. The smell, his natural scent, filled her nostrils. She loved the aroma, but hoped that one day he would allow her to buy him some of her favorite colognes. Then again, she knew it would be hard to ever capture the smell of a man who grew on her day by day.

"Keep your elbow higher." She studied the light touch of Lester, the dance instructor coaching her. "Back straighter." Okay, she tried, but if she couldn't see her feet, how in the hell could she ever avoid stepping on his toes?

"This is a waltz, and to win a competition you need to dance as one. Carlos, you've mastered a perfect frame. You must have taken dance lessons before."

Carlos simply smiled, and as usual, he didn't fill in anything about his past. Instead, he kept his eyes fixed on Rachel's eyes.

"Remember it's simply one, two, three . . . one, two, three . . ." He moved in behind Carlos and watched them dance. "Keep your head up."

She continued to dance with Carlos, as the attention coming from her instructor encouraged her. Maybe she was dancing better than she thought, or then again, maybe it was the fact that she simply had a great dance partner. Either way, she loved the dancing . . . and the attention.

The lesson lasted an hour, moving from the waltz, to the cha cha, and finally to the salsa–the dances selected for the competition. "I think with a little practice you two will walk away with the contest."

Rachel knew he probably told all of his clients the same. Only time would tell. "I don't know. We only have a few more weeks to prepare."

"Then I suggest you practice a lot. You still have two more lessons with me also. However, I think you've found a great dance partner." The instructor stopped to study Carlos's face. "I think I've seen you before somewhere. Have you ever danced professionally?"

"No. I dance at many places, and I have for a long time. Perhaps you saw me out dancing one night."

The instructor kept staring. "Perhaps, but maybe it'll come to me later."

She watched Carlos face turn solemn for a minute. "Thank you for the lessons, and the use of your dance floor."

Lester pointed to Rachel. "She's the one paying for this, and I want to make sure she receives her money's worth. I hope to see you two again soon."

They left as soon as Carlos retrieved her coat and they changed out of their dancing shoes. She loved her shoes. As she studied Carlos taking off his shoes, she wondered how much dancing he really did. She didn't think that most guys own their own ballroom dancing shoes. She needed to ask him about this later.

***

The lights flashed as the music continued to play. The shoes hurt her feet, but rest wasn't on her mind. While they had danced several times a week, they still needed a lot more improvement to have any chance in the dance contest coming up in a few days. While she watched him introducing new movements and followed as best she could, he never said how he learned to be so damn good. He seemed to avoid the question, and in return, she never pushed him hard for an answer.

He sent her spinning and moving in circles, as the sweat made her clothes stick to her back. Fortunately, the fans above circulated any foul smell she might have created. If she concentrated, however, she could smell the beer and various cheap colognes or perfumes as the case may be.

She didn't mean to limp on a turn, but he stopped her, as he glanced at her feet. "Are you getting blisters?"

She moved closer to his ear to be heard easier. "I think I'm working on one."

"Here, we need to stop. A blister is one problem we don't need to contend with on the dance floor at the competition." He squeezed her hand and led her to the table, where drinks were waiting on them.

Rachel glanced around. She hated to sit for too long for one reason. She was always scared that one of his friends would come by and ask him to dance. "Thank you for dancing with me. I know I need a lot of practice."

Carlos smiled and pointed to the floor. "Most of the people here go dancing almost every night. Lots of practice is the only way to become this good."

"Every night!"

"Yes, trust me. Most of these good dancers concentrate only on one thing night and day." He raised his glass and saluted her before finishing the last drop. "I've enjoyed working with you, and I hope to not let you down at your competition."

"I doubt you'll ever let me down."

He smiled, acknowledging the evil implications.

Chapter 20

Rachel shuffled through several papers at her office, looking for someone to work with. While the amount of calls she received was high, the trick was trying to decide which one was gold, and which potential buyer would simply be wasting her valuable time.

Cindi answered another call before she walked over to the entrance to her office. "I have Aaron Bank on the line. He wants to know if you have time to meet him at your boat. He's at his boat right now."

"I might as well, especially since all of these look useless." She started pulling them together. "Tell him I can leave here in a few minutes."

Cindi left to relay the information. Rachel thought about how much she paid Cindi. Her salary wasn't much, but every dollar she spent now pulled her under more. She thought about the monthly bill from the broker she had received early that morning. *How did I spend so much on advertising?* Perhaps she could do with a smaller office. If something didn't break soon, she would need to start cutting more corners somewhere.

Cindi reemerged. "He said he would wait on you."

"Very good." Rachel stood and glanced at her listing board. It remained full, but she had no buyers. "I'll be back shortly."

***

The seagulls squawked above Rachel as she walked along the dock toward her boat that she hardly ever took out any more. She used to love to take clients to her boat to impress them with cocktails on the lounge area on top of the boat, but with cash short, this might be a good time to think about selling her boat. While she wasn't sure what it was worth, she knew Aaron would have a good idea since he was much more into boats than she was.

Aaron's boat was docked not too far from her own. She had always envied his boat and how impressive it looked. She knew he worked on his boat often, doing small maintenance projects. He enjoyed scuba diving and prided himself on cleaning the bottom of his boat himself. She knew she should clean her hull, but that was one cost she would put off until later.

Rachel saw Aaron waving long before she reached his boat. He wore a safari hat she remembered seeing him wear many times before. It must be part of his good luck superstition, she thought. She knew some men horded hats they should throw away. This appeared to be one of those.

"Hello, Rachel, it's good to see you." He reached over and kissed her cheek. "Come on aboard, and I'll show you what I've been working on."

She accepted his hand and walked aboard. "Your boat looks as great as ever."

His chest must have swelled. It should have. "I like this boat." He followed her to the galley. "What do you want to drink?"

"Well, it's a little early. I still need to go back to work." She glanced around at the perfect order on the boat.

"Here, one glass of wine never hurt anyone." He reached into the refrigerator, retrieved a bottle and poured two glasses. "I've been meaning to talk to you."

"Really, what about?"

He handed her the glass of wine and raised his in a toast. "To life . . . and what we make of it." He touched her glass. "We've been friends for a long time, haven't we?"

"Yes, for many years. I think it's because of times on this boat I decided to buy one." She enjoyed the wine, and as usual, he stocked some good wines on his boat.

"I met your friend at the wine auction. He's much younger than I had anticipated. How old is he?"

So . . . Carlos is why he wanted to see her. Word must be circulating about her and Carlos being together lately. "He's much younger than me."

"I know he is. He looks like he's twenty."

Rachel laughed and looked him directly in the eyes. "Close, he's actually twenty two, I think. Why do you ask?"

"Rachel, people are talking. You know how it is." He motioned for her to follow him on top.

"Aaron. Let me ask you something. Why is it that successful men can date younger women and no one ever says a word, but when a successful business woman has a younger boyfriend, the world feels like they have the right to pass judgment?"

"What can I say?" He walked over to the edge and looked over. "I don't want to see you get hurt."

"I do appreciate your concern." She glanced toward her boat. "So, what are you suggesting?"

"I guess I'm curious, that's all."

"I've been through a lot lately with all of the deaths at the condo complex I'm trying to sell. The authorities think the murderer is still on the loose, and I feel safer with a man nearby right now. You need to admit the fact he's in good enough shape to take care of any problems coming our way."

"I think I can understand, but what about your future plans? You're not getting any younger. Do you feel like you have a future with him?"

She raised her glass and finished her wine. "I don't think I've thought about the future lately. Let's face it, I don't exactly have men knocking down my door."

"I do have one question. Are you seeing each other exclusively right now?"

Rachel thought hard about her response before she answered. She knew her answer represented a double standard, but she hoped Carlos wasn't seeing, or at least not screwing anyone else. On the other hand, she considered her options open, that is, if she had the opportunity. Deep down, however, she worried if Carlos had other friends and perhaps . . . lovers. She had forced herself, most of the time, to ignore these suspicions. "I barely have time to see Carlos. I don't think he's seeing anyone else, but then again, I don't own him."

"That's about what I thought. How would you like to have dinner with me later?" He managed a twinkle in his eyes she hadn't noticed earlier.

"Dinner might be interesting. I'll let you know." She titled her head and enjoyed the flirty attention.

"Fair enough, since I know you need to work out things with Carlos. I, for some reason, don't think it'll last too long." He reached over and hugged her shoulder. "Okay, now you wanted to ask me about your boat."

After arriving at her boat, she turned to ask Aaron the one question she had on her mind. "I'm thinking of remodeling, of course, but also thinking I might need to sell it."

"Really, why is that?"

"As you know, the real estate market isn't doing so well right now, and a sale would be nice to free some money." She glanced at him to watch his reaction.

"I understand fully since I've several properties now that are upside down. However, let me ask you what you owe on the boat right now. As you might not know, the prices of boats are falling just like houses."

She had heard the same, but hoped maybe not as much. "What do you think I can sell the boat for now?"

He stepped on board as Rachel reached for her keys. "Let me see your boat again, and give me a few days to ask around."

Rachel intentionally didn't answer his question concerning the amount she owed on the boat. She had refinanced her boat a year ago and had never told him that she had used the money to buy yet another condo, thinking the prices had bottomed out. Instead, they had kept falling. "Okay. I'm not planning on selling today, but I need to know, just in case."

Aaron nodded his head. "I understand. If you're thinking about selling your boat, the work you do in remodeling it will help you sell it as well. I do most of my own work. You might want to do some of the work on your own. It's a great way to get some exercise and keep some of the money in your pocket."

Rachel smiled at the thought of working on her boat, knowing that she had no clue where to start. But . . . with his help, it might be possible to do some things. "I'll think about it."

He smiled as he started studying the cabin inside. "Besides, it might give us a chance to become better friends." He winked playfully, as he continued to examine the galley.

Rachel's phone rang and she excused herself to walk away from him. "Hello, this is Rachel."

"Hello, Rachel, my name is Eric. I see your name on the sign in front of some condos I'm standing in front of. They look like what I'm interested in. Can you come show them to me? I'm only going to be in town for a little while." His voice resonated deep and low–spooky.

Rachel's mixed emotions played havoc with her

immediately. She knew she needed to sell them, but at the same time had a growing fear of meeting men in vacant condos that she didn't know. "I'd be glad to show it to you. Can you meet me at my office first?"

A long silence increased her apprehension. "I don't know where your office is, and I don't have much time. How long will it take you to come here?"

"I'm sorry. I really need you to come to the office first and–"

"Forget it." He hung up.

Rachel glanced at the incoming number, and knew it wasn't local. While she really needed to call him back, she hesitated, as she wondered if she really wanted to. She froze, trying to decide. Perhaps she could call Carlos and ask him to go with her. What to do?

Chapter 21

As the dinner cruise ship picked up speed and entered the shipping channel, Rachel fought the tightness in her stomach, knowing the lessons and practice over the last few weeks wasn't nearly enough. She remembered watching some of these women dancing at the studio. They danced as if they had been taking lessons forever. When she sized up their dates, however, she knew she had an ace in the hole. Carlos looked stunning tonight in the outfit she had purchased for him–one he had actually accepted with little reluctance.

Lester, the dance instructor, soon walked over to them. "I'm so glad to see you here tonight. It's going to be a great evening." He looked professional and full of energy. This was a big deal for him since this dance cruise represented the culmination of a lot of dance lessons that he had talked these women into. The night had to be fantastic, or they wouldn't sign up for more lessons. Rachel knew Lester depended a lot on the evening being fantastic.

Carlos reached over and shook Lester's hand. "I think you did a great job in preparing this boat for dancing tonight. The floor looks great."

"We're going to start the music in a few minutes so you can work in some last minute practices. Please . . . help yourself to the champagne." He pointed to a station on one side where a private bartender who was hired for the event worked.

After Carlos excused himself and walked over to the bar to retrieve two glasses of the champagne, Rachel soon followed him. The bartender smiled and welcomed them with a deep French accent. Rachel watched a large smile cross Carlos face as he asked the bartender, "*Ca va* (How are you)?"

Carlos had a French accent that sounded astonishing, as the Frenchman acknowledged his question immediately. "*Tres bien, et tu* (very good and you)?"

Carlos accepted the glasses and raised them to salute the bartender and say without words that with champagne, all is good, a motion that the bartender acknowledged gracefully.

Accepting the glass from Carlos, she smiled. "Where did you learn to speak French?" As usual, he smiled and ignored the question. She decided to push this time. "Really, where did you learn?"

"From friends. I think many people know more than one language. If they don't, they need to."

"Okay, so how many languages do you know?" Rachel asked.

"I know the romantic languages like English, French, Italian and Spanish, but I know none of them really well." He raised his glass to hers. "To victory in dancing tonight."

She touched his glass. "To victory." Again, he had managed to avoid talking about his past.

Before she could push him about his knowledge, the music started. Another man walked over and introduced himself before asking Rachel to dance with him. Rachel turned toward Carlos, hoping he would rescue her, but instead, he extended his hand toward the floor, giving his permission to the stranger. "Have fun."

Shortly, she saw Carlos dancing with someone else. This wasn't the way this dance was supposed to be. She wanted to keep him all to herself. The girl he danced with smiled too much, and she was also very skinny.

Lester, joined by most of the other instructors at the

studio, constantly worked the group, making sure no one felt jilted. They all had clients attending. He finally walked to the center of the floor as the music faded. "Before we start tonight, we've some special entertainment. My cousin from South America is joining us tonight with her partner. They own a studio in Argentina and consented to demonstrate for us what it's like to dance tango–Argentina style." He pointed to them on one side of the floor as everyone clapped.

They moved to the center of the floor and assumed their positions. As the music played louder as they started to dance, Carlos reached for her hand and squeezed. The performance was incredible. She glanced at Carlos and studied the way he concentrated on their dance with such intensity.

When the dance finished, Rachel knew Carlos would be dancing with this girl before the night ended. However, he was her guy for now. "You enjoyed watching them dance, didn't you?"

"Of course, they're very good."

She glanced at him, as the warmth in his hand radiated into her own. Tonight, she knew his interest came only for a love of dancing, and not a special girl with a past she needed to worry about. She would let him enjoy his fun.

The instructor walked back to the center as the contest began. While the others danced good–very good, she quickly told herself, win or lose, she intended to have a good time tonight. She allowed herself to curl into Carlos's arms and relax, much like an actual couple tonight. Age didn't matter; the only fact that counted was that she was having fun.

After all of the dances, the crowd voted on the winners for each dance. They didn't win the first two, but on the waltz, she screamed as they announced the winner. A trophy, she won a trophy! Sure, it wasn't like winning at Blackstone, but it was a trophy. She hugged Carlos and kissed him on the lips in front of everyone, as they all clapped for them.

New rounds of champagne and toasts circulated around the floor as the various couples continued to dance. While she danced with various men, she glanced around for Carlos. Their attention made her feel strange. *Now where is Carlos?*

Soon the music stopped, and she saw Carlos walking on the floor with the girl from Rio, taking their positions as a tango song began. Since most of the clients of the dance studio had never learned such a dance, they cleared the floor. Rachel held her breath and watched Carlos arch his back straight, and increase the intensity in his stare before moving in sync with the music.

With each passing minute, Carlos's movements became more intense and dramatic, as this girl matched his movements almost as if she had danced with him for all of her life. *How did he learn to dance like this?* His moves became more sensuous as the dance continued. It looked almost as if he was having sex on the floor. She wished she could dance like this girl, but knew with her big cahootus, she would never be able to bend or flow like a professional dancer. While part of her felt depressed, another part of her yearned for the time when she would have Carlos alone to herself later tonight. She wanted him more now than anytime she could remember. Tonight would be special, very special. She knew it.

Chapter 22

"I brought you some lunch back. I hope you like it," Cindi stated, as she walked through the door to Rachel's office, carrying a small sack from a Chinese carry out restaurant.

With hunger pains increasing, Rachel wished she had more time to go out to eat. "Thanks. I'll eat in a minute." She flipped through the stack on her desk. "I can't find the file on the Italian couple I worked with last year. I heard they're coming back to look for something next week, and I need their number if you can find it."

"I remember them. Their English wasn't that good, and I remember how frustrated you were with them. Are you sure you want to work with them again? They had wasted a lot of your time."

"They're planning on paying cash, which is exactly what I need."

"Okay, just asking. Have you called Carlos back yet?" Cindi smiled and pointed to the clock on the wall.

Rachel breathed deeply. "I know he wants to go out tonight, but I've too much to do. He'll need to be understanding. Can you call him for me and tell him I'll make it up to him later?"

Cindi looked shocked. "Sure, if you want me to. This is the third time this week you've put him off."

"I know, but he's such a sweetie. He'll understand." She quit hunting in the files. "What time is Michael Penske supposed to be here?"

"He said around lunch." Cindi retrieved some of the files

on Rachel's desk. "Here, let me arrange these for you."

"Fine, I'll need the file on the condo complex also. I think the condos might be why he's coming by today. I know he has an interest in them. We also need to talk to the attorney today that's handling the estates of the two deceased owners again. I'm not sure how long this will be tied up, or how much more time I have to sell these."

Rachel looked toward the door to find Michael standing there and listening. "I think I can answer some of those questions for you."

Rachel stood, embarrassed by being overheard. "I didn't see you waiting on me."

"Relax. I understand the predicament you're in. I'm afraid, needless to say, I'm in the soup with you." He slowly walked into her office as Rachel motioned for Cindi to shut the door behind her as she left.

"I'm glad you came by. I was about to call the attorneys office to obtain an update."

He lifted his hand. "I've some facts you don't know. As you remember, I was a silent investor in the condo project. What I didn't mention was the amount of the investment."

Rachel leaned back in her chair, since this information really didn't matter. While the investment was something for the courts to worry about, she now worried about the fact he could foreclose on the property and really tie up any sales. "No, you never mentioned the extent of your investment before, and I guess it wasn't my business to know."

"I just left a meeting with all of the attorneys and the court a few minutes ago. I didn't want to make this too public, and I hope you can help me keep this quiet."

Okay, he captured her interest. *What was going on?* "What meeting?"

"The property was owned jointly by the three of us with

the right of survivorship."

It took a minute for his words to sink in. "You're telling me you own the project, free and clear?" She knew her face reflected the stunning news.

"It was never my intentions to own this project, or to let anyone know I had purchased an interest in it." He leaned back in his seat and crossed his arms. "The attorneys are working out a compromise where I can keep this fact from becoming public knowledge, and I hope I can count on you to do the same." His eyes remained penetrating, waiting on an answer.

"It's my responsibility as a realtor to maintain confidentiality with my clients." The thoughts of the various implications bounced around in her head. She needed to think fast.

"As of right now . . . I actually own the property, but not the corporation managing the units. We worked out a deal this morning, however, for me to also buy out that corporation."

"I see. So, am I still the agent on record on the project, or are you going to be selling them now?"

"Are you kidding? I want no one to know I own them. I've had the detective investigating this pouring through every transaction I ever worked right now. I don't need the investigator to work harder. I want these remaining units sold as fast as possible."

"You know how hard it is in this market right now."

"I know, but I'm going to lower the prices dramatically. I'll submit the new numbers to you soon." He paused. "I hate to lose money, but I know that I may have no choice now."

"I understand. The other problem hurting sales is all of the murders happening in the building."

He leaned forward and glanced around before he

whispered, "What makes you really think they have been murdered?"

"Everything looks to be pointing that way. If Jody ever comes out of her coma, we might get some answers."

She watched Michael take a big breath. "How is she doing?"

"I've been told she's showing no changes. They really don't know if she'll ever come out of it." Rachel knew she needed to try to see Jody again, but every time she tried, the police blocked her. The police wanted no one to visit Jody until she came out of the coma.

Michael hung his face for a second before looking back. "Do you have any idea who might be behind all of this?"

"I wish I knew. The murders have really scared me a lot lately. I know I'm turning away showing appointments I used to take all of the time, much like the one I turned down earlier."

Michael glanced at her with renewed interest. "Do you feel like you have a stalker?"

"I sometimes think I do, like when this caller earlier wanted me to meet him at the condos right then and not come to the office to register. You know this procedure is one of the rules we've established until all of this is over."

Michael let out a big sigh. "I can understand. I don't want you to put yourself in any danger. If you need backup at any time, call me and I'll be glad to meet you."

"Thanks, I might take you up on the offer sometime." She glanced around. "The broker is willing to help, and I have a guy I'm seeing who is more than willing to help. I think we have it covered."

She watched Michael attempting to hide a smile. "I've heard you still have the young stud you're running around town with." She felt like he was examining her, much as if a father might be, hoping to protect her from a bad experience.

Rachel leaned over her desk. "You're the second person to tell me about hearing about us today."

Michael stood. "Do your best, and let me know if you have any ideas at all on how we can move these last units fast. I'll give the new prices to you as soon as I can also. I've some serious calculating to do." He turned to leave, but stopped. "I also heard the guy you're seeing has some loan contacts for developers. The news of a loan Carlos was in the process of having approved had never reached me before. I think they were trying to see if they could buy me out. It would've been great if they did, since I wouldn't have been in this position if they had."

Rachel slightly bit her tongue before she asked another question. "How much time do you have to sell these before the banks come after you?"

She could tell he hated to admit it, but could see the writing on the wall. "I think you now understand. Before, I was a silent partner with limited liabilities. Now, I'm a prime owner with all of the risk." He remained standing. "If I don't make some sells soon, I may be in a very difficult position. However, a few sales can free up the cash to hang in there."

"I promise . . . I'll do my best." Rachel drew on a new reserve to push on. "I've been thinking of one point I want to discuss with the detective. Since the deaths occurred in the building, and no one has ever seen anyone leaving, then just maybe the killer lives in the building."

"The thought has occurred to me as well, but considering the owners, none of them fit the description of what you would consider a murderer." Michael reached over and rubbed his chin. "I should also let you know that I've hired a private detective to look into this. Not, mind you, that our finest aren't doing a good job, but I now have a much higher need to know the truth."

"I'd love to help anyway I can." She understood his situation.

"Thanks." He smiled and walked out.

Chapter 23

"What? I can't hear you." The background noise continued to be too loud for Rachel to hear Carlos clearly on her cell phone. "You need to speak louder." Rachel still could only hear a few words. "Where are you?"

Shouting continued as she started to hang up. Then she heard him yell, "—sports bar."

Rachel could hear the sounds of many people yelling and laughing. "Call me later."

The background cleared for a minute. "Now, how is this?"

"Much better. What's going on?" Rachel asked.

"I went with some friends to a watch the game on the screen at Hooters."

"I see. Don't you have some clients you need to be working with?" She shouted as loud as possible to be heard.

"It's seven o'clock and nobody calls me at night. If they did, it can wait until tomorrow. Why don't you join us?"

She really had no intentions of watching some soccer team playing on a screen in a sports bar, especially at Hooters with all of the skinny young girls walking around. "I don't think so. I'll be home soon. Why don't you come to see me in an hour or so?"

"Okay, I'll see you later." The phone line died.
***

Rachel pulled into the garage at her condo. *Where is he?* She reached for her phone again and dialed Carlos's number. No answer. She knew there was a strong possibility that he was still at Hooters enjoying himself, but damn it, she needed him.

Since she couldn't remain in the car all night, she opened the door and walked fast. While she couldn't believe she had stayed so late working, she knew that she needed to find some good clients, and especially someone who could buy anything–now. After moving to the elevator and looking back over her shoulder at all of the vacant cars which looked suspicious, she wished she had paid more attention to them earlier. A few she recognized, but many she didn't.

Minutes later, she locked the door to her condo behind her as the racing of her heart reminded her of what danger she might be in. How ridiculous, she thought. She needed to handle this mounting fear of being stalked.

After glancing at her home phone and scanned the calls, she saw where one of them had come from Carlos. She hit the play button. "Hi. This is Carlos. I've been waiting for you for about an hour. I tried your cell and had no answer. I'm going back to Hooters to see my friends. Call me later."

"Damn." *Why didn't he wait for me?* She quickly called him as she reached for the brandy. This is what she needed now, she thought, as she made her way to the balcony. She started to hang up when he finally answered. "Hello."

"Well hi. Why didn't you wait for me?" She tried to restrain her anger, but knew she failed.

"I'm sorry. I left you a message. I thought you might've become tied up with a client for a long time."

"I'm home now. I wished you were here." She forced her voice to sound as pathetic as possible.

"Why?"

"I know I'm becoming paranoid with all of the murders lately, but I need you to look out for me."

She heard him sigh. "I'll do the best I can, but you know I can't be with you all of the time."

She knew she came across as demanding, but she knew

he was right. However . . . she thought he owed her since she generally took good care of him. "I thought you would be more concerned for my safety."

"I think we need to talk about this."

With her control disappearing, she knew to end the call as soon as she could. "Okay, I'll call you."

She didn't wait for a response as she decided that she would deal with him later. For now, she gulped down a large swallow of the strong brandy and slid into the lounger. Perhaps she would find a blanket and sleep out on the balcony tonight.

***

Rachel shifted through the stack of showings she intended to present to her couple from Dallas who were sitting in her back seat. She had their nine year old in the front seat with her. The time for lunch was approaching quickly and she hadn't heard from Carlos. With the clients hanging on to her every move, she had no way of calling him. She needed to find a way to slip away from them for a minute to call him. He worried her.

She pulled into the lot near the next showing and turned to smile at them, hoping to read their reaction to the outside. They flashed a smile, a good sign. "Who knows, maybe this is the perfect one."

Opening the door using the key in the lock box, she stood to one side and motioned for them to look around. "I need to make a few calls, so check this one out and I'll be with you in a minute."

The nine year old ran down a hallway with the father quickly chasing him, hoping to keep him out of trouble. The wife turned to Rachel. "I like this one so far, take your time."

Rachel walked out to a side balcony and called the office. "Hello, Cindi, I'm still showing. I've three more to go and hope to be finished by lunch. I'm not sure if I'll take them out to lunch, or come back to the office to write up one of them."

"I understand; how's it going?"

"Everything looks good."

"I'm glad. You received a call a few minutes ago."

Good, Rachel thought, assuming the call was coming from Carlos. Hopefully he called to apologize for the night before. She had agonized all night trying to decide if she should call him. He had never called her back.

Cindi continued in her normal chipper attitude. "Aaron called, asking about you. He acted friendly and asked a lot of questions about you. You know, I think he's interested in you."

Rachel caught herself laughing. "He said he would call me, but I didn't think he would get back to me this quick. I have his number, but it'll be a little later before I'm free to talk." A thought floated inside her head. She knew Cindi hoped she would like Aaron, since the arrangement would free up Carlos. Right now, however, she wasn't too happy with Carlos, and how could he just leave her stranded like that? She needed to call him next.

"Is there anything else I can do for you until you return?" Cindi managed to know most of the time what she needed before she asked, which had created such a good working relationship.

"I know you're preparing for the state realtor exam. How close are you to being ready to sit for it?"

Cindi laughed. "I think I'm close. I just need to get my nerves ready to take the exam."

"See if you can take the test soon. By having your license, you'd be a big help right now in showing some properties as a licensed assistant."

"Okay, I will."

After disconnecting, Rachel located Carlos' speed dial and clicked on it. He answered immediately. "Hello, Rachel, how are you today?"

Rachel forced herself to remain cheerful. "I'm doing great–showing houses. How about you?"

"I've been busy doing some research on loans for some friends."

Good, he was busy with clients, and perhaps not avoiding her as she had feared. "I'm sorry about last night. I'll be free tonight, and after working so late last night I need to relax."

He cut her off. "Tonight . . . I'm going to be busy with some clients. I'm sorry."

A shock of resentment shot through her body. *Is this the truth or a brush?* "I see . . . . What time do you think you'll be through?"

His voice remained steady and slow. "I'm not sure. We're going out to eat."

She forced her voice to be as charming as possible. "Will you call me when you are through?"

His voice returned to the pleasant voice she loved. "I will, but it might be late."

Rachel saw her clients walking her way. She definitely didn't want to allow them to overhear her talking to Carlos. "Okay, I hope it's not too late." She hung up.

***

Rachel leaned back in the chair at her office. "I'll have Cindi bring you the offer in a minute, and I hope you can present it soon." Rachel knew the offer her clients had made a few minutes ago would be accepted. In this market the seller would be a fool not to take it.

"I'll present the offer as soon as I get it, Rachel. I feel like I can have you an acceptance shortly." The excitement in the other agent's voice was contagious as Rachel quickly celebrated with her. "I'll be right here, waiting on it."

After saying goodbye, Rachel walked out to Cindi and handed the offer to her. "Be sure to make some copies and take this to Beck as soon as you can."

"Great job!" Cindi raised her hand in a quick high five. After all, she received a bonus on all sales as well. If she obtained her license, Rachel knew Cindi would make much more.

"Thanks, I've some more calls to make."

Cindi handed her a call slip with Aaron's number on it. "I know you don't want to forget this one."

Rachel smiled as she accepted the note. No, she hadn't forgotten. "Thanks, I'll call him in a minute." She didn't want to tip her hand to Cindi, but she knew Cindi was trying hard time to determine her interest. Rachel walked into her office and closed the door behind her.

She studied the number for a few minutes, thinking about what she would say to him. She made her mind up and called.

"Hello, this is Aaron." His voice sounded professional, almost like a paid spokesman for a commercial.

"This is Rachel. I've a message you called."

"Yes, I was thinking about you, and I've some numbers to go over with you on your boat, if you're interested."

That was fast. He must have worked hard on it. "That's great. I hope they're not too bad."

"Well, they are what they are. The great thing is the fact that I know I helped you buy your boat at a great price. So, I think you'll be okay."

Rachel's heart sank slightly as she thought about the refinancing she went through a year ago. She owed more than he thought on the boat. "I hope so."

"Anyway, when can we get together?"

With a mixture of feelings, Rachel knew it would be great seeing him. What the hell, Carlos was going to be busy tonight with clients. "If it's not too quick of a notice, I'm going to be free tonight."

"What about your boyfriend?"

"You know I'm dating Carlos, but he's busy tonight, and we're not engaged or anything." She couldn't believe she used the word *engaged* and wished she could retract the comment.

"Great! I'll pick you up at six, if that's okay with you."

"Sounds great!" She smiled at the prospects of going out on a date. Carlos didn't own her. Yes, she really liked him, but he had been mean to her by leaving her all alone last night. Perhaps, this would teach him a lesson.

Chapter 24

The café at the marina looked crowded for a weeknight, but it was one of those places Rachel enjoyed experiencing the special fares of the awarding winning chef who recognized her as she walked to her favorite table. He had come out to greet her many times in the past. "Hello, how are you tonight? It's good to see you again."

"It's good to be here, as well." She motioned to her date. "This is —"

"–Hello, Aaron." The chef interrupted, apparently recognizing him instantly.

"I'm looking forward to some great food tonight, Andrea." Aaron glanced at the unobstructed view of boats and the clear sky above. "It's going to be great weather this evening."

"Yes, and I've some fresh Grouper in. I know you'll love it." Andrea turned to make his way back to the kitchen and left the waitress at their table.

Rachel heard a large group speaking in perhaps French, she thought, behind them. She hoped they wouldn't be so loud as to be distracting, but her only choice was to change tables. No, she wanted to sit here.

The night progressed as Rachel listened to Aaron talking about boating. His interest and knowledge fascinated her. While the French group behind her continued to have fun, she did her best to ignore them.

During dessert, Aaron turned his attention to questions he apparently had on his mind—Carlos. "I've been thinking about this guy you've been dating . . . ." He allowed his word to die on purpose, as if he wanted Rachel to respond.

Rachel laughed as she sipped the last of her wine, washing down a great crème d'mint. "I thought you would have questions about us."

Aaron remained quiet, intentionally waiting for her to volunteer information. His smile stayed pleasant, but his eyes became penetrating, almost haunting.

"Carlos is a great guy. Yes, he's young, and sometimes immature, but you know the saying, he's great in bed." She couldn't believe she told him this. "I think this is the kind of affair all women dream about at one time or another. Now, tell me, Aaron, you really can't blame me, can you?"

He let a little devilish smile pass his lips. "I guess I'm not one to cast stones."

This confession confirmed what she had heard about him and some of the parties on his boat. "Believe me when I say that I've been teased many times about hauling him around like a boy toy."

"I understand." She heard him laugh loud, which felt good. She knew it would be good to see Aaron again, and she didn't want to scare him off with the notion Carlos had her all to himself.

As the wine continued to relax her, she noticed the French group behind her stand to leave. When she turned to glance at them, her eyes suddenly locked in on Carlos. *Had he been in the group behind her? Did Carlos hear her talking about him? Ohmigod!* His face frowned at her.

One of Carlos's friends, or perhaps clients, slapped him on the shoulder and broke the concentration between her and him. After Carlos spoke French, sounding almost native in his accent, his friend laughed before yelling back at him in French. She wished she knew what they had said.

Rachel watched Carlos glance over at Aaron and smile before he nodded his head toward her and turned back to his friends. *Was that it?* Embarrassed, she turned toward Aaron who was studying the situation. Moments later she turned back around and watched the French group proceeding toward the front of the restaurant, and still yelling to each other in French. *How did Carlos learn French this well? And who were these clients of his?* She studied the group as they left. They all looked to be in their early or mid twenties. All of them stood tall, even the girls. She would guess over six feet tall or they wore high heels. Their clothes looked great, designer quality at the least.

So Carlos had some sophisticated clients, clients with money and style. *Who were they? How did he know them?* She needed to ask him later. That was later, if he wasn't too mad at her. She hoped that she could explain the date as a business dinner. If he had overheard her, that would be another story.

She turned back toward Aaron, the expression of helplessness written all over her face. "I'm sorry. I didn't expect to see him tonight."

Chapter 25

Rachel stopped by her real estate agency's kitchen to pour a coffee. She hadn't slept well at all last night. She never heard from Carlos, but she had expected as such. The coffee smelled so good. Now, if the magical liquid would only refresh her like she hoped.

Cindi smiled and jumped to her feet as soon as she saw Rachel. "How did your date go last night?"

Rachel thought the dark sunglasses being worn inside should tell it all. She forced a smile. "I've a bad headache. Do you have anything I can take?"

Cindi raised her fingers to cover her mouth as a playful laugh escaped. "Was the night that good, or that bad?" Cindi continued to bounce as she stood in front of her.

Rachel lowered her sunglasses. "Carlos saw us last night."

"Ohhhhhhhhhhh shit!"

"My words exactly, and he may have overheard me talking about him. I need to talk to him and explain."

Cindi started searching in her desk for something for Rachel's headache. "Well, you'll have your chance soon. He's coming by here before lunch."

Rachel knew she had a dumb look on her face, kind of one of those deer in the headlights types. This wouldn't be a good place to talk to him. "I need to call him." She walked toward her office and closed the door, almost slamming it.

She waited for several minutes as she tried to calm down and decide what she wanted to say. As she reached for the phone, she heard a knock on the door before she dialed.

"Yeah, come on in."

Cindi peeked around the corner as she opened the door. "I've good news. We received a fax. They accepted the contract from yesterday."

Good, good, good. That was great. She really needed this sale–especially considering the news of what her boat was worth last night. Aaron had told her the boat had a value of twenty thousand less than she owed. "Fantastic. I'll give the buyers a call now."

The call lasted a long time as she answered one question after another. They were really ideal clients. Rachel heard Cindi knocking on the door, seconds after she hung up. Apparently Cindi had been waiting on her. "Carlos is here."

With her lifted spirits she could face him, so she motioned for Cindi to send him in. As he walked in, he closed the door behind him, which was something he never did before.

Rachel raised her hands in self defense before he could say a word. "I can explain."

He looked puzzled. "Explain what?"

He either didn't hear her, or he was acting dumb. She decided to play along. "I was referring to the guy I was with last night." He kept the puzzled look, waiting on her to continue. "He's the guy who talked me into buying my boat, and I needed to know what it is worth now."

"I understand. I was going to call you last night, but we all went to see my boat last night and we stayed onboard until early this morning."

"Boat, you own a boat?"

"Yes, but I've been having the inside remodeled and updated, and they just finished the work yesterday. They did a great job and I can't wait to make a trip in it. In fact . . . the boat's why I stopped by. My friends are only going to be here for a few more days. We're going to the Keys this weekend and I want you to go with us."

"This weekend! I don't have time to take such a trip. It takes a day to drive to the Keys and a day back. Add any time in the Keys at all and before you know it, you wasted most of a week."

A large smile crossed his face. "How long it takes all depends on the boat, I guess. I can be in the Keys in less than four hours . . . and from what I hear, the water is going to be perfect. Listen, we plan on stopping by Naples for dinner on Friday night and heading down as soon as we climb back on board. My boat sleeps eight, so I've plenty of room."

"How big is your boat?"

"It's a sixty-five foot powerboat."

"Wow . . . that's impressive."

She started to ask him how in the hell he could afford such a toy, but he pushed her again on a commitment. "We'll be back late Sunday night. What do you think?"

"I can't. I wish I could, but I can't. I need to work on the weekends, especially this one. I have an open house on Sunday at the condos. If I don't, the new owner, Michael, will be mad. I could lose the listings."

Carlos looked stunned. "I'm sure you can find someone to cover for you."

There was a slight chance, naturally, but this is one Sunday that she needed to go all out. "I'm sorry. I can't."

"Okay, but you're going to miss a great time." He walked toward the door, but turned before he left. "I heard you made a nice sale yesterday. I'm glad for you."

Smiling, he pulled the door behind him as her eyes shed tears. She couldn't ever remember crying like this. Well . . . at least in a long time. She wiped them with a tissue and straightened her back. She had plans to make and work to do.

She paused and thought about his friends–his *French friends*. *Who are they?* She concentrated on their images from the night before. The two great looking guys about the same age as Carlos looked to be good buddies of his. She wished she had studied the three girls with them more. They were also young and she had to admit beautiful, almost like super models. The numbers quickly calculated in her mind–three guys and three girls on a cruise to the Keys. Surely, he wouldn't . . . .

Chapter 26

Rachel rushed through one of Michael's condos that she had for sale, letting her mind plan the staging. "I think we need to really dress this room up. What do you think?"

Lisa, an interior decorator followed behind her, making notes. "We've something in the warehouse I think will do great. I wish we had more time."

"Sorry, I do also, but I need to finish this tonight. We recently changed our mind and decided to make this an all day Saturday and Sunday open house." She breathed heavily, but knew she would be at the open house until late, working on all of the final details.

Cindi rushed in from the kitchen. "I think we have all of the food here we need for tomorrow. I'll bring some more ice in the morning."

"Thanks, I hate to ask you to work over the weekend, but I'm going to need you some."

"Not a problem. I know you have several condos open at once. With the ads we're running and the amount of publicity you've paid for, the traffic should be great."

Rachel glanced around. "I hope you can stay until we're finished tonight. This place brings back some bad memories."

"I understand. Don't worry." Rachel knew she had asked a lot of Cindi. She probably had plans of her own for the weekend.

Rachel opened the refrigerator and examined the wine inside. "I hope this will be enough. I sure don't need to spend any more money on this."

"It should be more than enough. If the food or wine runs out, I can go for some more, or we can just quit serving." Cindi walked around the kitchen, waiting on further instruction on how she could help.

Lisa walked back into the kitchen with the phone stuck to her ear. "We'll be right down." She pocketed her phone. "I have more boxes and pictures downstairs. The men will bring up the furniture, but they want us to help with some of the smaller items."

Rachel led the way. "Let's get to it. I want to finish up as fast as we can."

Cindi followed her, leaving the door open behind her. Rachel stopped and looked at it. "Perhaps we need to lock the door."

"Sorry." Cindi turned to pull the door shut. "I know you're concerned about safety. Have you heard from Carlos?"

"No. I'm sure he's on his way to the Keys by now. I still can't believe he's abandoning me this weekend." Rachel forced herself to remain strong. She had already cried all she wanted to the last few nights.

***

Rachel placed all of the food and wine on the counter, rearranging it several times for the perfect style. Putting out the open house signs required more time than she had thought. She assumed the traffic would be slow at first, but she would never know for sure. She walked through the condo, turning on lights.

While the quietness of the condo haunted her, she knew her nerves would be much better once people started showing up. *Where is Cindi?* She stopped to adjust the temperature as she studied one of the flyers before walking back into the kitchen.

With her eyes studying the wording, she didn't notice a

man standing in front of her at the kitchen until she almost walked over him. "Ohmigod!"

Rachel jumped backwards, dropping the stack of flyers to the floor. "Damn, you scared me." She raised her hands to her throat, trying to catch her breath.

"Sorry, I didn't mean to scare you. I thought you would like a little company this morning." Michael reached over to pat her on her shoulder. "Are you okay?"

"Yeah, I'm fine. I guess I wasn't expecting anyone yet." Embarrassment replaced the fear. She needed to act more professional.

Michael glanced around the condo. "Wow, it looks like you've been busy. The place looks great."

It should, Rachel thought, she had worked on setting it up until late into the night. With the presence of someone all night haunting her, she enjoyed having others with her now. There was no way she could stay here on her own. "Thanks, I appreciate it, but I've received a lot of help."

"I can't stay long, but if you need me to do anything at all, please let me know. You have my number." He picked up one of the flyers. "Is it okay if I keep one of these?"

"Sure, help yourself. If you have any suggestions on improving the ads, let me know. Cindi, my assistant, did the work on this one. I think she did a great job."

Michael smiled as he studied the work. "You're lucky to have someone so talented. You need to make sure you hold on to her."

Rachel knew she made a good choice in hiring Cindi and she hoped to hold on to her for a long time. However, the salary Rachel paid her hurt when sales fell to this level. While it would be great to give Cindi a raise, Rachel just hoped that she could just keep paying her right now. Maybe when Cindi obtained her license, she would be able to generate more sales and help pay her way more. She remembered promising Cindi some bonuses when she obtained her licenses. "I think she's happy."

"Good. Call me if you need me." He turned and left, allowing the eerie quietness to creep back in.

She thought about Carlos again, probably having a blast with the group of skinny French girls. *How is he able to own such a boat? Did his parents have money?* Considering all of the time they had spent together, he still remained a mystery to her. She ran the scene of the night she went out with Aaron through her head over and over. *Did he hear me talk about him?* He had sat directly behind her. He should have let her know he was behind her.

During the night she constantly went from being mad at him to missing him. And now . . . he was partying with these girls. She tried to force herself to quit thinking about *these girls*. Feeling the tightness, a slight ache in her muscles from exercising the night before, she thought there must be a way she could lose some weight.

Rachel opened her purse and retrieved the pages she printed from the internet last night. The thoughts of having liposuction scared her. With the procedure so barbaric to her, she could feel the pain this had to inflict. Knowing she would be alone for most of the day, waiting on prospective buyers to come by, she decided today would be a good time, however, to read more about the procedure.

***

Rachel could hear them coming, laughing and having fun. Mary Jane, Margaret and Gloria walked through the door and headed for the wine. They had dressed to impress tonight. Apparently they had made big plans on going out later. While she knew they heard about Carlos's trip, she enjoyed knowing that they, at least, cared about her. With Carlos partying with the bunch of skinny girls from France, she needed their support. It made little sense trying to impress them with how she had him in tow as a boy toy.

"This condo looks almost exactly like Jody's." Mary Jane glanced around the kitchen. "Of course, she did have a much different decorating style. Does someone live here?"

Rachel smiled as she poured some wine for her friends. "How do you like the way we staged the condo? I think the decorator did a great job"

"Well yeah, the floor plan has a great flow to it." Gloria examined some of the pieces scattered around the kitchen. "I might have to get her name from you."

Margaret remained quiet as she studied the room. "Has anyone heard how Jody is doing?"

Rachel dropped her smile. "I've tried to see her many times. She's being guarded, and they're not letting anyone in to see her. I've heard the only one to be allowed in is her sister."

All eyes quickly darted around. Rachel knew they all had heard about the tragedy of Jody's sister without saying a word. The thoughts of what Angela had been through flashed across Rachel's mind. Ricky, the masseur, the boy toy passed around by the group earlier, had been caught having sex with Angela three years ago when she was sixteen. To her it was love, but to the district attorney and the court it was statutory rape. Ricky had been sent off, never to have been heard from again.

Margaret broke the silence. "Is Angela still going to school at the University of Miami?"

Rachel answered. "I think so. She'll eventually have access to her sister's condo above us, but for now the detective has the unit sealed off and hasn't allowed her into it."

"Didn't Angela stay with her sister from time to time?" Mary Jane asked as she reached for a piece of cheese.

"I'm sure they saw each other some, but Angela didn't

like living here since she had been treated like a tramp by her friends. I can understand why she wouldn't want to ever return." Rachel suddenly wondered how much contact, if any, the other girls had with Angela.

Rachel allowed her eyes to drift from one girl to the next. While they had joked about Ricky for several years, she knew she would never know the truth. Yes, they all received massages by him. How much of a massage remained a guarded secret, and probably would always be.

Mary Jane, an attorney with a reputation to protect acted like he performed great. Perhaps she had overplayed reality in order to divert the truth. If anyone had full sex with him, Rachel considered her to be the most likely one. But . . . Ricky wasn't caught offering male prostitution; he was caught with a sixteen year old.

There was also Margaret, who also had a professional reputation to protect. Whiles she was normally too reserved to be that daring, she had been talked into having a massage several times.

Gloria, the youngest of the group and perhaps the wildest, owned a spa, and she could've hired Ricky to work for her, but never did. Rachel knew of Gloria's attraction to Ricky. She may have been avoiding a working relationship with him on purpose because of this.

In looking around the room, Rachel assumed all of the other girls were doing the same thing as she was–trying to guess Ricky's history. While the group talked openly in many ways, this one secret separated them.

Rachel poured herself a glass. "Everyone, please enjoy the wine and cheese; I'll be back in a minute. I need to retrieve the open house signs outside."

Several asked at once. "Do you need any help?"

"No. It'll only take a second." Rachel left the kitchen and walked fast toward the elevator, which arrived promptly.

Being vacant, she stepped inside and pushed the button for the first floor. The elevator, however, stopped on the third and opened to a vacant floor. Rachel pushed the button to close the door and continue. It next stopped on the second floor, another vacant floor.

Rachel peeked around the edge of the elevator before exiting on the first. A side door leading to the beach outside closed as she stepped out of the elevator. She walked in the other direction, and toward the front of the building, where she needed to walk to the street and retrieve the open house sign. She reached in her pocket, checking to make sure she had carried her phone with her.

As she almost reached the door, it swung open. "What are you doing here?" Rachel asked.

Aaron pushed the door open further. "I wanted to stop by and check on you."

"Thanks, I could've used some company earlier. If you don't mind, you can walk me out to the curb to retrieve my signs. The open house is over now."

"Ooh, I'm sorry I'm late." He turned to walk with her.

"I'm really glad you came to check on me. There's something about this place making me feel uneasy. I know it has to be all of the deaths occurring here lately."

He smiled and offered his arm as they walked–a true gentleman, she thought. "I know you'll be glad to sell these remaining units. How did the open house go today?"

She started to lie, but changed her mind, hoping she could trust him. "Not good. I hope tomorrow will be better."

"I'm sure it will be. What are you doing tonight?"

She knew she already got in trouble once by going out with him. *However, who am I kidding? Carlos is the one down in the Keys, doing who knows what.* Still, she hesitated. He may be in the Keys because of her treatment of him, and he did invite her to come along. "I've several of my girlfriends upstairs for a little get-together."

"I see–perhaps later." He reached over and pulled the open house sign out of the ground.

"Perhaps." She smiled, as she decided to keep her options open.

He stopped as he reached the entrance. "I'll call you. Who knows, I might stop by and check on you tomorrow." He followed the comment with a small wink.

Rachel laughed. "A little company would be good. I'll see you tomorrow."

Rachel walked back to the elevator and hurried inside. As the elevator lifted, she closed her eyes to think about Ricky. He wasn't really a bad guy. Yes, he had made a bad mistake . . . and it was great that the police didn't push too hard on fully investigating his business. Rachel knew all of the girls owed him for not mentioned them or calling them to his defense. The truth could've ruined their careers. Angela had scared all of them. Jody had done the smart thing by moving her to a different city.

Rachel's thoughts floated to the one time she had allowed Ricky to give her a full massage. When she turned on her back, his hands caressed her. He slowly explored more and more of her body, and was always so close to the bottom of her stomach. With each breath, she thought he would slip lower to her pussy.

She remembered him talking to her, asking her if she liked the massage. She remembered groaning, only groaning and nothing more. He slipped his hand lower. Years later, she still remembered wanting his touch. When he finally asked if she wanted more, she groaned, giving him full permission to massage her. Damn, she loved it.

The bell announcing the floor arrival startled her out of her daydream, slightly scaring her that she had let her guard down. Rachel walked out and toward the condo where her friends still laughed loudly. As she entered she heard them talking about a cruise they were leaving on tomorrow, and one that she wished she could go, but there was no way. If Cindi had obtained her license and could cover for her, she could go on the trip, but Cindi hadn't even taken her test yet. Perhaps next week she would. She would think about going on a cruise as soon as Cindi could cover. She needed to escape from work, just like her friends.

Rachel entered the room and walked to the counter, pouring herself a full glass of wine. She needed to forget her problems and just hope she could drive home later.

Chapter 27

The next day Rachel sat by a small table in the den, waiting on traffic to come to her open house. She knew Sunday morning would be slow, with the church group coming more in the afternoon. She flipped through her information on liposuction again and saw where it wouldn't cost anything for a consultation. This was crazy. She was too much of a chicken to go through this, especially with no one to go through the process with her.

Rachel heard a knock on the door and saw Aaron entering the condo. She slid the papers into her case before he could see what she was reading. "Hi."

"I hope I'm not too early." He glanced around the den. These units are a little smaller than I thought."

"You know how it is. Places on the beach are limited, and they try to build as many units in a building as they can to keep them affordable. Most of the units in here are one bedroom units, with a few two's, and only one floor with three bedrooms."

"Have you had anyone looking yet?" He walked over and examined some of the pictures on a wall.

"You're the only one so far." She hated to admit it, but that was the way things were in the real estate business now.

"I'm going to take my boat out this afternoon, and I hoped you could come along." She watched him standing still, looking like a puppy dog, waiting on an answer.

Her thoughts cluttered her mind too much as she failed to answer him timely. She smiled, hoping she reached the right answer.

***

The day dragged, allowing too much time for Rachel's mind to conjure up scenes of Carlos playing in the Keys with his stable of skinny French girls. She missed him and wished she had gone with him now. The open house had wasted her time, but perhaps her efforts would satisfy the new owner for a while.

She heard a small knock on the door and quickly forced a smile, one which faded as soon as she saw Detective Lindstrom standing in the doorway. She strained to remain her smile, in spite of her growing distaste of the problems he reminded her of. "How are you today, detective?"

He strolled in, glancing around the room. "I'm fine, for a Sunday. I was going to call you tomorrow, but when I saw the open house sign I decided to stop by and ask you a special favor."

"I see, but of course it depends on what kind of favor you're looking for." She studied his face for any kind of a clue.

He stopped in front of her. "I know this is asking a lot from you, but we're still unable to obtain any breaks in these cases." He paused to take a larger breath. "I have to release Jody's condo upstairs soon, and I hoped to talk you into coming to take a look at it with me, just to see if you notice anything all of us professionals are overlooking."

Oh hell no. The images of Jody trying to commit suicide flooded her mind. Her face tightened.

He raised his hands as if in self defense. "I know what you're thinking. The room has been cleaned, but we still have her personal effects in the condo. I think Jody would appreciate it very much if you helped us find her killer."

Visions of Jody in bed at the hospital materialized in Rachel's mind. Yes, Jody would appreciate it. She bit her lip, but remained still. "I'm not sure I can do this."

His mannerism stayed controlled, but insistent. "We'll not stay any longer than you want."

Small beads of tears formed in the corner of Rachel's eyes. She needed to turn from him to save face. "Okay, but I can't promise I can stay long. I need to concentrate on my open house."

He placed a hand on her shoulder. "I understand. I'll be in her condo waiting on you." After he removed his hand, she soon heard his withdrawing steps.

***

Rachel's heart beat hard as the sweat beaded in the palms of her hands. I can't do this, she repeated in her mind. Each time she made her mind not to show, she saw Jody in the bed, lying still and unable to help herself.

She soon noticed the door open as a rush of fear overtook her. With the detective standing slightly inside the doorway staring at her, it was too late to back out now. He waved at her to come on in.

Rachel forced her eyes to behave; she knew they were darting around, wildly allowing her to scan the condo. She breathed easier as she observed the clean organized kitchen. Good, no blood stains, yet. "Detective, I'm not so sure about this."

He moved closer to her to offer his assistance, apparently hoping she could control the faint feeling fighting inside her. She smiled in appreciation of his concern, as he spoke slowly. "We've been over and over this room. I know it's a long shot, but it would be a big help if you can tell me anything that you see that is out of the ordinary here. Please, take your time."

Rachel walked around the kitchen, thinking of the last time she had visited Jody. Visions of her friends having a party played through her mind. She blinked her eyes, attempting to erase the images. The room looked too straight, too perfect. "Was everything like this when you discovered her, or did you have this room cleaned?"

"This is the way we found the kitchen. Why?"

"I don't remember Jody keeping her place this organized." She swallowed hard. "Where did you find her?"

"We discovered her at a small desk in the bedroom. We'll go there when you're ready."

Ohmigod no, she thought. She looked for a reason to stay in the kitchen. A picture of Jody's sister, Angela, stood on the back of the counter. She looked to be fifteen or sixteen. This sordid past must have played hard on Jody. Rachel wondered before if it had any connections, but surely not since the scandal had happened so long ago.

The detective followed her gaze and reached for the photo. "Angela has wanted to take over the condo and prepare it for sale. She said she has no interest in living here."

"I can understand. I know she visited Jody some, but not too often at all." Rachel hung her head slightly.

"I know the story, and I talked to Angela about the past extensively. One fact we've not released to the general public, and one I trust you'll keep confidential, is that Angela is the one who discovered Jody here."

Rachel raised her hands to her mouth. "I never heard this before. In fact, I'd wondered who found her."

"The shot was heard by many of the neighbors, but no one could tell exactly where it came from. It was later when Angela arrived to find her sister dead." She watched the detective's steady examination of her face.

"It had to be terrible for her." Rachel studied Angela's photo and how similar Angela and Jody looked as sisters. "How is she?"

"She has been in therapy since this happened. On the advice of her psychologist, she hasn't been allowed back in the condo."

Rachel thought about Angela; she should've been there for her. She owed this much to Jody. "I need to see her. Jody would want me to."

"Is there anything else you notice different about the room?"

Rachel studied the room, but had trouble focusing. "I don't know."

The detective reached out and squeezed her arm. "I know this is hard, but let me help you to see the rest of the condo. I'll be right here with you."

They walked into the bedroom where a sheet covered the floor. Rachel could only guess what the carpet looked like under the sheet. The rest of the room looked to be clean and in perfect order. This looked strange, but Rachel didn't say a word.

The Detective stood still, patiently waiting on Rachel. "I'm sure you've been in this room before. Can you think of anything missing?"

Rachel thought of the designer clothes and accessories Jody liked, but nothing really came to mind. The door to the closet had been left slightly open. She decided to open the door and see what she left hanging. The clothes were packed in, much like she would've expected. She recognized several outfits as well as shoes carefully placed in a floor to ceiling holder. How was she to know if anything was missing?

The detective stood quietly, watching. "We're going to release this condo soon to Angela. I think this is a mistake, but the judge told my boss to expect the order soon. I hope you understand why I'm asking you to help me."

"I understand." Rachel reached for the clothes and parted them, hoping to recognize some of them. Almost at the back of the closet, she stopped. Two outfits appeared to be too large for Jody and still had a crisp new look to them. Thinking fast, she moved past them–the last time she had seen these was when she had purchased the same. *What are they doing here? Did the killer place them in the closet for me to find later? Was it a sign? Oh my God! Should I tell the detective?*

Rachel forced her hands to remain stable. "Jody . . . always had good taste." Her voice trailed off with a sob.

"I can tell. Angela will, of course, have all of these shortly." He helped stabilized Rachel as she weaved. "Are you okay?"

"Yes, but I need to get out of here. I need some fresh air." A sick, light headed feeling passed over her.

Her vision blurred as she relied on the detective to lead her out of the room. "I'm so sorry. I wish I could help you more." Her vision returned to normal when she returned to the kitchen.

Another thought occurred to Rachel. Maybe she had overreacted. Perhaps Jody had purchased two identical outfits to give to Angela. She knew Jody shared a love for a lot of designer styles that she also loved, and Angela was close to the same size as Rachel. She breathed deeply, allowing her head to clear more.

Rachel glanced at the photo on the counter one more time. "I hope you get to the bottom of this soon. I'm turning into a nervous wreck. Everywhere I go, I feel like someone is following me."

His face reflected a cold stare. "If I were you, I'd be careful until we do. We still don't have a suspect, and the motive is anyone's guess. Have you ever purchased a gun?"

"I'm working on it. It takes some time."

"Call me if you need some help. I might be able to push your gun permit through faster if you encounter a problem."

"Okay, I need to buy one, but I know nothing about guns,

nothing at all."

"Well, If I was you, I'd not go anywhere by myself. You know you can call me if you feel you're being followed. I want to solve this case, much like you do."

Rachel smiled and turned toward the door, saying nothing else since she needed time to think. She wanted to go home, to close out the world, but as she reached for her phone, she stopped. There had to be someone she could call; someone to talk to. *Damn it! Why did Carlos have to go to the Keys this weekend? Damn him!*

Chapter 28

The escrow agent slid the commission check over to Rachel as the relief flowed through her body. This transaction had been difficult, but finally, yes finally, the deal closed. She smiled at the new owners and placed the check in her folder. "I think you'll be happy with your new home."

The couple glanced at each other and smiled. "We hope so. This is the last time we'll ever go through this."

Rachel forced herself not to show how much she agreed with them. This closing pushed everyone to the limits and beyond. The requirements of the mortgage company kept changing. Yes, they were being careful, but this was ridiculous. This was definitely a commission check she wasn't going to spend until the contract closed. She smiled, knowing that this check would cover many of her problems. Generating almost thirty thousand in commissions, it represented a great sale. She had earned more than this amount many times before, but not lately.

Rachel stood and thanked everyone as she moved toward the door. She knew the broker would cut her a check for her part by tomorrow if she hurried to turn the paperwork in. While she knew most of the money was accounted for, she needed to celebrate some. It was so bad that her friends were still off on the cruise. As far as Carlos was concerned, she hadn't heard from him all week. Well, tough luck for him, she thought. She felt in the mood to spend some money and have a great time.

On the way to her car, she flipped open her phone, but

walked with it inactive in her hand. There must be someone she could have a good time with tonight. She finally decided to wait until she returned to the office to make some calls. She had not heard from Carlos for a while now.

***

Cindi flashed Rachel a big smile as she walked in to her office. "Hey, I heard you closed."

"Ohmigod, yes. I don't remember the last time I put so much work into one sale." She staggered to her desk, reiterating just how exhausting this case had been.

"Here, give the file to me, and I'll prepare it for turning in. If I hurry, we can receive the check back from the broker by tomorrow."

Rachel pulled the file from her bag. "Thanks, I appreciate your help very much."

Cindi continued to smile. "I have also obtained some good news–I passed the exam this morning!" She jumped up and down in a victory dance.

Rachel became so focused on the closing she had forgotten all about Cindi taking the real estate exam. "Wow, that's fantastic! I knew you would. You know more about real estate than most agents." Rachel turned and gave Cindi a hug.

"I hope I can take some more of the pressure off of you now. I know how exhausting cases like this can be." Cindi jumped up and down as she shared her youthful celebration with Rachel.

"Yes, I can use your help, especially in showings and doing open houses." This would be a big relief to Rachel. If Cindi had passed her test earlier, she could have gone on the trip to the Keys with Carlos. Also, if she made this closing earlier, as originally scheduled, she could be on the cruise with the other girls. It would be a few more days before they returned.

"My parents are taking me out to eat tonight to celebrate." Cindi handed Rachel the paper showing where she passed.

"That's great." Rachel glanced at the notification and gave the paper back to Cindi.

"Rachel, what are you going to do to celebrate this closing?"

"I'm not sure. I still haven't heard from Carlos, and my girlfriends are all gone. I might go shopping."

"If you do, be sure to be careful. I'm still worried about this killer."

Rachel wished Cindi hadn't reminded her about this. "Trust me, I will be."

"Why don't you call Carlos?" Her eyes reflected a more than unusual intuitiveness.

"He's the one that disappeared to the Keys. I think he needs to call me." She forced her head high.

"Hmmm. If it was me, I'd call him."

Rachel studied her statement. She might be right, but she had waited this long. She knew she played a silly game, but it was the only way she knew how to stay in control. If only it hadn't been for those silly, skinny French girls. "I don't think so. I think he'll call me soon."

"Okay . . ." Cindi walked off with the files, examining them as she left.

Rachel rested, unable to take her mind off of Carlos and his trip. She ran her hand down to her legs and around to her large cahootus. She had thought about taking care of this forever. She opened a drawer and hunted for the file on the liposuction she had been accumulating information on.

The most important consideration for her was down time. Since Cindi had obtained her licenses, she would have some time now. While she had seen different reports on how long the surgery would take to heal, she assumed at least one week. She would stay at home, and maybe do some light work. The bruising could last for as long as two months, but good clothing could cover this, she thought. Total recovery could take as long as six months–a fact which scared her more than she wanted to admit. At thirty-eight, however, she thought her skin was still young enough to recover quickly. Yes, she knew the surgery must be painful. However, she could deal with the pain if she received the results she wanted. She smiled as she realized the check had just given her the money she would need for the procedure.

Rachel retrieved her phone and called one of the recommended surgeons. She would owe it to herself to at least check out the full details. Ohmigod, she couldn't believe she was really considering doing this.

***

Damn, Rachel cried softly. *What in the hell was I thinking?* Her legs and butt hurt like hell. While the drugs sedated her, making her feel woozy, it was not enough to take away all of the pain. Another nauseous wave passed over her. "Ohmigod." She mumbled enough to catch the attention of Gloria and Margaret who had agreed to come with her.

A light cloth applied to her head comforted her. "I know the surgery has to hurt, but the doctor said you did great." She heard Gloria's smooth voice attempting to make her feel better, but still not fully convincing her she hadn't made one terrible mistake.

"Thanks for being here." Rachel's voice sounded weak and her mouth dry.

"Just relax. Margaret has gone to find the nurse to get you some more medicine."

***

She remembered nothing more until she woke later the next morning. She groaned and looked around at an empty room. Finding the call button, she called for the nurse who responded immediately. "Can I help you?"

Since Rachel couldn't say a word, the nurse rushed into the room in seconds. "I see you're awake. How do you feel this morning?"

"Morning? I feel tired."

"I understand. You'll feel much better today and you'll be able to leave shortly."

Home. Mixed feeling entered her mind. *Who would take care of me at home?* "When?"

"This afternoon. Your assistant came by a few minutes ago. She said she would drive you home."

Rachel relaxed for a minute. "That's good."

"I've a lot to teach you today about taking care of yourself. You need to wear compression garments for at least the first few days following your surgery. This will decrease your recovery time."

Rachel remembered reading about this. The operation had happened so quickly. When she went into the office for a consultation, she had no idea she would be scheduled for surgery in a few days. "Okay."

The nurse smiled. "I think you're going to love the new you."

"I hope so."

"Now remember, you're going to be swollen for a while, and you'll not see the full benefit until later."

"I understand." Rachel twisted in the bed, hoping to feel the difference. "When can I get up?"

"I can help you stand right now, and the sooner the better." The nurse lowered the side rail.

With her resolve vanishing, Rachel pulled hard to attempt to sit. The cool air of the hospital registered on her back. "Where are my friends?"

"They had to leave, but your assistant has been here the

entire time. She's a real nice girl."

Rachel stood and for the first time really noticed the handiwork. She looked different, much different. "Wow."

The nurse's white teeth glistened in a large smile. "I take your smiles as a good sign."

Rachel stood in front of a large mirror, trying to ascertain how good the doctor matched her two legs and butt. She knew having them match perfectly was one of the main objectives. She saw the swelling and hoped it would dissipate soon, but both sides appeared to be the same. "What do you think?"

"The doctor will be in here shortly, and I think he'll be happy with the results." She helped Rachel to walk a little more. "This is good for you. You need to move around some."

After helping Rachel back into the bed, the nurse checked the sheets covering her. "I'm going to go over a few things with you. Your doctor has specialized in this procedure for years. Unlike other doctors, he used a three millimeter rod to perform the liposuction. Many use a six to eight millimeter rod. The larger rods are faster, but they can also leave more divots and other type puckers in the skin. He also places compression devices on your legs during surgery to help reduce the risk of blood clots developing."

"I appreciate his expertise very much. He told me most of this before we started. Call me a chicken, but I wanted to know what I was getting into." While the smell of the hospital left much to be desired, she enjoyed the feeling of the pillow under her head and the warm feeling of the covers.

"I know you feel like you have a lot of bruising, but the tumescent fluid the doctor used prior to performing the liposuction contains epinephrine, which is the same as adrenaline. This helps to restrict the blood vessels and thus bruising. The fluid also keeps the skin much smoother.”

“I hope so. I had no idea this procedure would hurt so much.”

“I know it does, but the good part is that the pain will not last for long. In fact, your major pain should disappear by tomorrow. The doctor will give you something to take with you, just in case you need it. You’ve already received some decadron, which is a steroid for the nausea.”

“How long do you think it will be before the bruising will be gone?”

“Usually, the bruising takes a few weeks to a month. To obtain the best results from your procedure, you should consider having some endermologie sessions.”

“What exactly are they?” She had gone this far and wanted to be sure to make her transformation the best she could.

“Relax; it’s an easy procedure where I use a hand suction device to smooth out the skin. Consider this a final ironing of the skin.”

“How often do I need to do this?”

“Obviously, the more treatments the better, but I think usually four to six times will do it.”

Cindi suddenly knocked on the door, smiling broadly. “Well hello, sleeping beauty.”

Rachel smiled when she saw her. “I heard you came. Who’s minding the office?”

“You amaze me, but don’t worry about a thing. As I told you, I’ll take care of everything until you recover.”

“I’m counting on it.” Rachel tried to sit as the nurse helped her with the controls on the bed and raised her higher.

“How long do you think you’ll be out?” Cindi asked, as she slid into a seat next to Rachel.

Rachel glanced over at the nurse. “I think I’ll be at home

for most of a week. If all is going good at the office, I've been thinking of taking another week off and spending some time on my boat. I want to take the boat to Naples to have some remodeling work."

"Wow—those plans sound ambitious." Cindi looked skeptical.

"I think it will be good for me to disappear and come back in full shape. This way you can tell everyone I'm off on vacation. I'd prefer if they didn't know I had this procedure until I return."

"I understand. I think I can cover for you so don't worry. You need to enjoy yourself."

The nurse looked puzzled. "Are you going sailing?"

"No, it's a power boat I seldom take anywhere."

The nurse pushed on. "Can you handle a boat on your own for a trip so far?"

Rachel laughed. "I think I can, but I'll hire a ship hand to help me. I know to be careful. However, a friend of mine says working on a boat can be great relaxation. I'm thinking of selling the boat and I need to make one good trip on it. Also, if I'm going to get top dollar for the boat, the interior needs some updating." Both the nurse and Cindi maintained a cautious eye on Rachel. "What? I know what I'm doing."

"I hope so. I don't need you turning too wild on me." Cindi allowed a smile to return. "Have you heard from Carlos?"

"No and I don't want him to know about this until I recover. If he calls, put him off for me. Tell him . . . I'm on vacation this time."

Cindi smiled, but Rachel realized she knew the truth. Rachel missed him, and it would've been nice to have him by her side now. She hoped this procedure made her as appealing as the skinny French girls she last saw him with.

Chapter 29

Rachel walked around her boat, a Sun Chaser, examining every inch as if for the first time. The ten year old fifty-five foot Neptunus Sedan Motor Yacht appeared to have not been used much; in fact, Rachel had only taken the Sun Chaser on three or four trips. She thought she could drive the boat, but why bother when she had a guy hired to help her? She owned the license needed, but knew a boat this size required more than one woman on board. He had also agreed to help her with some of the repairs she had planned.

She retrieved her phone and called Cindi. "How's it going today?"

"All is good; not much happening." Rachel expected her to say such. Without being in the office to generate business, she knew her sales would slow down. She hoped Cindi could keep the real reason she stayed out of the office quiet.

"That's good. I think I'm going to be leaving Saturday, the day after tomorrow."

"Are you sure you're ready for this?"

Rachel wished she knew for sure. "I think so. Staying inside all of the time is driving me crazy, and I need to complete this work on the boat."

"I meant to call you. Carlos called a few hours ago."

The rush of adrenaline surged through Rachel's body. "Really, what did he say?"

"Carlos keeps checking on you. He said he had tried to call you several times, but you never returned his calls."

Yes, he had left several messages, but since they all sounded professional, she had ignored them. "If he calls back, tell him I'm out of town." Her words sounded hard and cold, especially since she really wanted to see him. After considering all she had endured, she wanted to make sure that the next meeting was perfect.

She soon saw the hired hand, Jeff Brewer, lumbering toward her boat. While not a real go-getter, he was affordable. He had worked around boats most of his life, and he was apparently content to work part-time here and there. "Hello, I hoped you would be here soon." Rachel lifted an index finger to indicate she needed a moment. "Cindi, the guy I'm hiring to help me with the boat is here. I'm call you later."

"Okay, but be safe since you know the killer's still out there, and I'm worried about you." Rachel heard the line go dead.

While the deck hand's slim size made her wonder if she had made the right choice, his body showed signs of a rough life, one where he had worked on boats, clearly pulling his own weight. She guessed him to be around fifty. A Ray's baseball hat covered his head, which appeared to be almost bald from the side views. "Sorry, I'm late. I thought I had a ride, but I had to take the bus instead."

Rachel smiled. "No problem. I was examining the boat and trying to decide what all we can do ourselves."

"I've done some work before. What did you have in mind?"

"It all depends on the guy in Naples and what he charges. He'll do most of the major work."

"I see. When are we leaving?"

Rachel knew she needed to rest as much as possible before leaving, but she had watched all of the TV shows she could handle, especially the news channels which kept repeating the same specials over and over. "I'm thinking of two days from now."

"That sounds good to me. I can use the money." He walked on the boat. "Yeah, I can help you with some on the repairs. Depends on what you want to pay me."

"I'm sure we can work something out." A slightly uneasy feeling scared her as she planned to go off with a strange man, but he was a hired as a hand to work on the boat. She might even need him for some protection. "Do you own any tools?"

"I can come up with a few." His voice, which was rough from too many cigarettes, sounded sincere. She knew smoking wouldn't be allowed on her boat, and hoped it wouldn't be a problem.

While being proud of the contemporary styling and the functional layout, Rachel walked through the boat, talking to him about her plans. The radar arch added a special look, as well as the custom fly bridge enclosure. "I think a good coat of wax can improve the appearance greatly."

"I agree."

"Good, we can work on waxing the exterior while we're heading to Naples. I'm also thinking of doing several changes in the galley. I never liked this counter top. It should be an interesting two weeks."

He glanced around at his new home in the guest cabin. "I agree. Thanks for the job."

***

Rachel listened to Carlos's message several times. "Hi, call me. Cindi said she was covering for you. I didn't know you had planned a vacation." She knew if she called him, he would have many questions for her. She still wished she knew if he had heard her talking about him at the restaurant the night she went out with Aaron. She also wanted to know about his trip to the Keys, but she needed to be in control when she did. It wasn't the right time now, but it would be soon.

She packed all of the clothes that she thought she could handle. Since all appeared ready at the boat, she hoped to relax and allow her body time to recover more. The special sessions had helped as she thought about the last one she had received yesterday.

Rachel yawned as she thought of the little sleep she had gotten last night. The afternoon naps had upset her sleeping schedule. After slowly moving in front of the mirror, she dropped her skirt and examined her legs and rear one more time. They still looked swollen. She fought the depression overtaking her, wondering if she had made a good decision or not.

Mary Jane had promised to take her to the marina. Rachel smiled as she appreciated the offer. She could have asked Cindi, but her little car carried almost nothing. Mary Jane, by contrast, owned a large SUV with lots of room. She hoped all would be perfect when she returned, and just maybe they could find out who had committed all of the murders while she disappeared. For some reason, she considered her boat much safer than her condo. Every strange sound, every creak, or bump in the night sent panic through her nerves.

She smiled as she thought of the pistol she had purchased. The store owner showed her how to load and shoot it, but she had never fired it. She had packed the pistol and thought about firing the damn thing for the first time out at sea.

She heard a knock on the door. Even while expecting Mary Jane, her heart suddenly raced. "Hi, I decided to come on up. Did you know the front door below was left wide open?"

"What? Who would do something stupid like leaving the door unlocked?"

Mary Jane lifted her shoulders. "Sounds like you need to

schedule a meeting with your owners."

Rachel made a mental note to arrange one when she returned. Since security in her building is one item she thought she could count on, this needed to be handled immediately. "Did you close it?"

"Of course." Mary Jane walked over to examine the amount of luggage involved. "Wow, your boat must be larger than I thought."

"It's fifty five feet but has a lot of storage, which is one reason I like it."

"Okay, it's going to take several trips to the car. I don't want you extending yourself anymore than necessary."

Rachel smiled. "I'm really healing much more than it looks." She reached over to lift one of the bags.

"I wish I could go with you, but after going on the cruise I have my hands full now. We'll need to plan a party when you return."

"Yes, you can count on it. The boat should look great, and I should be recovered much more than now." She certainly hoped she would feel much better. "I'll talk to you more about the party over the next few weeks."

"Tell me what I need to do and who I need to . . . invite." She slowed her speech as she muttered the word "invite".

Rachel smiled. "As you know, I'll want to reintroduce myself to everyone, and I can think of no better way than this."

Mary Jane pressed on. "And I assume reintroducing yourself includes your *boy toy*." Rachel stopped walking. The use of the word to describe Carlos didn't seem to fit any more. Rachel knew Mary Jane sensed her feelings as she smiled back at her and said, "Don't worry. I'm good at keeping secrets."

Rachel replaced the frown with a smile, but offered no comments as to acknowledge or deny the inference.

***

With a hood over her head and wearing heavy glasses, Rachel walked to her boat as her hired hand, Jeff Brewer, rushed out to help retrieve the luggage. He had cleaned up his appearance from what she remembered from the last time she had seen him. Good, he considered the job to be serious. "Hello, Miss Contino, how are you today?"

Rachel smiled at his polite mannerism. "Better every day, thanks." She glanced around the boat. All looked secure–great. "I've more bags in Mary Jane's car you can help us with."

While not formally introduced to Mary Jane, he still nodded his head toward her. "Is the car unlocked?"

"No, I'll go back with you. I've something that I want to give Rachel before she leaves." Mary Jane glanced at Rachel with a devilish smile.

As she waited on them to return, Rachel walked around the boat, making final inspections in anticipation of leaving quickly. The thoughts of Mary Jane finding her condo building main entrance left open bothered her. She walked to her stateroom and lifted her bag onto the bed. The short twenty-two Smith and Western special she had purchased still scared her. She left the pistol in the holster as she placed it in the drawer beside the bed.

She soon heard Mary Jane and Jeff returning. Knowing Mary Jane maintained a busy schedule, she knew it would be a short goodbye. Curiosity made her hurry above to see what she had retrieved from her car.

Mary Jane walked toward her with a package in her hand, professional wrapped. "I think you might like this one day."

Rachel accepted the gift. "You shouldn't have." She ripped open the package to see a small sundress-type outfit. It looked so . . . small.

Mary Jane laughed. "I think it's going to take you some

time to get accustomed to your smaller size. We'll need to do some major shopping when you return, girl."

Rachel returned the laugh. "Yes, it's going to take some time. I'm so accustomed to hiding my cahootus that it's going to take some time to buy clothes to show my new one off!"

Mary Jane leaned forward and gave Rachel a hug. "Have a great time and call me if you need anything."

"Thanks, we'll be back in about two weeks."
***

The sweat rolled down her back as Rachel pushed herself to complete another workout. The library of tapes steadily increased as she became more and more obsessed in keeping the body she had purchased by way of the liposuction. She relaxed some, but spent many long days working on the boat and exercising. "I'm going for a quick swim," she said as she saw Jeff look up from the front of the boat.

She moved to the side and jumped in before he could say a word. The cove she had selected for the day provided the perfect end to the day. The water, slightly cold and refreshing, wrapped her body in a chill she knew would only be temporary. She returned to the top of the water and started swimming, feeling more alive now than she had in a long time.

After returning to the boat, she climbed the ladder and shook her head as she reached for her towel. She saw Jeff watching her. The sensation felt strange but good–even if he was simply hired help. She considered herself safe with him–more now than the first few nights where she had some misgivings.

"Are we still planning on going back tomorrow?" His voice indicting he enjoyed the trip and the work.

"Yes, I'm afraid so. Paradise can only last so long." She wrapped herself in her towel and decided to call Cindi.

Cindi answered in her usually cheerful voice. "How are you?"

"I'm doing fine. All of the work is complete, and we'll be leaving tomorrow morning. I know I need to work a lot when I return."

"Well, you know a lot of people have been asking for you. Angela did come by today and sign the papers to put Jody's condo on the market. She said the work will be completed by tomorrow on erasing all signs of her sister's death."

Rachel listened to the words carefully. "How is she with all of this?"

"To me, I think she's trying to act professional and uses this as a way to hide her emotions. She volunteers nothing, and she went back to Miami as soon as she left the office."

"I understand. She has a lot on her mind, I'm sure. I can't imagine being left with no one to turn to. She has no family left now."

"Also, you need to call Carlos. He stopped by the office a few hours ago."

"Really, what did he want?"

Rachel heard Cindi clear her throat before answering. "He's leaving for Europe in a day or two."

Chapter 30

After walking past the wine cooler, Rachel located the vodka. Hell, it already came flavored with some kind of strawberry shit, or maybe kiwi–whatever. She located some ice, a shaker and a glass. She studied Jeff watching her movements, but keeping a safe distance as she waved the bottle at him. "I'm going to leave you in charge of the boat for tonight. I want to see or talk to no one."

He smiled, but maintained a 'what the hell' look on his face, "I'll start getting ready for our trip home tomorrow."

"Don't worry about it. We'll do it tomorrow morning. There's no hurry since I don't think I'm going to be getting up too early." She headed for the top.

"Is everything alright, Miss Contino?" His eyes darted around.

"Hell no! But that's life. Don't worry about me. I'll be fine."

Rachel reached her favorite seat at the back of the boat and placed the bottle of Grey Goose on a side table. A shaker and glass soon found room next to the vodka. After realizing that she had forgotten the ice, she stood to make the trip back to the galley when she saw Jeff moving toward her with a bucket of ice. "Thanks, Jeff." Rachel smiled at him. Since he had been attentive to her on the trip, he definitely deserved a good tip when she returned to St. Petersburg.

"You're welcome. Can I bring you anything else, maybe something to snack on?"

"Maybe, but I want to be left alone tonight."

"As you wish." As he turned and left, she knew he would disappear for the night. She uncapped the bottle and poured the vodka over the ice in the shaker. *What is Carlos doing going to Europe? Is he going to see the French girls, those skinny little bitches?*

She shook the canister, releasing her rage. *How could he?* Almost to the point of pain, the canister turned colder and colder in her hands as she continued to shake until condensation covered the outside of the canister, glistening in the afternoon's display of colors scattered across the sky. Of all days, this sunset had to be one of those where the colors covered not only the area of the setting sun, but highlighted every cloud in the sky.

She knew most people would die for the setting around her. With the weather in the eighties and soft breezes full of the smell of fresh sea water, she forced herself to relax. She breathed deeply, taking in the essence of the good life. She closed her eyes and listened to the sound of seagulls above mixed only with the low rush of the winds blowing in from the gulf.

Rachel eventually poured her first drink as she studied the slivers of ice dancing on the top of her martini. The words of an old tune, *One is the Loneliest Number*, played in her head. Oh how true were the words. What the hell, she turned up her drink. The taste of strawberries and kiwi resonated on her tongue as the strength of the vodka soothed her. She anticipated the rush of numbness that would come soon.

As she heard the sound of a plate being laid beside her on the table, she focused to see a plate of cheese and crackers Jeff had prepared for her. "Thanks."

He smiled but didn't stay. He apparently knew she had problems she wanted to drink away.

She reached for her glass again as she analyzed her new

look. "Carlos, eat your heart out," she whispered. *Will I ever see him again?* A rush of small tears attempted to form in the corner of her right eye. She quickly wiped them clean before finishing her first glass.

The chill of the sides of the canister shot through her hands as she reached for it. However, the warmth generated by the golden liquid inside flowed through her body as the treasured concoction spread. While feeling the slight rocking of the boat caused by a passing boat, Rachel steadied her glass as she poured.

Rachel used her hands to explore the areas where she had the liposuction. The skin felt soft to her touch. She thought she still looked young for her age. She smiled as she considered the stares this would generate. Yes, for the first time ever, she imagined walking on the beach in a bikini–maybe not in St. Pete, where many people knew her, but definitely in Miami. She would need to make the trip to South Beach one day soon.

As the next drink started working its magic, she thought about her life and asked herself the *what if* questions. *Why did I wait so long to consider having this procedure done?* She had avoided the beach most of her life. Before, she had never wanted to be seen with all of the skinny girls in their bikinis. Now . . . yes, damn yes–it was now her time to shine!

Her mind flashed back to the times she had pretended not to hear the passing comments about her weight. Revenge was going to be sweet. She knew that her resentment over this longstanding issue wasn't a good trait, but from the years of abuse, she thought she deserved her one vindictive moment. More importantly, she looked forward to having fun shopping. The thoughts of going from a size twelve to a size four made her smile again.

"Carlos, damn you, I wanted you to see the new me."

While her whispered words spoken only to a half empty glass appeared half-lifeless, they reflected her challenge, to herself if no one else. If it takes making a trip to Europe to find him, she would track Carlos down. She finished her second glass.

Rachel glanced at the fading clouds above her as the breezes whipped cooler winds across her boat. She had one more drink in her shaker before she needed to add more vodka. The condensation on the side of the canister dripping on the table, reminded her of the first time she saw Carlos on the beach. From that first moment, she knew she had her hands full. Yes, she enjoyed pretending with the girls that she could control him–to make him into a boy toy. After all, her money provided everything she ever needed . . . until now.

A warm feeling crossed her body, partly fueled by the vodka and partly from memories of her times with Carlos. With her drink in one hand, she used her left hand to rub her legs and reaffirm the small size of her rear. She imagined his hard muscular body next to her and how he would treat her. She would not allow any more awkward positions designed to accommodate him. She glanced where her stomach hid her legs before as the thrill of seeing the transformation sent waves of ecstasy over her. She could see the top of her pelvis bone. She closed her eyes and imagined Carlos on top of her again. She ran her hand up her legs to her crotch, slightly massaging herself. She needed to have him again–at least once.

With her mind drifting off into a light sleep, she fantasized about the ways that she would make Carlos her boy toy for real. With this body, she would regain control, she told herself. She would make him beg for it.

Chapter 31

Rachel maneuvered through the marina, glad to be home. With a pounding headache for most of the morning, she had allowed Jeff to do most of the driving. She, however, wanted to be at the helm when she passed the other boats. As the afternoon quickly came to an end, Jeff moved around the boat and prepared to tie on.

Approaching her spot, Rachel smiled as she saw Cindi standing on the dock, waving. She knew Cindi had worked hard while she had disappeared on her trip. It would still be another week until Rachel thought she would be at full speed, but she intended to work as much as she could next week.

As soon as they pulled in and Jeff tied on, Cindi jumped onboard. "Hi, it's good to see you. I know you must have had a great time."

"Well . . . it helped a lot to vanish for a few weeks." Rachel stood to allow Cindi to see the new slimmer her. "What do you think?"

"Wow, you look great!" Cindi moved around Rachel. "I can't get over how much you look different. How do you feel?"

"I feel fantastic!" Rachel walked toward the boat and her stateroom. "We need to place some of my stuff in your car. I'll come back for the rest later."

Jeff returned from his cabin, carrying his small bag containing all of his belongs. "I have it all locked down." He glanced around the boat. "I'm going to miss this boat."

"You did a great job in the galley and I really appreciate

your help very much." Rachel reached for an envelope she had already prepared for him. "I think this will make you happy."

Jeff opened the envelope and a flood of emotions radiated through him. "Wow. This is too much . . . too much."

"You earned it. I hope you don't mind getting some more business, because I'll tell many of my friends about you."

Rachel thought she saw a small tear in his eye as he reached over and gave her a small hug before jumping off the boat. He never turned around as he walked toward town. She knew showing emotion was hard for him, but he acted happy, which also made her feel great.

After locking the door, Rachel and Cindi headed for the car. "So, tell me about last week."

"It was a normal week. All's going smooth, so don't worry." Cindi's smile faded. "However, I do have something I need to tell you."

Rachel braced herself. She didn't know if the news was going to be from a bad contract, or the murder investigation, but could feel the bad news coming. "What happened?"

Cindi walked quietly for several moments keeping her stare straight ahead before she finally spoke. "I spent some time with an old friend yesterday, and I discussed my options with my parents for a long time last night."

Rachel stopped walking. "What are you talking about?"

"I know this is bad timing, but I might never get a chance like this again." She paused and bit her lip. "I know you know Linda Durant. She has been a friend of mine for a long time, and she wants be to me her partner at her real estate company."

"What–you're leaving me?"

"I'm not leaving right now. It'll take a few weeks to get everything in place. I know you need me right now, and I feel really bad about this."

Rachel's heart pumped hard. "You just obtained your licenses and you have to know that you can make much more working for me than her. She has almost no listings."

"Trust me, I've thought about it. We both know your sales are falling and I know you need to start watching what you're spending. My parents agreed to help me until the market turns around." Cindi pulled away from Rachel.

Rachel thought fast about what to do. She didn't like the idea of her assistant leaving her. *Would she take some of my business with her?* She knew by working without an assistant, she would need to do all of the time-consuming work of the office, leaving her with much less time to actually sell. The thoughts of training someone else scared her.

Cindi stayed still, waiting on Rachel to cool off. "I'm so sorry."

Rachel knew she needed to put her best foot forward, so to speak. "We need to talk about this." She decided to turn and walk forward. "You know how much it cost to get started in real estate, and right now is a terrible time to do so."

"Yes, I've thought about it. I know you taught me a lot, and I'll stay until you find someone new." Cindi hurried to walk beside her.

Rachel thought about the three thousand she paid Cindi each month. Perhaps she could hire someone cheaper. *Who am I kidding?* It would cost her a lot to train someone new. "You know I just had this surgery. How long are you planning on staying?"

Cindi stopped walking and faced Rachel. "I think two weeks would be good."

"Two weeks." The unexpected pressure closed in on Rachel. "Okay, if working as an agent is what you really want." She wished she had the guts to call her a traitor to her face, but knew those comments would be scattered all over town.

Cindi smiled and walked on. "There's one more thing. Detective Lindstrom wants you to call him tomorrow. He has some new information for you on the murders."

"What information?"

"They expect Jody to come out of her coma in a few days with the use of a special drug they're going to use on her."

***

While answering the phone at her office, Rachel soon regretted allowing Cindi to take off the day to make arrangements for her life at her new real estate firm. Rachel now had to answer her own phone. While she realized Cindi was serious, she had retained the hope that Cindi might change her mind. "Hello, this is Rachel."

"Rachel, this is detective Lindstrom. How are you today?" His voice never failed to send chills up her spine, even when he tried to be friendly.

Rachel unloaded on him and spoke before she realized how her attitude must have come across. "Well to tell the truth, sales stink, my secretary is leaving me to go into competition against me, and my desk is a mile high due to a small vacation I went off on. What else do you want to know?"

She heard him breathe hard into the phone. "I'm glad you're in a good mood. I need you to come into the office for a minute. I've some questions I need to ask you, and I've some news you might not have heard yet."

"What news?"

After a long pause, he continued, "I think it's better if you come here."

A rush of images raced through Rachel's head. "What time do you need me to come to the station? I'm covered up this morning."

"I think the sooner the better. If you can't make it, I'll need to come see you."

The detective had been to her office so much lately she knew that it would be better if she went to see him. "Give me about thirty minutes." She glanced at her watch.

"Okay, I'll be waiting for you."

Damn, she had forgotten about Aaron coming by to see her. She needed to call him to let him know she had to reschedule. The thoughts of Aaron helping her plan a party forced her to smile, slightly forgetting the problems she faced. She could hardly wait to see the look on his face.

Rachel's phone rang again. Now what? "This is Rachel." No answer. She waited, holding her breathe. Time slowed. A faint rustling in the background, followed by a small thud ended the call. Rachel hung up, shaking.

***

After walking into the station, Rachel hurried to the back office where Detective Lindstrom smiled as he met her at the door. "I'm glad you could come see me. Please come in." Rachel walked past him without shaking his hand or saying a word. Lindstrom walked over to his chair behind the desk, as he glanced at her, allowing his gaze to study her. "You lost some weight." His eye brows arched as he continued to study her.

Rachel smiled and shifted in her seat. "Yes, a lot of weight. I had liposuction and left for a small vacation to recover."

"Hmmmm. Well, you look great. How are you feeling from it?"

"I'm still recovering. I hope to be operating at full speed soon." She watched him stalling, a trait he exhibited many times before as she stared quietly at him.

"I'll get straight to it. How well do you know Mary Jane

Allison?"

Rachel swallowed hard. *What is he trying to prepare me for?* "She is a friend of mine." She lifted her hand to her mouth, anticipating bad news.

"Mary Jane's secretary called us when she got to work this morning, she had an e-mail waiting for her from Mary Jane."

"What kind of message?"

"We're still analyzing the e-mail, checking to determine if it's authentic, but she stated that she felt scared of being murdered and was leaving. Since she left no way of getting in touch with her, we have decided to process this as a missing person for now."

"Ohmigod, do you think she has been kidnapped?"

"We've no proof of any foul play. Apparently, she thinks she's in danger. We're also trying to determine if she did send the e-mail."

Shock settled in as Rachel stared forward. "I talked to her a few days ago. She acted tense, but not much more than usual. She always has clients under extreme pressure. You know she practices as an attorney here in town, right?"

"Yes, I've worked with her before on some other cases. She's a good attorney." He lifted his cup of coffee and sniffed the aroma drifting out of the cup. "Would you like a cup?"

"No. Tell me more. What did her note say?" She knew he held back telling her everything.

"I can tell you this. She wrote a note stating she knew she had been followed and stalked. She thought she was being targeted and had to leave before it was too late. She instructed her law partner to take care of her cases until she returned. The letter also made her appear to be suicidal."

"No. This isn't like her." The anger boiled inside of her.

"I have to agree with you. She is a fighter."

"What's being done to find her?"

"We're making calls and checking with all of her friends, like you, trying to obtain an idea where she might've gone."

"I see. I know some of her friends, and most of them know her like I do. All I know is she used to be married, but she hasn't seen her ex-husband in a long time. I think he moved to New York. She works all of the time, like I do and I don't think she's dating anyone now."

"I understand. Why do you think she thought she was being stalked, and do you have any idea who this stalker might be?"

"I didn't think she had any problems. Yes, she heard us talking about the killer out there, the one killing the developers. I know she felt upset about Jody also. But . . . I've no idea why she thinks she's a target."

"I think there's a connection here somewhere. Let me say I see some similarity to the notes typed by the two faked suicides." He lifted his cup of coffee to his lips again, patiently watching her.

"You've got to find her." Rachel brushed her tears from the corners of her eyes.

"Trust me, we're working on it." He retrieved his pen and doodled. "I need you to tell me of any connections between her and the other victims."

Rachel touched the corner of her eyes again, allowing the rest of the tears to escape, but hoping not to ruin her eye shadow anymore than possible. Her mind searched for answers. Who else did Mary Jane know that she knew?

The detective appeared to know she was concentrating on his question and allowed her time to think. "We're a small group of women who gather together from time to time. There's, of course, Jody in the hospital, Margaret Barrington, a stock broker and one other–Gloria Sanchez– who runs a large spa here in town."

Detective Lindstrom made notes as she talked. "Have any of these other women said anything about being stalked?"

"Being single women, we're constantly on guard concerning predators out and about."

At the mention of the word 'predator' he continued, "Is anyone coming to mind that would make any of these women apprehensive?"

Rachel thought hard for a minute. "No one comes to mind."

"I know you've been seeing a Carlos Martin for a several months now. Are any other men seeing any of these women?"

"I was seeing Carlos. He went to Europe for a few weeks, and I've not heard from him since he left. As far as the others, I know of no special men around."

The questioning lasted for over an hour. Rachel grew tired as the fear increased. *Why did Carlos go to Europe right now, of all times?* She missed him and needed him. "I wish I could tell you more."

"You've been a lot of help. I do need to ask you one more question."

Rachel shifted in her seat, relieved that the questioning would soon be over. She wanted to talk to Gloria and Margaret as soon as she could. "Which question?"

"Jody's sister, Angela has an attorney, one appointed by the court, who keeps calling me. I've learned Jody is behind on the payments on her condo and they need to sell the place as fast as possible. I also understand you're the agent handling this listing. How long do you think it'll take you to sell it?"

Rachel let out a gush of air from her lungs. "In this market, who knows?"

"I understand. You would think Angela would be more cooperative in getting to the bottom of her sister's problems, but perhaps she's still in shock. And . . . she's only nineteen now."

"Angela has always been a little strange and a problem for her sister. I think the move to Miami was a good one. I heard she's doing well in college."

"I know she appreciates all you're doing for her. There's one last thing. The doctors treating Jody are thinking about using a special drug to bring her out of her coma."

"I heard." Rachel leaned forward as she forced her attention on him. "Is this safe?"

"I'm sure the doctors know what they are doing. They feel like they need to do this now since they think that a prolonged coma will only make things worse. And, of course, if she regains consciousness, we want to ask her a few questions. Her answers can help us tremendously, as you know."

"Yes, it would be great if she could tell us what happened."

"They're planning on doing the procedure sometime soon, depending on how she's progressing." He stood to signal that the interview was over.

"Please call me to let me know of any news on Mary Jane."

He walked around the desk, studying her as she stood. "I still have a hard time believing how much weight you lost. I know you're happy with the results."

Rachel smiled. "Yes, very happy. Thank you."

Chapter 32

"Come take a look." Rachel moved to one side, allowing Aaron Banks to examine the remodeling work she had completed in the galley. While studying his face, she waited on an honest opinion. She hoped the work would raise the price of the boat to where she could at least break even on it. "Okay, tell me what you think so far?"

"It's amazing how much of change of style this makes. You did great." He continued studying the counter and new leather seats. "I didn't know you planned on doing all of this."

"Once I started, I couldn't stop. Well, Jeff kept going. He did almost all of the work."

Aaron turned to face her. "And I still cannot believe how much of a change you went through. How long has it been now since your surgery?"

"I think about four weeks now." She turned sideways to flirt with her new body. The Armani outfit set her back, way back, but this represented a special night. Many of her friends had already boarded, but not the one she held her breath for–Carlos.

"Well, you look great." He had sparkles in his eyes.

Rachel glanced over her shoulder. "Would you like some more wine?"

Aaron noticed the glance. "Do you think Carlos will come?" Rachel knew Aaron had Carlos on his mind since she had given him the list of people to invite to this party. Yes, she owned the boat, but he insisted on throwing this party for her.

"Since he returned to the States a few days ago, I hope so." She knew her voice reflected her feelings as he smiled softly at her response.

"I talked to him. Has he not talked to you since he returned?" He stood still, waiting on a response.

"No. Not yet." She bit her lip and hoped to hide her feelings.

Aaron reached over and hugged her. "Don't worry. I'm sure he'll come. I know he means a lot to you." Rachel started to speak, but he lifted a finger for her to stop. "I cannot say I blame you. He's an intriguing guy–young, but interesting." He smiled and pointed at the stairs. "Yes, I think another glass of wine would be great."

While she knew most of the people walking around, her two friends, Margaret and Gloria sat at the rear of the boat quietly chatting. Rachel could easily guess what they were talking about. She glanced at her watch. It was almost eight.

Thirty minutes later, she saw Carlos walking along, carrying a small package. Even from this distance, she knew he had dressed in a suit, much more formal than usual. She watched each step, waiting on him to notice her. *What would he say? Did he know anything?*

After walking onboard, his face beamed a large smile full of brilliant teeth reflecting the sparkling lights above them. His dark suit had an Italian cut, perfect for his ripped body. With the brilliant colors of the tie highlighting the dark colors of the suit, he looked fantastic. She realized she was holding in her breath as she eventually gulped in new air. He hadn't noticed her yet. *Should I turn around and surprise him as he comes on board? Why not?* She turned momentarily, waiting on him.

Aaron walked over to Carlos as she heard him welcoming him. "Hi, Carlos, it's good to see you. I hoped you would make it."

Carlos deep and smooth voice sounded so familiar, yet so different. "Thanks for inviting me. I've been sleeping most of the time since I returned to the States." His voice grew louder as he came closer.

Rachel turned at the last moment, hoping to be as dramatic as possible, eager for praise. She saw his mouth drop as the conversation with Aaron stopped. "Well, say something." She turned to the side allowing him another view.

Carlos smile grew like a sunrise which keeps growing and growing in the morning. The glow increasing steadily, reminding her of the moment of the sun's final appearance exploding over the horizon. Finally, his face shined as she studied each perfect feature. Ohmigod, say something, she begged him with her eyes.

"Wow, you lost a lot of weight." His glaze flickered around her body, examining her in detail. At any other time, she would be totally self-conscious, but not now. This was the moment that she had dreamed of for weeks now. Well, at least one of the moments she had dreamed of.

"Yes, about forty pounds, to be more precise." She turned around for him again, hoping to excite him more.

"I can't believe how slim you are. How did you do it?"

She knew to be honest with him. She also wanted to see how he would react to the news. "I decided to have liposuction. I followed up with a lot of exercising, but the hardest part is my newest diet." She smiled broadly, forcing a sexy curl to the side of her lips.

Chapter 33

Rachel turned the lights on to her condo as they walked in. The fresh linen smell of the air freshener she had used earlier lingered, perhaps too much so as she ignored the urge to mention it. His touch behind her back glided her along, as if she needed the help. This time she had avoided the excessive amount of wine.

She stopped and turned to face him. "It feels good to have a man walking in with me. The thoughts of this murder still on the loose are scaring me more and more."

He stood and adjusted his eyes, those deep-brown, puppy dog eyes, before he spoke. "I can check around the condo if you want me to."

She breathed easier as he made the offer. She wasn't going to turn him down, but gladly accepted his offer as she nodded a definite yes for his benefit. "Thank you."

He smiled, kissed her forehead and walked to the back of her condo. "It's a little warm in here. Do you want me to adjust the temperature?"

"Only if you want to, I'm fine."

When he returned, she moved to the sofa, the same one where they had first become intimate. She forced her mind to focus, fully confident that this time it would be different. She knew it. Her new body made her happy, and she just knew she had to look hot. He had to want her now, he had to. "Come on over. I want a big hug."

He smiled and slid in beside her. He lifted her and placed her on his lap, turning her slightly to face him. This would've been hard before, but now she knew he had to love it. "I think you like the new me, huh?"

He said nothing as he reached over and edged closer to her lips. The thoughts of him so close thrilled her and teased her too much. While he still maintained the dominate force in their relationship, she forced herself to concentrate.

Rachel pulled away from him, and stared back into his eyes that radiated so rich, so powerful that she knew it would be a useless battle to resist him for too long. She could feel him breathing softly and controlled, not like hers at all.

Carlos pulled her back closer, stopping inches from her lips. His eyes drifted lower as she watched him studying her lips. His scent filled her nostrils–exciting her. He smelled so good, so damn good. A soft moan escaped her lips.

"I missed you." His words soft and sincere vibrated through her head. Should she wait on him to kiss her or quicken the process?

"I missed you too." She lost the ability to resist and leaned forward, letting her lips brush against his. With the warmth and moisture reminding her of times before, she paused, waiting on a response. His nibbling lips teased her upper lip as she rested, fully taking in the moment.

She allowed him to explore her upper lip, as she knew he had mastered the game of taking his time. She had mentally prepared herself for this. She was as ready as she'll ever be, she told herself.

His tongue worked its way along her lip. Ohmigod, not his tongue! He slid it lower and enjoyed her lower lip at will. It soon darted quickly, penetrating her mouth. She closed her lips around his tongue as it became stronger, blossoming inside her mouth, digging deeper, ravishing her as she allowed another moan to escape.

She twisted the strands of his hair between her fingers, but couldn't remember placing her hand to the back of his head. His smooth hair felt almost like silk. She pulled his head lower as she buried his head in the softness of her breasts, and the gentle smell of his shampoo filled her soul with new memories.

The kisses of his restless lips explored her throat, another super weakness she'd revealed many times before. He knew exactly how to excite her. *Why did I think I could resist him?* He owned her and she knew it. Still . . . she forced her mind to fight on.

Carlos's lips slipped over to her shoulder, sucking tenderly as he progressed. A gentle tingling shot through her spine. She knew the slight difference in being teased or being erotic to being annoyed. He worked the line like a pro. His fingers gently massaged her shoulder as he followed with his kisses. The slight sound of the sucking on her skin drove her crazy. It had been too long, way too long, damn it!

As she ran her hands over the lapel of his coat, she thought how unfair this was. He wore way too much clothing. She pulled away slightly as she looked at his face. He had his eyes closed. Funny, she couldn't remember him having them closed before. Good, very good.

She ran her fingers through his hair again. "Don't you want to take your coat off and make yourself a little more . . . comfortable?"

He rose on his elbow before answering. "I was thinking. With a perfectly good bed here, why are we still on the sofa?"

His assessment represented her thoughts completely; however, she wanted to at least appear to be in control. She thought about teasing him, finding some way to make him want her, to desire her like she did him. "I thought you would never ask." She forced her voice to be deep, sultry, and of course, teasing. She knew she failed miserably as he smiled, almost mockingly.

He pulled her beside him and stood before lifting her off the sofa. She knew she had to feel much lighter to him. It felt great to be lifted, much like a dream–the one most girls dream of–the one where the girl is carried across the threshold. She snuggled next to his shoulder as he walked with her in his arms. His muscular body protruding through his suit reassured her of his control in walking with her.

He laid her on the bed and smiled before pulling off his jacket and starting to work on his tie. She didn't recognize the designer, but it had to be one of the most beautiful ones she had ever seen. She thought, perhaps, he had purchased the tie on his trip to Europe. Oh yes, Europe, she needed to talk to him about the trip later.

He gently laid the tie on the counter. "Are you going to join me, or do I need to undress you also?" he asked, as he reached for the buttons on his shirt, working them slowly, seductively. *Damn, he is good. How does he maintain such control*?

She slithered in the bed. "Which would you prefer?"

He leaned over and kissed her lips again, his presence shocking her with the quickness of his moves. His smell quickly refilled her nose. She wondered if he knew how fast her heart was beating right now. Oh shit, he had to know. "I think tonight . . . yes, it would be great to peel a banana. That is, if you want me to." His teasing tone worked much better than her imitation. How could she resist?

"You think you know exactly how to drive me crazy, don't you?" Her eyes remained half closed.

"I think only you can answer that question." He stood and removed his shirt, laying it beside the tie on the dresser.

She forced her eyes to open wider as he lifted his t-shirt over his head. The sight of his massive chest muscles sent her heart racing even harder. She thought how the words *six pack* did little to describe the muscles in his midsection.

Without surgery, his stomach looked so damn flat–firm.

She glanced at his face covered in a sheepish grin. Yes, she studied every move he made. He looked great. "What?"

"Nothing." He reached for his belt and unfastened the latch.

She didn't mean to, but her mouth felt dry as she licked the corner of her lips. She knew he saw it. Being eager to give him a blow job wasn't the message she wanted to send. Control, she had to be in control–damn it!

His dress pants contained an unusual pleat in them, and the fabric looked expensive. She wanted to ask him later who made it, as she caught herself glancing over at the jacket. Perhaps she would sneak a peek later. They slid to the floor, revealing an intriguing set of boxers with strange cross patterns, ones she didn't recognized at all.

He stood and walked over to her, stalling for a minute, she thought. Yes, she wanted to see him totally naked. *Is he already hard? Does he want me like I want him?*

He leaned over the bed and cupped his fingers around her face, gently massaging the skin with his warm smooth fingers. She moaned again as his fingers slipped down her chest to the first button on her blouse. She bit her lip. She had to control the moans.

He worked slowly down the line of buttons. At the bottom, he reached for her arms, lifting them. The blouse fell to the floor. He lifted her arms and reached behind her to unlash her bra, allowing it to fall freely. She opened her eyes to study his reaction. She knew they were perhaps too large for her new body, but she wanted to see his reactions before she considered further improvements. His steady smile sent new waves of shudders across her body.

He ran a finger, one simple finger, up her stomach toward her breasts, allowing the finger nail to glide along her skin. The teasing sensation became too much for her as her body immediately trembled, causing her to pull her shoulders forward. "Stop that." Her voice sounded more like a giggle. Finally, his finger reached a nipple, where he circled the edges, but never allowed his finger to touch it. She thought he would, but instead he ran his finger back down her stomach toward her skirt. "You're a big tease, you know it?"

"Me . . . never." He stopped at the top and started searching for the latch.

"It's on the side, big boy." She managed to tease one time properly, she thought.

He rolled her to one side and managed to unsnap the latch with no further problems. The zipper hummed as he pulled it down. For the first time, a pride in the way she looked registered. No more large stomach. Every crunch was well worth the effort as he lowered the fabric. The panties she picked for the night were nothing to speak of, but a lot to talk about, she thought. She wanted to watch his face–to read his mind, right now.

He pulled her skirt lower, fully exposing her panties, where he stopped briefly before pulling them lower. She knew her legs were where most of the weight loss had occurred. He had to be happy with the difference as she stepped out of her dress. He slowly smiled as he straightened and place it next to his pants.

She glanced at him standing, watching her. He reached for his shorts and smiled. She returned the smile and fixed her glaze as he lowered them. Yes, his dick stood rigid, looking much better than she remembered. The thoughts of previous nights flashed in her mind. She knew he loved oral sex. Why not, most guys do. *Should I do it for him again tonight?* She had told herself no earlier. Now, she wasn't sure. She would decide later.

He leaned forward and ran his fingers gently up her

thighs. The result immediately made her shiver violently. "Stop that." How could such a simple act excite her and drive her crazy. He had learned her weakness and used them without mercy.

He latched a finger under the thin sides of her panties and pulled down. They lowered easily. He allowed the sensation to linger, dragging out the feeling. She allowed another moan to escape. What the hell, he knows she was excited. She moaned louder.

Finally, her panties slipped past her toes. The cool sensation of being totally naked and with the lights on overtook her. She would had never allowed the lights on before, not knowingly anyway. He gently kissed her lower leg and slid upwards. Yielding to his touch, a spasm of pure ecstasy flooded her body.

His exploring fingers worked on spreading her legs further apart. He apparently wanted a good view of her. At first she resisted. Maybe she did need the lights turned off. However, he persisted until she relented. He pressed two fingers against her cleft, exploring her folds. She felt wet–HELL–she had felt wet a long time ago. His thumb circled around her.

She wanted him now, right now. Yet . . . he continued to tease. She moaned again, louder and much clearer than before. *How did he maintain so much control? Doesn't he want me like I want him?*

Wave after wave of pure passion ran through her body. She had to have him now. She spread her legs out as wide as she could, allowing for full exposure. His fingers explored deeper, but she wanted more. She wanted him. Yet, he remained in control.

She knew what he wanted. He wanted her to beg for it–that had to be it. She was too far gone to fight. "Please. I want you."

He didn't respond as a new wave of shudders flooded her. *Didn't he hear me?* "Please. I have to have it." *There, I admitted it.* However, he still waited, lingering.

Chapter 34

"Gloria, I'm so glad you could meet me at the mall today. I feel like I'm wearing the same clothes over and over." Rachel walked in front, dragging her friend with her.

"Slow down, girl. You need to remember the old saying that Rome wasn't built in a day." Gloria struggled, carrying several of the packages with her. "Slow down, really."

Rachel took a large breath. "Okay, okay." She stopped to look at the packages. "Well, maybe you're right. I think I need to check my balances on my cards also. I never realized this new body would cost me this much in a new wardrobe."

"I keep hearing how bad business is in real estate right now. Are you sure you need to be spending money like this?" Rachel studied her focused stare.

"I know you're right." Embarrassed, she thought about the few sales she had closing recently. She had convinced herself that she could use the money saved by not paying an assistant. She knew, however, that not having an assistant would force her to spend more time in the office, doing work an assistant should be handling. "Maybe I'll take some of this back." In fact, she had held several pieces to the side at home, just in case she needed to lighten her load.

"How are things going with you and Carlos?" Gloria dropped the packages next to her.

"I'm so glad he's back from Europe." Rachel never asked him to explain the trip and too scared he would mention the skinny French girls if she did. She knew she had to one day. While now wasn't a good time to discuss these girls, she wanted to ask him about them soon.

"Does Carlos know you're buying clothes for him again?"

"Well . . . it's a surprise. He looks so great in good clothes that I've a hard time resisting."

"I hope your *new romance* works out for you. You appear to be happy. I never thought you would be the one to find love."

Rachel allowed the word *love* to resonate in her mind for several seconds–a word neither she nor Carlos ever used or approached. Their relationship had been more about sex. Rachel pushed the thought aside as she continued to urge Gloria on by grabbing some of the packages, lightening her load. "Thanks, I think he's happy. He should be, since I take good care of him and yes . . . the sex is great! Now, come on, let's finish."

Gloria resisted, standing her ground. "Are you telling me the two of you are having sex, and there's no mention of love in the relationship?"

Rachel's head hurt. She needed to be in control, and allowing anyone to think she had fallen in love with him would destroy that. After all, she knew he enjoyed the sex. She hoped the tightening muscles in her face didn't show that she wanted sex much more than he did. She would love to see him beg for sex, just once. She forced a straight face, but she knew before the night ended, every time, she was the one begging for more. "I think love is overrated. You know, sometimes you need to just do what feels good. Do you know what I mean?" Rachel tried to sound confident, but knew she didn't believe the bullshit she spread. She turned to cover her mistake before Gloria pushed her again.

Gloria retrieved the remaining packages from the floor. "I think you're wrong and I also think that you know it. When are you going to see Carlos again?"

"I'm not sure. I might give him a call later today." In fact, she needed to call him. He hadn't called her in a few days now. She called his office yesterday and was told he was at a closing. Good for him. She hadn't closed one lately. She knew she should've left a message, but decided not to do so.

"Good. I hope he likes these clothes. You need to tell him next time he has to carry them." Gloria smiled and struggled to stay even with her.

***

Rachel packed every available inch of her BMW before moving into the driver seat. How ridiculous, she thought. She checked her phone. No one had called. While she had hoped Carlos would check on her, she also hoped her latest ads would make the phone ring.

As she pulled out of her spot and glanced at the rear view mirror, a dark sedan pulled out behind her, slowly following her. She knew she had seen this car before. She reached for her phone and pulled off of the ramp to circle the floor of the parking deck, allowing the car to pass her.

Feeling safer, she hit the gas and made the circle, hoping to catch this strange car. She needed a license plate number, but the car surged as she raced around one corner after another one. The last turn, however, put her back on course. *Now, can I catch this car?* The motor roared as she hit the gas again.

After reaching the exit, she glanced around–the car had vanished. Damn! She rushed toward the entrance of the International Plaza, hoping that was the way the car had disappeared. She saw nothing and slowed since she didn't need a ticket. Her heart started beating harder as sweat from her hands stuck to the steering wheel.

With the packages blocking the view from her rear view mirror, she leaned forward to use the mirror on the right side of the car. She really needed to cross the bridge heading back to St. Petersburg before the after-work crowd.

On the bridge connecting Tampa with St. Petersburg, Rachel glanced out at the choppy water being disturbed by the high winds of an approaching storm. A car with tainted windows passed beside her. The dark sedan roared to pass her, changing lanes before it was fully advanced in front of her. She hit the brakes and swirled to the right, almost losing control. "Damn you!" Rachel yelled at the driver.

While this type of driving often happened on the roads around Tampa, she wasn't sure if the movement was intentional or not. She hit the gas and quickly approached one hundred, but it was still too slow to catch him. She thought about calling 911, but she knew this car would be long gone before the police ever responded.

Her breathing slowed. *Who is the driver in that car?* She needed to call the detective later. This car was a Lincoln, a dark green Lincoln, and there couldn't be too many of them around. She needed a drink, and she needed to talk to Carlos. Damn it! She needed him around right now. Her sexy new body should convince him to come see her again. Damn, Damn, Damn. *Why is this happening to me?*

Rachel considered a new thought as she exited off Highway 275 and raced to her condo. Her new body could be attracting interest. This might not be such a good idea right now. She knew she needed to be careful as she retrieved her phone again to call Carlos.

***

Rachel rushed to the door of her condo, glad to have Carlos waiting for her there. The thoughts of being alone tonight scared her. Detective Lindstrom had also called. He would be by soon to talk to her about the results of the experimental drug they would be using on Jody. She knew they hoped to find out about her attempted suicide.

Carlos smiled and lifted a bottle of wine. Dressed in blue jeans and his Texas style buckle made her laugh inside, but she managed to maintain her outward composure. Apparently, some things about him would never change. The pullover t-shirt stretched over his muscular body looked new as she remembered how much she had craved him all day.

"Hi, you look comfortable," Rachel said, as she moved to one side and allowed him to enter.

"Thanks." She saw his eyes glance over her body. "I still can't believe how different you look."

He leaned over to kiss her on the cheek. His smell immediately filled her memories with times of him coming over a few nights ago. After walking to the kitchen, he placed the wine, apparently a white, in the refrigerator.

"I'm so glad you came over. I need your advice." She waited for him to turn toward her. "I know I keep my mind working over time thinking about this, but I feel like I have a stalker following me all of the time now."

He smiled softly. "I understand what kind of pressure all of the murders are causing you. I think you need to relax."

"I know what you're saying. It's just that I haven't seen you in several days, and I hate being on my own." She studied his eyes, waiting on a reaction. "I need you."

"If you ever need me, you know all you have to do is call me." His calm, cool, collective manner infuriated her at first, but she fought back for control.

"I know that." She moved over closer to him and snuggled against his chest. "What have you been doing?"

He massaged the top of her head. "Working mostly . . . some of my friends have been calling me, wanting to do things. I've enjoyed hanging with them." The gentle touch of his fingers had a mystical magical feeling. She knew it would feel so good to fall asleep in his arms; even better to wake next to him.

She wanted to ask him, "You're not screwing anyone else, are you?" While she held her tongue, she still wanted to know; but no, she didn't want to know either. She wanted to own him, to control him, but she knew if she pushed too hard she could lose him as well. "I see, but before I forget, Detective Lindstrom's coming over shortly."

Carlos released her and pulled back showing his face. "Why is he coming here?"

"I haven't had a chance to tell you something. They're going to use an experimental drug on Jody soon to see if they can bring her out of her coma. They hope the procedure works so they can find out what happened to her in her condo." She continued to study his face as it signaled mixed emotions.

"Is this safe?" His dark-brown eyes maintained their focus on Rachel's own eyes. "It sounds dangerous."

"Her safety is my first thoughts as well. I hope they know what they're doing." Rachel's thoughts of the last time she saw Jody returned. She didn't appear to be overly bothered or apprehensive about anything.

"I hope so too." He pulled her back into his chest. "It sounded on the phone like you missed me."

Yeah, she had, but admitting this fact would give up too much control. She had the body now. She's the one that needed to be desired. She decided to see how much of an influence her body actually had on him. "I thought you might be missing the new me."

She heard a small teasing like laugh coming from deep down in his throat. "You are definitely different." He reached under her arms and lifted her to his height, kissing her lips lightly. His eyes locked on her eyes, mesmerizing her. Damn, he was good.

She decided to tease more, to test him. "I don't know.

You seem to have many friends taking your time up. As far as I know, you might have a girlfriend in every corner of town."

She heard him laugh as her heart sank. "I see . . . checking on me, are you?"

"It does make one wonder." She reached over and placed a hand on his chest. His heart beat remained normal. "Let me just say I'm getting used to your being around."

"Hmmm, is that a good or a bad thing?" Damn, he turned the tables on her again. She refused to answer.

She massaged his chest, waiting on words of inspiration. "I'm not worried. I think you enjoy having sex with me."

"Yes, sex is always good. I never hear you complaining." His hand moved to her neck where he started gently massaging. The familiar rhythm resonated across her body, sending waves of heat deep into her core.

"No, I've no complaints, and you?"

She waited for his response, listening to his breathing. *What is he thinking about?*

Ring, ring, ring, the lobby bell sounded, announced a visitor below. "Damn, that must be Detective Lindstrom. He's early." Rachel pushed past Carlos and walked over to the talk box by the door. "Yes . . ."

"Hi, I'm early I know, but this is Detective Lindstrom and I need to talk to you."

"Yes, I've been expecting you. Come on up."

Carlos moved to the kitchen counter and straightened some plates Rachel had left out. You would think he was straightening his own place. "Is there anything else I can do for you?"

"No, all is fine. I don't think he knows you're here, but it'll be alright."

"Okay. I can leave for a minute if you want me to."

"No, I want you here. Please." She reached for his hand,

squeezing it tightly while waiting for the detective.

The expected knock on the door sent another shudder across her body. *What kind of news is he bringing?* She reached for the door as Carlos stood behind her.

"Hello, Rachel, I'm glad you could see me." He glanced behind her and apparently recognized Carlos. "Hi, I'm glad you're here also."

The silence soon filled the room as she shut the door behind the detective. With his grim smile signaling the news she fully expected one day, she prepared her mind for the worst.

Carlos reached over, extending his hand to the detective. "How are you?" The detective accepted his shake without comment, waiting on Rachel to face him.

Rachel's impatient nature moved her along. "How is Jody?"

The detective glanced first at Carlos then at the floor, his face stone cold. "I hate to have to inform you—"

"—Ohmigod!" Rachel cried into her hands. She knew.

She saw Carlos rushing to her as the light heading feeling overtook her. He grabbed her arm and pulled her to his side to steady her as the fading world around her escalated. She needed to find a seat. Carlos reached under her, lifting her off of the floor as he carried her to the couch.

He laid her down and disappeared, only to return with a damp cloth. "Jody . . . why, oh why Jody?" She continued to cry.

The cool cloth washed away the fading lights around her. Rachel reached for Carlos hand. The strength in it made her feel better. She studied his face as the world around her refocused.

"Rachel, it's going to be okay. I'm here." Carlos voice, so slow and deep, gave her some comfort.

"Yes, I'm feeling better now." Rachel tried to sit higher

on the couch. She swallowed before she continued to talk. "What happened?"

The detective kneeled closer to her and glanced over at Carlos. "As you probably know, the doctor gave Jody a drug to attempt to bring her out of a coma. All went smoothly, and she soon regained some degree of consciousness. The medical staff thought the procedure was successful." He lowered his head again.

Rachel sniffed as tears made their way down her face. Carlos wiped her tears as he turned toward the detective to ask, "I assume something went wrong."

"Yes, she recovered slowly and the doctors knew regaining consciousness would be traumatic on her. However, she appeared to be so cool and relaxed at first. I know my thoughts may sound strange, but I think she must've thought she was waking up in heaven."

A small smile crossed Rachel's lips as she tightened her grip on Carlos's hand.

The detective continued, "It was the reality of the hospital which made her snap. She yelled at all of us, saying that she wanted to die. There's no doubt she had wanted to commit suicide."

Rachel's chin trembled, but she needed to know. "Why?"

The detective placed a hand on Rachel's shoulder. "The doctors realized from her reactions that reality was too much of a shock for her and started inducing the coma again. The last words she said before she went under were screams that she had to die so no one else would, and that everything was all her fault."

Carlos spoke first. "What fault?"

Rachel watched the detective inhale deeply before answering. "Her meanings are what I need to find out. I was in the room while she was awake. I think she died trying to protect someone from something, but I don't know what or who."

Rachel tried to comprehend the information. "What else did she say?"

"That's all. She arrested a few minutes later. I heard the doctor say it looked as if she had forced herself to die. They did all they could for her, keeping her on life support for a long time, but in the end . . . . Jody was pronounced dead a few hours ago."

Rachel closed her eyes. *What is Jody hiding? Why did she think she had to die?* This wasn't like her. "Who else was in the room when she died?"

"Other than the medical staff, it was just me and her sister Angela."

Rachel glanced at him. "How is she taking this?"

"About as you would expect. A lot of pressure is being placed on her right now, and much more than any nineteen year old deserves. The hospital is providing some psychological support, and I think she'll be okay later. I sure hope so."

The detective stood. "I'll have some more questions for you later, but I know this isn't a good time. While her words gave me a lot to consider, I think Angela needs your support now."

"I'll try to call her in a few minutes." Rachel thought about how this must be affecting her.

The detective reached over and shook Carlos' hand one last time as he turned to leave. "If either of you can think of anything that can help me to solve this case, please call me."

***

Rachel stretched on the sofa as Carlos gently massaged her scalp. The detective had left hours ago, and the bottle of wine Carlos had arrived with had also disappeared. With the conversation sparse, allowing for drifting thoughts and fears to mount, Rachel snuggled deeper into his lap.

She saw Carlos glancing at his watch before he spoke. "I think you need some sleep."

Rachel snuggled deeper. "I feel good here."

"I understand, but I know you need some sleep. Tomorrow will be a big day for you. Are you sure you don't want to call Angela tonight?"

Rachel thought about it. "No, I need to make sure I'm composed. I still don't know exactly what to say to her."

Carlos stopped massaging her scalp. "Do you think she knows who or what is behind all of these deaths?"

"I don't know. Yes, I've been thinking about many possibilities, but nothing makes sense."

Carlos squirmed and placed a hand behind her shoulder, lifting her slightly. "Come on, you need to make it to the bed. I'll help you."

A small wave of delight passed through her mind as she envisioned Carlos helping her remove her clothes. She hated to stand, but knew he was right. It was critical that she land some closings soon and thus extremely crucial for her to work hard tomorrow to make some sales happen. "Okay, I know you're right."

Carlos gently pulled Rachel as she staggered to her feet. His arms guided her to the bedroom where she stood like a zombie waiting on him to undress her. She wanted to give him the appearance she became more incoherent than she actually was. She wanted to know, or rather see what he would do, and how he would react to seeing her new body again.

Carlos lifted her hand and placed it on his shoulder. "Here, steady, I'll have you in bed in a moment." He unbuttoned and unzipped one piece of clothing after another until she stood in front of him with only her panties remaining.

She peeked at him, hoping he didn't realize she slightly

cracked her eyes open. "What do you think?" She realized she must sound like she was begging as soon as she asked. *Why do I do that?*

Through her squinted eyes she watched him smile, a gentle warm caring smile that had captured her emotions from the first day she had met him. "Rachel, I think you look fantastic, and I know you're proud of the results, but you also look tired." He helped her to sit on the edge of the bed before he left for the closet to retrieve one of her night gowns.

"Thanks, I wanted to do this a long time ago. You gave me the motivation to do it."

He returned with a nightgown and lifted her hands high to slide the material over her. She knew she acted lazy, but she enjoying his attention. "Why? How did I motivate you?"

She decided to confess some of her feelings. "When I saw you with some of your friends, you know, the ones from France, I knew I needed to do something about my body."

"Which friends from France?"

She studied his eyes as she opened her eyes slightly fuller. "You know, the ones I saw you having dinner with one night."

She watched him smile softly, as he appeared to slowly remember the night. "They weren't French, but their French is much better than their English," he responded, as he moved to the side of the bed and pulled back the covers for her without offering any more comments on the skinny girls he had dined with.

She decided to let the explanations pass for now. "I really don't want to be alone tonight. Can't you spend the night with me and forget about working out this one time." She saw him waver and pushed on. "Please."

Carlos gently touched her. "I didn't think you wanted sex tonight."

He was right. Tonight she wanted to be hugged and held tight. "I want you to keep me safe tonight."

She heard him breath long and slow before he answered. "Okay, I think I can go during my lunch tomorrow."

Rachel stood and walked to her side of the bed, crawling under the covers. "Good, I was hoping I could talk you into it. By the way, I purchased some presents for you."

"Presents–for me." He stood in front of her, waiting on her to continue.

Damn, she hoped he would be happy. Perhaps she should've waited for another time to tell him about them, but too late now. "Yes, they're in a sack inside my closet. Tell me what you think."

His voice turned stern, not a good sign. "You don't need to be buying me presents." He walked toward the closet as she held her breathe. Rachel moved over as he returned, making room for him to sit on the bed beside her. His stern, deep voice returned as he turned to face her. "Rachel, you know I appreciate the thoughts, but I'm completely capable in shopping for myself."

Rachel's heart hurt from the immediate pain caused by his reprimanding. "Don't you like them?"

His words sounded much colder than usual. "They're nice, thanks."

Rachel worked on making her words as pleasant as possible. "I love to see you dressed nice. You have a great body, and I love buying for you."

"It's not that I don't appreciate the presents, I really do. It's that . . ." She watched him lower his head. "Thanks." He carried the clothes back to the closet and reached over, turning out the light, robbing her of the chance to watch him undress.

As he slid in next to her, she knew he had become upset. While she had him with her tonight, she knew he would leave if she pushed him any further. For tonight, she pressed in as close to him as she could, enjoying his warmth. *What is it with him?*

Chapter 35

Rachel changed her dress again as she tried to decide which black dress to wear to Jody's funeral. She knew Carlos would come by her condo soon to pick her up, but since the night he had spent with her, he has been too busy to see her; at least, that's what he's been telling her. In any event, it allowed her time to work hard, which wasn't too bad a thing. While she had been trying her best to make one more sell, and she did have several closings in the works, in this business she never knew what would work until the deal closes.

Rachel stepped into a pair of black Prada she had stashed away in a box. They fit good at the store, but felt a little too loose now. It might not be too late to exchange them. If she was careful with them today, perhaps she could later. She glanced at her watch, a David Yurman she owned forever, but still looked stylish. She knew he would be arriving soon.

She wondered what kind of mood Carlos would be in. She thought back on the morning he had left a few days ago, and how he had forgotten his gift of clothes she had purchased for him. Most guys would die for such a gift, she thought.

She hadn't slept much the night before. She thought about calling him, but she didn't know how she would handle the news if he had gone out with his friends. She wasn't seeing anyone else, and she knew he understood. *Why can't I get the nerve to ask him? Surely he isn't.*

She reached in her jewelry box and selected a black pearl necklace. This piece looked expensive and could fool most people, but the necklace remained a cheap piece she had lucked upon while out shopping once. She glanced at her watch again. He was late.

After placing the necklace around her neck, she mentally relived the day when she had purchased it. She had been shopping with Jody in Miami the day she had talked her into buying it. *Well, maybe it's fitting that I wear this piece today in her honor, so to speak.* However, she would keep the reasons for wearing the piece a secret. Rachel had searched her mind extensively over the last few days, trying to determine what would make Jody want to take her own life.

Rachel heard the knock on the door. It's about time. She moved to the door and looked out the peek hole. Carlos was dressed in a black suit, one she hadn't seen before—fascinating. As she opened the door, he stretched out his arms and turned his head to one side. "I think this will do. What do you think?"

She examined him. The white shirt had an Italian cut to the collar, allowing plenty of room for a large folder tie, of which he had chosen an intricate gray and burnt orange design. She hadn't seen the style before and thought she would wait and check the back label later for the name. His belt buckle caught her attention, making her smile broadly. "Where did you purchase a Gucci belt buckle? It looks great with your suit."

"I went shopping, hoping to make you happy. I don't want to fight today."

Rachel's mind went to thoughts of the funeral. "Fighting—I don't think we fight over clothes, do we?"

"At times you think you can control me and make me dress the way you want me to. I'll assure you I know how to dress, but like I said, I don't want to fight today." He stepped forward and reached for the door behind him.

Rachel decided to smile and walk back into the center of

the room, where she turned to show him the one black dress she had selected. "And . . . what do you think of this?"

He smiled as he studied her. "I think you look good, as usual." He glanced at her shoes. "How long have you had these?"

"Why, are they bad?"

"No, no, not at all–it's the first time I've ever seen you wear them." She turned to her side, but she studied him out of the corner of her eye. If she didn't know better, he appeared to know that this was last year's style, but how would a Texan know current styles in women shoes?

"Well, I'm sure I own several items you've never seen before." She glanced at his shoes. "For example, I've never seen those shoes either."

"I think you have. They're a pair of Kenneth Coles I wear often." He stepped over to her. "I think we need to hurry."

Rachel moved closer to him, as the last few days away from him had made her miss him more than she had realized. "It's good to see you again." Damn she wanted to tell him how much she missed him, but such a confession would lead to too much loss of control for her.

He leaned forward to touch the side of her face with his. Apparently they both knew a kiss would destroy her makeup. His smell, his awesome smell, as always, overpowered her senses as she inhaled in deeply. He spoke in a whisper. "I'm sorry about the other morning, and not being here much for you the last few days. Being gone on vacation has caused my work to back up on me."

"Oh, that's fine. I needed to put in some long hours myself." She thought about how late those hours have been lately. *And what for, I want to know?* Nothing was working out right. In fact, she had lost one of the closings she had hoped for and another one had been postponed again. She wished she could tell him all about it, but not now. Perhaps one day she could. "Okay, let me turn the lights out and find my jacket."

As they left for the funeral in silence, Rachel appreciated the safe feeling of having him with her and never thought about the perceived evil which might be following her. She needed to talk to him, to tell him her feelings and the way her life was now. *How would he react when he finds out I'm facing a serious financial situation?* Unless something changed soon, she knew she wouldn't be able to hide the fact much longer.

***

The parking lot next to a small cemetery at the funeral home had half-way filled. Jody had many business associates, but not much in the way of family. Rachel had seen Angela at the funeral home last night for a few minutes and they had discussed this in detail. Angela planned on staying in school in Miami, and she needed the condo sold as soon as possible to give her the funds she needed to finish college. She had no money to make payments on the condo, and hadn't heard from the attorney who was handling the estate as to how much monetary assets Jody actually had. As far as Angela knew, Jody had no life insurance.

Carlos had agreed to drive Rachel's BMW without any fighting or arguing. She appreciated his calm cool mannerism today. "I think over there will be good." She pointed to a shaded parking place under a large tree. From living in Florida, she knew that a large tree like this was one of the first choices of everyone.

He parked the car and moved around to open her door. She reached out her hand, allowing him to be the gentleman. Her smile, out of habit and years of training, quickly formed; after all, she never knew who might be studying her at a distance. She reached under his arm and stepped beside him as they walked. She knew from experience that he much preferred to simply hold hands as they walked, but today he continued to offer no resistance.

Rachel stopped at the front door and checked her outfit before studying Carlos. "You look great today–thanks."

While he smiled without saying a word as he opened the door, she saw a slight tightness in his jaw, as if he was fighting back a desire to do so.

Although several people were walking about as they entered, Gloria made the first move over to them. Her red and swollen eyes, an apparent result of crying, told a heartbreaking story of their friendship. "Rachel, I'm so glad you're here." Gloria gave Rachel a large hug which lingered for several minutes.

When she finally pulled away from Rachel, she glanced over at Carlos, studying him in silence. "Hi, thanks for coming." She extended her hand to him, but didn't offer him a hug as she forced a smile.

Rachel saw through the hidden meaning and hoped Carlos didn't. To Gloria, Carlos was a boy toy; after all, that's how Rachel had always explained him to the others. If that was truly the case, she suddenly realized how it could be perceived to be in poor taste to bring him to a funeral with her.

Rachel watched Gloria glance around as she made it obvious she hoped to find a way to move from them before she said the wrong thing. The sounds of others chatting in the line to sign the registration book gave the correct amount of distraction as Rachel continued to hold her head high and flash her smile.

"I'll catch you later." Gloria gave Rachel another quick hug and left without even acknowledging Carlos.

Rachel strolled toward the registration table with Carlos slightly behind her. The warm temperature inside the funeral home made Rachel uncomfortable. She decided to remove her jacket and hand it to Carlos as one older lady walked over to them. It took a minute for Rachel to recognize Jody's secretary, Freda Brentwood.

Freda's eyes showed signs of crying as Rachel approached. "Hello, Freda. How are you holding up?"

"Not real good, but I suppose I'll make it." Freda must be close to sixty, and wore round eye glasses which were much too small for her face. Her bad posture and swollen eyes reflected how bad her health must be.

"I know how rough this must be on you. You've worked as her secretary for a long time, haven't you?" Rachel talked much softer than normal, hoping to keep anyone from talking about how loud she normally talks. "She always told me how great of a job you did for her." This was a lie, but Rachel knew how good the comment would be received.

Freda glanced over at Carlos, waiting to be introduced.

Rachel had placed her body between the two without thinking about it. She moved to one side. "Freda . . . this is . . . Carlos." She talked slowly as she thought of the words she would use to introduce him.

Before she followed up with the proper word, Carlos stepped forward and extended his hand. "Hi, I'm Carlos Martin, and I'm sorry for your loss. I can only imagine how you must feel."

"Thank you so much for your concern." Freda glanced back over to Rachel as she continued to study the situation. "She's going to be missed very much."

Rachel glanced across the room to see Gloria talking to a small group of women; her hand covered her mouth as if she was trying hard to not be heard. She glanced at Carlos and saw him studying them as well. She spoke quickly, diverting the attention back to Freda. "I'd love to talk to you later, if you have some time." She handed Freda a card with her number on it. She did need a new assistant, since Cindi had abandoned her.

"Sure. I'll need to find a new job soon." Freda also noticed the conversation on the other side of the room. She turned to Carlos. "It was nice meeting you, Carlos. Jody thought a lot of Miss Contino."

"It was nice meeting you also." Carlos stood still beside Rachel, but stared at the crowd across the room.

After reaching the registration table, Rachel signed for both herself and Carlos. She next moved toward the chapel and the waiting line to shake the awaiting hands. She knew it would be a slow line, as she glanced at Carlos. "Don't worry, this will be over soon."

He only returned the smile.

"Carlos, I cannot remember. Have you ever met Angela?"

"No, I never have. It'll be nice to finally meet her. Is she anything like her sister?"

"No–not at all. You'll see in a few minutes."

Several women from the crowd talking to Gloria earlier joined the line behind them. Rachel glanced at them, but failed to recognize any of them personally. She watched the intense stares at Carlos coming from all three of them. What did Gloria tell them?

Enduring the glances for several minutes, Carlos finally turned to speak. "How are you doing tonight?" While he obviously directed the question to all three, he maintained a steady but inquisitive look on his face.

The first woman, one with big brown eyes and long matching brown hair, intensive concentration left little to doubt that she wanted to meet him. "Hi, I talked to someone who knows you and told us about you."

Rachel saw him glance over at her. "Really. That might be fascinating to hear about."

Rachel stepped forward quickly to introduce herself. "Hi,

I'm Rachel Contino. I don't think we've met."

Yes, Carlos watched her intensely. Her heart raced. What did Gloria, her friend, tell them?

Carlos continued his stare for some time before he turned around to study the girls behind him. "I take it you know my name already."

"Yes, I heard your name is Carlos Martin. My name is Nancy, and this is Megan and Maria." She pointed to the girls behind her, offering small waves.

Rachel didn't like the fact that the group ignored her. "I think I saw you talking to my friend Gloria a few minutes ago."

Rachel saw them glancing at each other. "Yes, we met her a few minutes ago. She told us about you two."

Oh shit, what did she say? "That must have been a fascinating conversation. So, I assume you've heard all about my love life. She has such a big mouth." She reached around Carlos and gave him a small squeeze.

Rachel knew the girls would take her signal as a sign to back up, but she wasn't sure how Carlos would take this sudden show of ownership. While she knew he would have questions later, she continued to direct her attention at Carlos. "We've been dating for several months now."

She breathed easier when he returned her smile. "I think it's almost six months now." He stayed close to her–good.

The girls glanced at each other with questioning looks on their face. Megan spoke first in a Spanish accent. "I'm sorry. I think we misunderstood what your friend Gloria told us."

Rachel had to think fast. *What did Gloria say?* "I'll need to talk to her about this later. She has a remarkable sense of humor, and one which can get out of control at times."

The women smiled at each other and exchanged small laughs. "We'll do it for you." They made their way to the back of the chapel, looking for Gloria.

As soon as they moved out of hearing distance, Carlos turned to face her. "What was all of that about?"

She knew Carlos could see through any lies she could offer. *What could I tell him–that my girlfriends teased me all of the time about having a boy toy?* Her smile turned to a frown. "You know we have a slight difference in our ages."

"Yes, does the age difference bother you?" His question penetrated her barriers she had erected to protect herself from answering this question so many times before.

"Me–no, but what about you?" She watched him study her question as she thought, how strange it was that after six months of being together this was the first time they had actually discussed this.

He leaned forward to whisper. "We share several clients and work together to close homes. I think we like each other's attention, and yes, we both enjoy sex with each other."

She glanced sideways at the mention of the word sex, hoping no one overheard them. This wasn't the time or place. She stretched her smile to the limit and glanced around the chapel. "I think we need to talk about this later, don't you?"

He matched her smile. "Maybe yes, maybe no."

Chapter 36

As she waited outside Mr. Langford's office, Rachel pulled the letter from the bank out again to study the wording. As a vice-president for St. Petersburg Trust he had managed her loan for the last six years, bundling all of her properties into one package. She returned the favor many times in sending them prime accounts from some of her best customers. However, that was then and this was now.

Two of her condo units had remained vacant for over three months now, and two others had slow paying tenants. Since her sales had fallen off by more than fifty percent, she had little cash left to spread around. The falling prices made liquidating some of the properties impossible.

The letter looked simple. They wanted reassurance her financial health was staying in good shape. She was late in making her payment this month. It wasn't over thirty days–yet, but it would be by next week. Mr. Langford had a large conference room next to his personal office. The letter stated that others would be in the meeting, but it didn't mention them by name.

Carlos had disappeared out of her life again. She knew he had realized he was being talked about and she needed some time to think about the situation. She wanted to talk to him, but this letter arrived the day following their big fight. Hopefully after this meeting was over, she could call him and work everything out. She didn't want to lose him–not now.

Rachel heard footsteps echoing off the marble floor as he approached. She forced her smile and concentrated on winning support as quickly as she could. He had two other men with him. She stood as they rounded the corner to the waiting area she had been confined to.

"Hello, Rachel." Mr. Langford stepped forward and extended his hand to her. "I hope you don't mind meeting with some of the other people at the bank today. This is Brad Comer, the controller and Richard Lios another vice-president here at the bank."

"Not a problem. I'm always interested in meeting new people. After all, I'm in the people business." At times she felt ready, but at others she felt insecure in her preparation for such a meeting.

"That's great. I told them you've always been one of the banks best customers. We can talk in the conference room, if that's all right with you." He turned to move in that direction, not waiting on a response.

Rachel grabbed her black business bag and followed them to her destiny. All three men who looked to be in their sixties wore nice suits and showed professional mannerisms. She knew what they would be asking, and she only hoped she could give them the right answers. It would be great if they could be a little lenient until the market turned for her.

The conference room had chairs for a dozen people with room for others to join if necessary. She knew the conference room was designed to showcase the bank's wealth and strength to encourage their better clients to use them. The art work and furnishings had a professional touch to them.

Mr. Langford stopped at the head of the table and pulled out a seat for her. "Here, I think this will be good for you to be here. I hope this will not take too long, but I'm sure you understand why we called you in here today."

Yes, she knew exactly why–they wanted their money and assurance she could keep paying them. "Thanks. I can understand your concerns." She pulled her bag open and removed some folders, placing them in front of her.

Mr. Langford had been carrying some folders with him and now started to distribute them to the two other men. All three men placed reading glasses on as they studied the papers in front of them. "I understand the total payment to cover your loans is over forty-two thousand a month and the payment due on the first is three weeks late. I also see where the payment has been getting progressively later each month." He stared at her over the top rim of his glasses. The other two continued to study the papers, staying quiet for now.

"I don't need to tell you what the economy's doing right now. It's lousy!"

Richard Lios spoke next. "That's exactly why we're having this meeting. What are you doing to correct your cash flow problem?"

Rachel knew they would center on this, but she felt somewhat surprised that they would descend on her this fast. "I'm working hard, and I hope to complete some good closings shortly." All three men remained quiet, waiting for her to continue. They all knew sales weren't dependable right now. "As you know, I'm having problems renting several condos. Hopefully this will be taken care of soon. I've remodeled my boat and plan to sell it soon. It won't generate much cash, but it will lighten my payments some. To survive through this time period, I might need to do some refinancing."

Langford spoke first. "Refinancing could be a problem."

"What do you mean–I've always paid the bank back before."

"These are difficult times, as you know. The values of your properties have fallen dramatically."

"Yes, the value has on everyone, but I don't plan on

selling in a market like this. Selling now would be crazy." She studied one man after another, looking for a sign of weakness.

Langford continued, as the other men watched in silence. "The problem is . . . you've nothing to refinance. You owe much more than your properties are worth." He leaned over and slid a paper to her. "We had BPO's run on your properties last week."

Rachel's heart fluttering since she knew banks ordered Broker Price Opinions mainly when they were considering the possibility of foreclosing on a property. "You know this is the business I'm in. If you wanted some opinions on price, I could've provided them for you."

Ignoring her, Langford pointed to the figures on the paper. "If you want to provide us with some more numbers, we would be glad to consider them, but for right now, it looks like you're very much under water."

"This market will turn around, and you know it."

"I wish we could believe you." Lios tapped his pen on the numbers. "For your sake, the rebound in prices needs to happen soon."

"What are you trying to tell me?"

"If you get further behind on your notes, we might have no choice but to take other actions." Lios voice remained cold and hard. "In the letter we also requested a current financial statement. Did you bring one with you?"

Rachel stared at one man, then the next; so much for loyalty and being available for you when you need them. "Yes, I brought one, but the end of the month's only one and a half weeks from now."

Langford grimaced before speaking. "That's why we're having this meeting, and we hope you can find a way to make your payments on time. We would really like to receive both payments–last months and this one–by the first, if possible."

"THAT'S INSANE!" All men pulled back and glared at her. "I'm sorry. I didn't mean to yell."

Lios stood. "I think we understand each other. Please keep us informed on how you are proceeding." He glanced at the financials Rachel handed him.

You bastard, she thought, but allowed her smile to cover her thoughts. "I will."

"I hope so, and I could only wish you could obtain such a price for your condos as you're showing on your financials." Lios appeared to be the main person pushing for the foreclosure.

She knew if they obtained control of the property and held it they would turn a large profit. *I can't let that happen, but how am I going to stop it? I need to do some serious thinking and get busy closing shit—now.*

    ***

Rachel turned her phone back on as she left the bank. Those dirty bastards weren't going to ruin her—not her! Not after all of the hours and sweat she had put into building her business. She needed time to find a source of funds. Several thoughts flashed in her mind. First, she might be able to borrow some extra money on the boat or sell it. Next, she might be able to obtain a commission advance. Several companies provided this service, and had sent her advertising on many occasions, but most of the time she had tossed them to the side. She knew of some hard money with high interest rates she could go to, but crazy people paid those kinds of rates.

Rachel stared at her phone, thinking about the numbers stored in it. She knew people with money, but who could she really ask for such an amount. The bank wanted almost forty-five thousand in less than two weeks. She had maybe five thousand dollars in her account, which she assumed the bank knew. She had closings in the pipeline for sure and rental checks coming in, but those funds would still leave her short. The scary part was the fact that the closing were set for the end of the month as normal and how many last minute snags could delay them.

She strolled through her missed calls on her phone. Carlos had tried several times, but he was another problem she had to deal with, just not now. However, she decided to listen to his messages. He sounded cheerful, but firm about wanting to talk to her.

She walked to her car and decided to return his call before starting the motor. With tears forming in the corner of her eyes, she dabbed at them with a Kleenex, hoping to avoid a messy problem.

The phone rang four times before he answered. "Rachel, thanks for calling me. I really need to see you."

She smiled at the word "need" that he used, but sex isn't what she needed right now. "I'm sorry I haven't talk to you the last few days; it's been busy."

"I understand, your office has told me you've been going crazy. Listen, I've been doing a lot of thinking lately, and we really need to talk."

Ohmigod, was he going to break it off with me? Damn, I need his support right now. "I don't know when. I have a major problem I need to handle."

His voice turned soothing, irritatingly soothing. "I'm sorry. What can I do to help?"

She couldn't help but laugh, and hoped he didn't hear. "I don't think you can help me with this problem." She started to add the words "lover boy" but stopped short.

His smooth voice persisted. "Why not? Maybe I can, and you know I will if I can."

Rachel wiped the corner of her eye again and thought that she might as well just tell him, since he would know soon enough when she loses everything. "I just came from the bank. I hoped to receive an extension on my loan with them until I got some of my properties under control."

"Oh, what did they tell you?"

She decided to level with him and slowed her voice as the embarrassment started setting in. "They told me I only had until the end of the month to make my payment on my loan and bring it fully current."

"I see. You sound worried."

"Yes, that's an understatement."

"Listen, I'll be glad to loan you some money to help you–.

"–Carlos, I appreciate your offer very much, but the amount I owe is much more than I think you can understand. However, I do appreciate the offer."

"I don't mind helping. I've heard you say before that you use St. Petersburg Trust. Who else do you owe money to?"

"They're the only one. I trusted them for years, and I have all my loans tied into one neat package." She bit her tongue, thinking about how stupid she had been in doing this now.

"Surely you can work out something with them."

"Carlos, I left the bank a few minutes ago. Don't worry about it; I'll take care of my problem." She knew she might be lying and started feeling bad about telling him about the bank.

She heard Carlos exhale. "I've a closing this afternoon to worry about. Let me take you to dinner tonight and we'll talk about your situation."

While drinking until she became absolutely drunk isn't what she really wanted to do, perhaps one drink with him before she went home would be good. She also wanted to make sure he told no one else about this problem. "Okay, but it'll need to be later, maybe nine. Is nine okay with you?"

"That will be fine. I need to do some work on my boat. Can you meet me at the Pier later? We can eat at the one of the restaurants there. I'll call you later to check on you."

"Okay, that sounds good." She dropped her phone in her pocket. She sat silently; feeling like her life was slipping away. Across the parking lot she watched a person vanish around the corner. She had the feeling a stalker was watching her and waiting for her to move, but right now, she didn't care. She stopped dabbing the tears with her Kleenex, as she allowed the tears to fall down her face.

***

The hostess greeted Rachel as she stepped off the elevator. "How are you tonight?"

Rachel thought about telling the bouncy little girl she felt like shit, but smiled instead. "Fine, thank you."

"Will you be dining alone, or are you waiting on someone?"

Thoughts of being asked this question so many times before flashed across her memory. She didn't know about the future, but for tonight she had Carlos. "I'm hoping my date might already be here."

The girl turned and surveyed the area. "I only know of one young guy here by himself. He's over by the corner."

"That must be him." She watched the young girl study her out again as she moved around the check in stand. Yes, she still had the large boobs, but no longer had the large cahootus. She smiled as she watched the shock register on the girls face.

Within seconds she saw him sitting at a chair looking out at the skyline of St. Petersburg. He had a glass of wine cradled in both hands as he appeared to be deep in thought. Rachel nodded at the hostess, letting her know he was her date. As the hostess flashed an approving smile and returned toward the reception area, Rachel walked slowly toward him and thought about sneaking behind him and placing her hands over his eyes. However . . . tonight was going to be too serious for such. She knew it as she stood beside him for most of a minute until he finally noticed her.

The shock of her standing next to him surprised him as he jerked forward before standing. "Hi, I didn't see you."

"I know, it was fascinating to stand here watching you. You appeared to be so deep in thought. You were posed kind of like the great thinker. Too bad I'm not a painter."

He stepped closer to her and leaned over to kiss her cheek. "I wasn't sure what time you would be here."

She wasn't either since she had worked all night on her finances, hoping to find a way to gather the forty-five thousand. She had some ideas, but would need to wait until tomorrow to see if she could obtain the help she needed. "Thanks for offering me dinner."

Carlos reached for her hand. "These chairs are very comfortable facing St. Petersburg. Would you like to sit here and enjoy a glass of wine, or are you hungry?"

Rachel looked over closer to the corner on the other side of the restaurant where the white table cloths covered the tables. "As late as it is, I think we might need to order."

He smiled and reached for her hand, placing it under his arm. "I'm hungry, so that sounds good."

"After we eat, I need to go to my boat for a minute. Do you have time to go with me?" Rachel asked in a pleading, pitiful manner, as she had two motives. First, he couldn't say good bye to her at the restaurant. If he planned to break it off with her, she could take it better with no one around. Secondly, she still didn't want to walk alone in the darkness.

He paused for a second. "Yes, I can walk you to your boat."

As they walked past the bar, she noticed one person

stepping away as if quickly to hide their face. She started to chase the stranger, but stopped. She had to maintain control of her fears of being followed. She had to convince herself that the whole world wasn't spying on her.

She watched Carlos study her stare. "What is it?"

Rachel blinked her eyes. "Nothing . . . I know it's me, but I feel like I'm constantly being followed and stalked."

He squeezed her fingers. "Relax, all will be fine."

As a waitress met them on the far side, Carlos pointed to the table in the corner with two glass sides, giving a great view of the bay as well as the skyline. "That table looks great."

The waitress nodded in agreement as they moved over to it. He escorted her to one side of the table and reserved the other chair beside her, making it possible for both to watch the view and keep their backs to the rest of the restaurant.

Carlos raised his glass toward the waitress. "This wine is great. Can you bring me a bottle of this?" The waitress smiled to confirm his request before she left.

While tired, Rachel needed to know what Carlos had on his mind. "You said you wanted to talk to me and you sounded serious."

"Yes, but first I want you to tell me what's going on with you." His eyes stared directly at her, demanding her to be truthful.

She knew she had to tell him sometime. She might as well do the unthinkable now. "This market is about to ruin me."

"I know the market is bad since I need to deal with falling prices every day." He moved his chair closer to her so their voices could remain low.

Rachel watched him closing in on her. She couldn't hide any longer. His face portrayed a guy much older or perhaps wiser than his true age. "I think I might as well tell you, since you'll know everything soon enough."

"You know, considering the time we've spent together, you would think you could tell me your problems. It's really a shame you think you need to hide everything from me."

"Okay." Rachel placed her hands palm down on the table. "Ask me anything you want, and I'll do my best to answer." She turned to return his stare.

"Your financial situation appears to be the most critical situation right now. I want you to start at the beginning and tell me everything." She glanced at him, attempting to resist or decide if she could really trust him. "Everything." He repeated with a deep voice.

For the next hour, she told him about all of her investments in condos, her car and her boat. She had little else, except for the designer clothes and jewelry. His only response during this time was to encourage her to keep talking. He didn't act judgmental or offer advice. He stayed on target like a true financial adviser would, indicating his training in finances had advanced much more than she had realized.

As the bottle of wine disappeared, he reached over and patted her on her shoulder. "Your investments are too much for one person to manage. I think you have many options, however, and I'll get back with you on what I mean later." He paused. "Now, I have some other questions."

Rachel thought she had laid out her entire history, but he gave her the indication he had only started. "Which questions?"

"What has caused you to be so scared to reveal who you really are?"

"What?"

"You have a great smile, but you hide behind it. I promise the face is capable of many emotions other than a frozen smile."

Rachel's muscles in her face tighten. She knew what he meant. Perhaps her smile was like her private, personal kind of poker face. She felt like she lost too much control if she ever let someone read her emotions. She decided to lie. "I don't know what you're saying."

"I think you do." He leaned in closer. "Would you like to try an experiment?"

She stared at him and he returned with a pout rather than a smile, mocking her smile. "Okay, why not. What do I have to do?"

"It's simple; force yourself to not allow your face to smile."

It sounded easy to do, so why not try, she thought. She allowed the smile to fade, and her face to relax. "Okay, now what?"

"We talk, we simply talk." His face remained serious. "Now, tell me why you think things are going so bad for you right now."

"That's easy. It's the market."

"Yes, the market is bad, but it's the same for everyone." He rubbed the back of her shoulder before he continued, "But . . . there's much more to life than work. What do you really want out of life?"

"That's a hard question to answer. What do you mean?"

"Surely, you don't want to work this hard all of your life, and we both know that life is much more than designer clothes and jewelry."

I always suspected that he resented my interest in designer styles. Is that what he's getting around to? "I like nice things, I think most women do."

"But . . . why is being successful so important to you?"

She started to smile, but his frown forced her to stop short. "I'll admit I like the way people look at me. It makes me feel important. It's also important for my business to let people at least think I'm successful. All buyers or sellers want to know they're using the most experienced and successful agent they can find. You know this."

"Yes, to a point. However, I think they also want an agent that's honest and trustworthy; even to their self." His words cut like a knife.

She started to smile again, but stopped when he pointed to her face. "Are you saying I'm not honest?"

He smiled this time. "Only you can answer this. So . . . tell me again, what do you really want out of life?"

"It's important, very important for me to be successful."

"Why?"

She stopped and thought about it. "I think it's the only way to secure my future. I don't think anyone else will provide for me in my old age."

He paused for a long time before redirecting his attention to the St. Petersburg skyline. "What about love?"

Oh yes . . . love, the one word I've sidestepped most of my life. Is that what all of this is about? "What do you mean?"

"I was wondering what's really important to you," he said.

He was digging deep, very deep tonight, but why? "I think love is one thing all of us want." He pointed to her face. "What?"

"The smile."

"Ohhh." She forced a straight face.

"Are you scared of being in love?"

"No, what makes you think so?"

"I think you're scared to not be in control." He nailed her, and she knew she could not lie to him. *How did he become so smart at such a young age?*

"You think so." She eyed him, forcing herself to be slightly angry. "You're the one who never loses control."

"And that frustrates you, doesn't it?" he asked.

"At times, I'll admit it. You know I had this liposuction procedure for you."

"Why? I never complained about your weight before."

"I wanted you to want me. I felt jealous of you and the skinny French girls I saw you with." She suddenly realized her voice rose in volume–perhaps too much. She glanced around to see if anyone overheard her.

She watched him laugh and his attempt to control it. "Skinny French girls?"

"Yes, don't deny it. I know you also went to the Keys with them."

"They're friends of mine. They're thinking of buying some property here, at my suggestions. And they aren't French. They're Swedish, but speak French. Their English isn't too good, and they prefer to speak French or Italian with me." He leaned forward to stare at her, as he continued to push. "Are you saying you became jealous of them?"

"I think any girl would feel threatened. Especially with the shape I was in." She knew she looked flustered. "And I remember a time I saw you out dancing with other girls. That's why I learned how to dance."

"I see. I wondered what made you interested in learning to dance."

She stared at him, looking for some clues as to what he was thinking. "I hate to say it, but I still don't know much about you. You never talk about yourself–ever."His smile faded as she knew she had hit close to a guarded secret about his past. "You seem to have no family, no past."

"That's true, and I told you before my parents died when I was young." He pushed his plate forward. "This grouper tasted great; however, I could use some desert tonight–how about you?"

"Not on your life–not after having to go through

liposuction to obtain this body."

He smiled as he glanced downward and back up. "Good for you."

"You don't have any weight problems, but eat all of the time."

"I pay for it. I work out every morning for about two to three hours." He lifted an arm to show a bicep as he laughed.

Rachel grinned. "Perhaps I need to exercise more." She lowered her eyes as she thought of her impending doom at the bank. "The way things look; I'll have plenty of free time when I lose everything."

"Do you really think the bank will foreclose on you?" He placed a hand on her arm, gently massaging it.

"I don't know. I'm working on a few plans, but nothing looks too good."

"I would be willing to help you if you let me."

"Carlos, I owe much more than you could possibly understand. One day you'll understand." She couldn't believe she said that.

"You mean much more than a *boy toy* can understand." He stood to leave. She now knew that he had overheard some previous conversations and the game was over.

"Where did you hear that term?"

"It's not a matter of where, but how often."

She knew their relationship had to be over. She didn't want their time together to end like this, not like this. "Please, I know you don't owe me, but I really need to go by the boat for a minute. Will you please go with me?"

He moved to the back of the chair to hold it for her. "Perhaps it would be good for me to walk with you."

She stood to thank him, but he simply backed away, waiting on her to walk out with him.

Chapter 37

They walked in silence past the strollers and joggers making their way back and forth from the pier. Rachel soon noticed the number of boats with for sale signs on them. In this economy she knew many people had fewer funds for such diversions as boating. Like her, they may also need the extra money to make ends meet.

Carlos walked beside her, but never offered his hand. His solemn face indicated that he was deep in thought and she knew why. She had hurt him and perhaps lost him as well, but she really needed him now, more than ever. *But how am I going to let him know?*

Remembering to soften her smile, she reached for his hand again which he accepted. The air, slightly cool in the evening, refreshed her, making her wish he would cuddle with her, but she decided not to push it. She squeezed his hand, hoping for a response–there was none.

She inhaled deeply before she spoke. "Why are you so mad at me?"

"I'm not mad, just thinking." He did, however, offer a slight squeeze to her hand. "Why is it so hard for you to just be you–rather than pretending to be someone else?"

"What do you mean?"

He kept his face looking forward as they made their turn to the left. "Never mind–I think it'll be too hard to explain that I want you to tell me exactly what you're thinking. You know, to simply be honest."

She swallowed. "Okay, what do you want to hear? You know I like being with you. I think we have great sex. We share an interest in real estate. I think we both want to be successful."

He looked straight ahead. "I understand what you're saying. However . . . we have other things to consider."

"What?"

"If you don't know, then I don't think we need to discuss it."

His comment frustrated her. *Is he talking about love, about marriage?* She quickly calculated the difference in their ages. While he had never said anything about the difference, she hadn't until recently even mentioned it. They had never talked about it. *Should I mention it now? And what exactly is it that he wants from me?*

Her mind accumulated several questions as they turned left again into the entrance to the pier where she maintained her boat. "Thanks for coming with me. This will only take a minute. Since I hope I can sell this boat quickly, I need some information on it that I keep onboard."

As they prepared to step onboard, a man walked up behind them. He had a dark hood covering the back of his head, allowing only the front of his face to be partially visible. When his quick movements startled both of them, Carlos moved between the stranger and Rachel.

In the dim light, they saw a pistol extend from under the jacket that he wore. His voice, loud enough to draw attention normally, became quickly muted by the ruffle of flags from the boat next to her boat. He repeated, yelling louder this time. "Raise your hands and walk onboard now."

She watched Carlos stand his ground. "Who are you?"

"That's not important–boy toy–walk on board now, or I'll shoot you right here, right now." The gun pointed directly at Carlos's chest.

Rachel knew this had to be the stalker, the killer. She thought about running onboard. *I need to call 911, but how?*

She panicked. *Would Carlos keep standing there and get shot?* Ohmigod no, she had to do something.

After she heard the command again to walk on board, she tapped Carlos on his shoulder. "Careful, he looks serious." She watched Carlos reach low and touch her leg, indicating she needed to move slowly.

The stalker pointed the gun again in his face. "I said . . . raise your hands and keep them where I can see them." They both complied and walked onboard, backing into the boat as far as they could. "Now, open the cabin and go inside. Don't try anything funny." He moved slowly in front of them, keeping his face directly in front of them. His heavy beard hid most of his features until they walked inside. "Turn the light on as you enter."

As he walked into the full light of the cabin, Rachel's voice squealed. "Ricky!"

He dropped the hood and pushed the gun further in Carlos face. "Yes. Surprised to see me, are you?" His blond hair shined in the light, matching the lightly colored beard. With several scars crisscrossing his face, indicating many fights, she could only imagine what had happened to him since the last time she saw him.

The shock of seeing him and the way he looked scared her. *What is he doing out of jail?* It was definitely him, but he looked so different now. She assumed he received the scars in prison. "What are you doing here?"

A smile oozed out of the side of his grin. "I can tell you really missed me, but who knows . . . maybe not. I see you got yourself another *boy toy* here." Ricky glanced at Carlos who was apparently sizing him up.

Carlos remained cool. "What do you want?"

Ricky raised the pistol to eye level. "You've no idea what kind of nest of bitches you've happened into, do you?" He glanced over at Rachel. "Perhaps, I should tell him, shouldn't I, honey?"

"Honey? We never had an affair."

"–but honey, you did like the way I gave you massages, didn't you?" He grinned fuller, apparently much for Carlos's benefit. Rachel's heart raced. Hopefully she could explain this to Carlos later, that is, if she had the chance. She watched Ricky explore her body with his eyes. "I'll have to say you look better up close."

"You've been stalking me, haven't you? But why? I've never caused you any problems."

"That's what we're going to find out tonight. Someone turned me in. I might not ever know the truth now, but since I spent years in prison for my sins, I think I need to know the truth." His voice spit the words out as he pointed to his face. "And this is nothing. Wait until you see the rest of their handiwork."

"I'm sorry."

"Sorry, my ass! Once word got out I was a masseur, I became the number one mark in prison. Everyone wanted a piece of me." Ricky's breathing raced as he let out the rage inside of him. She knew he had been abused and the thoughts made her close her eyes.

Ricky turned his attention to Carlos. "Have they started passing you around yet? They did me. I'm sure you meet them–you know Jody, Margaret, Mary Jane and Gloria–all of the bitches in this group. I gave all of them what they wanted and I forced no one. They asked me for sex, paid me for it."

The anger inside Rachel grew. "We never had sex."

"I guess it depends on how you define sex. You must have thought my dick was dirty, but you loved to be masturbated. Isn't that right?"

"What about Angela? Are you forgetting she's why you went to prison? She was only fifteen or sixteen when you had sex with her."

"At that time, I was only nineteen and that's not that large of a gap. We dated, and contrary to everyone's belief, we were falling in love, which is something you bunch of bitches would never understand."

"I never knew about you and Angela until your arrest. Also, the girls joked around, but they never admitted to having sex with you. I guessed they did, but I never knew for sure."

"Someone convinced the owners into pushing the charges. I know it had to be them. You were the agent in charge of selling the condos. You had to know something."

"Sorry. I can only guess. Jody is the one who caught you having sex with Angela."

"Jody tried to break us up. I think she thought I was trash, or as she put it, a boy toy, to be used at will." He paused to scratch his chin. "I also need to know where Mary Jane disappeared to. I know she is involved somewhere in this."

"What makes you think so?"

"She's the one who loved sex the most. She demanded not only sex, but she wanted me to spend the night with her. You didn't know that, did you? Let me tell you a few more things about your good friend Mary Jane that I think–."

A female voice shouting from behind him shattered the conversation. Rachel recognized the voice as well as Ricky.

Ricky reflected the shock and indecisiveness in his face as he pointed the gun at Carlos. "Mary Jane . . . it's good of you to join us." Ricky started turning slowly around.

"STOP! I have a gun pointed at your head and at this range and I don't think I'll miss at this range."

As Ricky became distracted, Carlos reached over and grabbed the gun from Ricky's hand. At first Ricky fought hard, but was quickly overwhelmed by Carlos, who wrestled control of the gun.

After being unarmed, Ricky turned to face Mary Jane, as he asked her in a slow deliberate tone. "So, my guess is right: you're the one who turned me in."

Mary Jane's face remained serious. "No, I didn't. I actually enjoying your attention until I heard you screwed Angela. I also thought, until a few minutes ago, that I was the only one you were truly intimate with. I should've known better."

Rachel had thoughts flying wild on her own. "Tell me something. Why did the two owners of the condo die?"

Ricky smirked and glanced around. "I guess they couldn't live with the fact they both also had sex with Angela."

Mary Jane shouted, as she clutched the gun in front of her. "You're a dirty fucking liar!"

Ricky responded as he dropped his hands. "Am I? Angela told me herself when she called me in prison."

"Do what?" Mary Jane screamed, as she lowered the gun in shock.

Ricky moved fast, taking advantage of the moment by grabbing the gun from her hand and rushing behind her. Carlos quickly trained his aim on Ricky, but Ricky had the new gun pushed next to Mary Jane's head. Ricky's eyes flashed wildly as he yelled at Carlos. "Put the gun down, or I'll kill her right now!"

Carlos didn't budge. "I don't think so."

Ricky tightened his grip as the veins in his neck bulged.

Carlos slowly lowered his gun. "Now what?"

"I don't know. I came here for answers, and I still don't have them. Everyone do exactly as I say and no one will die. I just need to make sure I can get away from here for now. There'll be another day."

Rachel spoke slowly. "How do you plan on escaping?"

"I'm working on a plan. I know if I tie you up it won't take long for someone to get free, or for someone to come checking on you. How much fuel do you have on this boat?"

Rachel looked forward. "Not much. I never refueled after my last trip."

His grin signified he had a plan. "It'll have to do. I know you have a small raft on board. Most boats this size usually do."

"Why?" Carlos and Rachel asked together.

"This is your only option. I'll leave you out at sea. The sea is fairly calm and you'll be fine as I disappear."

"You're not serious." Rachel's heart fluttered. Ricky had to be insane to think of such a thing. "Who's going to drive the boat? I own it, but I have never driven it." She lied, hoping he would believe her.

"I think I can manage. Wait, what's that?" A number of lights flashed from various windows in the cabin.

Rachel smiled. "Security system. Yes, even boats are armed with them."

Ricky acted desperate. "Nobody move." The sound of footsteps approaching confirmed that either the coast guard or the local St. Petersburg police were coming fast.

A voice boomed over the docks. "This is the police. Come out with your hands above your head. Do it now!"

Instead, Ricky yelled at Carlos and Rachel. "Turn around now." After they slowly complied, Ricky walked forward and hit Carlos on top of the head with the barrel. Rachel turned to face Ricky, daring him to hit her as he pointed the gun in her face. "Don't push me."

"You hurt him."

"He'll live." He shoved her on the floor next to him. "Stay put."

Ricky moved toward the door and pushed Mary Jane in front of him, using her as a shield, as he shouted toward the dock. "I don't think so. If you don't want blood on your hands, back up and get off this dock now."

Rachel's cell phone rang. They all looked at it. It had to be the police. Ricky reached for Rachel's phone and checked the incoming panel before smiling. "Yes?"

Rachel used the distraction to examine Carlos's head where he was bleeding and saw a lump marking the spot of the blow that rendered him unconscious.

Ricky walked over toward Mary Jane before yelling again toward the pier. "Who I am isn't important, but I want you to listen to me. I want you off this pier and I mean now!"

A bright light appeared from overhead. The police had a helicopter in the sky. Rachel knew Ricky had snapped, and she wasn't sure what he'd do next.

Ricky yelled back into the phone. "Kill that light." He walked over to Mary Jane and yanked her around in front of him by her hair as she screamed. He forced her to the door and positioned her where she could be easily seen. The overhead light died.

Mary Jane attempted to pull from him, only to have her blouse ripped before he pulled her on inside and closed the door. He immediately threw her to the floor next to the others. "Stay." Ricky moved back to the door, surveying the dock.

Rachel started to stand until Ricky leveled the gun toward her face. "He's not waking. I think you cracked his skull. If you don't get him some help, he might die."

She watched him bite his lip. "I didn't hit him too hard."

Rachel's phone rang again. Ricky clicked it on, and without saying a word, he listened for several minutes before responding. "Hello, Detective Lindstrom. I need some time to think. No, I don't want to talk about it. I don't need any more shrinks selling me down the river." He acted like he was going to hang up, but paused. "I have only one person I want to talk to–the one person you've denied me the right to talk to. . . . Yes, I want to talk to Angela, damn it, and no one else. Let me know when you can arrange it." After listening for a few more seconds to a response, he closed the phone.

***

Mary Jane continued to cry on the floor. Even after Carlos had gained consciousness, Ricky had made them all huddle close together on the floor, offering no assistance to the injury to his head. He especially enjoyed taunting Mary Jane. The more she cried, the more he smiled.

Eventually, the phone rang. Ricky grasped the phone in his free hand and answered. "Hello?"

Rachel watched the anger cross Ricky's face. He apparently didn't like the answer. He looked so much different than when she saw him the last time. The markings of over drinking or drugs registered on his slim pale face, not like the deep suntanned glow he had before. His eyes that once sparkled now looked dull and withdrawn.

Ricky began to shout. "No, that's not the way it's going to happen! I want her here now! I want to see her face to face. She's the only one who knows who sent me to prison."

Rachel had one hand on Carlos and one on Mary Jane. Their weakness gave her new strength to think of some kind of solution. Ricky had lost it and she knew he could kill all of them at any minute. She hoped the detective knew what he was doing.

Ricky continued to yell with his sentences becoming shorter and more vulgar. "Fuck you, I spent years in jail, and all I want is to know the damn truth!" He paced the floor, glancing out the window. "Good, I'll be waiting on you. What? Okay, I'll send one out–the guy. He needs someone to look at his head, but the girls are staying with me. That's the deal!" He slapped the phone shut.

Ricky walked over toward the group, addressing Carlos. "Can you stand?"

Carlos glanced at him, his head bobbling. "I'm not leaving the girls."

"Don't try to be a hero. I'm not going to hurt them. I need them for cover right now until I find a way to get out of here." For a minute, Ricky talked calm and collective. "Now, get on your feet and head toward the door."

Rachel leaned over to Carlos. "You know he's right. You need to go to the hospital and have your head examined. Please, do it for me."

Ricky pushed the gun closer to Carlos's face. "Okay, get up now, they'll be here in a few minutes."

Rachel reached under Carlos' shoulder and pulled. He struggled, but was unable to stand on his own. She tried again and he slowly complied as she pulled with all of her strength. On his feet, she walked with him to the door. She stopped and glanced at Ricky as he shouted instructions. "He'll need to walk out the door himself. I want you back over there." Ricky waived the pistol at her. As she edged closer, he continued, "Stop where you are and turn around."

She complied to feel him put the gun behind her head. He tapped her head hard; it hurt. "Don't move." He backed slightly.

He stood close enough for her to hear the dial tone as he made a call. "Okay, he's at the door. I'm sending him out now. I have a gun behind Rachel's head, so don't do anything stupid." He motioned for Carlos to start walking.

Rachel smiled at him as he left. Good, he was safe.

Ricky yelled back into the phone. "Now, I want to see Angela."

Mary Jane continued to cry on the floor, as he yelled at her. "Shut up, bitch!" He acted like he was going to kick her, but stopped and laughed.

Rachel saw him motion for her to turn around again. She complied as he grabbed her again, pushing her toward the door. "They're bringing Angela to the boat. Stay right at the door where I can keep an eye on you and hear her."

Rachel opened the door and looked out. She saw nothing, but heard various commotions coming from down the pier. She waited until she finally saw several people walking down the pier with two shields blocking most of the view. The top part of the clear shield allowed her to make out two men and one woman.

Ricky pushed closer to her with the barrel tapping her head. Oh god, she didn't want to get shot. She glanced down the pier as far as she could and saw no sign of Carlos.

Ricky leaned forward as the group reached the boat. "Stop there. That's close enough. ANGELA, CAN YOU HEAR ME?"

"Yes, I can." Her voice had a normal pleasing sound. Apparently she had been well rehearsed as to how to act and what to say. "You have innocent people in there. You need to let them go. We can talk later. "

"No, we can talk now," Ricky shouted. "I spent a lot of time in prison. I loved you and you know it. I need to know . . . why someone turned me in, and who it was."

"Ricky, you didn't love me. If you did, you wouldn't have been screwing my older sister."

"Angela, you know that happened before I met you. I told you that."

"I don't believe you."

"What are you saying?"

"Ricky, I'm the one who told the police. I'm the one who turned you in."

Ricky screamed. "No—you're lying; they're making you say this!"

"Ricky, listen to me. I'm the one who got hurt. I'm the one who had to leave and start over."

"Angela, I still love you, and I always will."

Angela didn't say a word. The silence appeared to last forever.

"You should've waited for me. I want to know one other thing Angela."

"What?"

"Is it true? Did you screw both of the owners of the condos? That's what you told me. Did you do that to get even with me, or did you make it up?"

Angela remained quiet again.

"I see–no answer. Well I know the truth and so do you. Listen to me–I always loved you and would've done anything for you. I know they're the ones behind sending me to prison. It's funny, they really only wanted to protect themselves. At least they received what was coming to them. I love you, Angela."

He backed away slowly, and cried loudly. BANG–the blast coming from the gun firing made her think she had been shot at first. She turned to see him falling–the side of his face missing, replaced with blood spurting across the room. The room swirled around her as she grabbed the door for support. She heard the sounds of Mary Jane's hysterical screaming as the world faded.

Chapter 38

Days later, Rachel worked fast at her office trying to finish a file on a closing. Good, this money would help, but she knew she was still short. The bank would be calling soon. She glanced at her phone again, since she had left Carlos messages all morning only to be transferred to his voice mail. The end of the month was tomorrow, and unless the bank changed its mind, she knew her career was over.

She heard a knock on the door as her broker walked in. Now what, she thought. "How are you?" he asked.

She forced a smile. "I have another closing."

"Good, you always work hard. The detective came by and saw me yesterday. It's amazing no one local knew Ricky had been released from prison. It makes you really worry about our legal system."

"Yes, it does. I'm sure the police are feeling the heat of this screw up. If the system had operated properly, the two owners would still be alive. They would've been warned he had been released and could possibly be looking for them."

"Exactly–I'm just glad this ordeal is over."

Rachel wanted to tell him about the bank, but decided to wait until the very end. Surely they would reconsider. "Thank you for everything. You've been a great broker."

Rachel's phone rang and the broker waved, indicating he'll talk to her more at a later time. She glanced at the caller ID and a sudden tightness shot through her body–the bank's name flashed on her screen. "Hello, this is Rachel."

"Hi, I hoped to catch you this morning. Something has come up and we need to see you at the bank as soon as you can make it here." His voice sounded amazingly friendly, which was totally unexpected.

"I'm in the middle of turning in a closing and can come after we finish. What is it?"

"I think it'll be better to tell you when you arrive. We'll see you soon." The line died.

***

Rachel soon walked into the bank with her case full of documents. She wanted to be ready for all contingencies. She had new financials, a list of her listings, her HUD from the closing earlier, and her listing on her boat showing where she was trying to sell it. She knew they knew the balance in her account.

Langford's secretary had a big smile on her face as Rachel approached. "Hi, it's good to see you today." She definitely had the look of the girl who couldn't keep a secret. Rachel thought about pressing, but didn't have the time as her banker walked out to meet her.

"Hi, please come on in." Langford turned and walked ahead of her as she followed and assumed the chair across from his desk.

She forced her smile and charm to cover the questioning look she knew she presented. "What is it you wanted to see me about? I still have one more day."

"I've some extremely good news for you."

"Really!" *Good, they must have decided to extend my loan and give me some time to work the details out. Good!*

"Yes. We meet with someone this morning who wants to buy your loans."

"What?"

As Rachel started to stand, he raised his hand. "Please sit and let me explain."

A thousand thoughts flashed around her mind. Now what? "Okay, I'm listening."

"I think you've attracted a white knight to look out for you."

Rachel smiled. "That would be nice."

"I'm sure you know a Carlos Martin."

"Carlos–sure. But what does he have to do with this?"

"Well, we've sold him your notes. He opened an account here for you to make payments into and we've also been instructed to tell you that all late payments have been waived."

"Wait a minute. Do you mean he has placed me with another lender?"

"No–what I'm telling you is that he's the lender. He used his own money."

"What money, he's only a young kid!"

She watched him reach over to the corner of his desk. "I'm not sure I would call him a kid, since he loans money to many investors around town. I also have another surprise for you." He tossed her several magazines. "Perhaps it would be good for you to take a close look at this. Of course these magazines are a few years old and people do age, but I think you might have a surprise in store for you, and especially since you pride yourself in designer styles so much."

Rachel knew her smile had vanished. *What is he talking about?* She heard him laughed as he left the room, leaving her with the magazines in front of her. She glanced at the cover. A young boy, perhaps in his early teens posed in a full tux. It took a moment. "OHMIGOD!" He looked younger, but Carlos smiled then much like he did now. She ripped through the other magazines. She saw his photos scattered on one page after another.

She jumped from the chair running out of the office, looking for the banker. "Are you telling me Carlos has worked as a model before?"

"Not simply as a model, but one of the top super models for a long time, that is until he quit a few years ago." His laugh turned serious. "Since he offered us full price for a loan we thought was going bad, we had no choice but to accept his offer."

Rachel remained in shock. "I think I owed the bank almost twelve million dollars."

He laughed. "Trust me; we decide to wait on calling you until the wire went through. He is wisely investing his money in loans around town."

"I need to talk to him." She stood to leave.

"I understand, but I think he's in the process of leaving."

"Leaving?"

"He said he planned to move back to Europe, I think Italy. I know he owns a place in Milan."

"No, he can't do that." She stood. "Please–I need to talk to him." She turned and ran out of the bank.

***

She flipped open her phone as she left the bank, calling his cell phone number again. Immediately, the call went to his mail box. "Carlos, I need to talk to you. Please call me." *Where can he be?*

Suddenly everything made sense, but he had deceived her also if he knew designer clothes. It also explained why he never talked about his past. She knew he must hate her, but if so, why did he bail her out? Damn, that was a lot of money!

Her phone rang. She answered before glancing at the ID. "Hello, Carlos."

The returning voice wasn't what she expected. "Hi, this isn't Carlos. This is Angela."

Rachel started to slap her own face. "Oh hi, I was expecting Carlos to call me."

"I understand. Listen, I've been meaning to call you

back, but haven't been feeling well. I'd love to talk to you about this condo some more. I really need to sell the place as soon as possible. I'm at the condo now."

Rachel glanced at her watch. While she really wanted to find Carlos now, she needed to keep this listing. Perhaps she could go by and see Angela while she waited for Carlos to call her back. "I can come by now if you need me to, but I'm not sure how long I can stay."

"Good, I'll see you soon." The connection died.
***

Rachel tried to call Carlos again as she reached Jody's condo complex. The thoughts of going in the room where she had died scared her, and especially not knowing how Angela would react in the room. She thought about the note she had left Carlos at his town house. Surely he would see the message and call her. His boss at the mortgage company where he worked also hadn't heard from him.

Rachel rode the elevator to Angela's floor of the condo and waited at the door, gathering her strength to knock. *Why does Angela want to see me?* She knew Angela had been under the care of a psychologist since Ricky shot himself. The question of Ricky's involvement appeared to be moot now that he had taken the truth with him when he shot himself.

Of course, the shocker was Angela's admission to witnessing Ricky have sex with her sister. Perhaps this is what Jody meant when she said the deaths were all her fault, but was this reason enough for her to commit suicide?

Rachel froze, attempting to think. Ricky had mentioned Angela had told him she had sex with the two condo owners. *Was this the truth, or did she tell him this to torment him? And, more importantly, should she ask Angela for the truth?*

When she knocked on the door, Angela opened it

immediately. "Hi, I hoped you would come by soon."

"Well you made it sound important. I also wanted to check on you. How are you handling everything?"

"Fine, I guess."Angela looked pale and tired with dark circles under her eyes suggesting days of crying. The blue jeans she wore fit badly. Much like her before the liposuction, Angela had many extra pounds and wore faded jeans which fit much too tightly.

Rachel cautiously walked around the kitchen. "I know you want to sell this condo as quickly as possible, but the only way to sell fast is to lower the listing to a give-away price."

"–I understand, but I want this nightmare behind me. I'm going back to Miami, and I don't plan on coming back again if I can help it."

"You don't really need to until the closing. In fact, I can send you the papers to sign in Miami if you wish." Rachel studied Angela who acted highly nervous. She floated around the room as her fingers tapped on the counter.

Angela turned to face her and added a new force to her voice which reflected the seriousness of her need to see Rachel. "I didn't know how much Ricky was involved with you until the other day."

Rachel thought quickly about the night Ricky died, trying to remember how much of the conversation Angela heard. "Ricky gave me some massages like he did many of the girls."

"–but did he give you other services like he did the other girls?"

Angela's question shocked Rachel in how blunt she was. Rachel had a feeling that Angela was perhaps more distraught than she thought over Ricky's death. "No, not like what I heard recently about the extra services he provided."

"But you knew."

"I suspected, but never knew for sure."

Rachel wanted to know if Angela really had sex with the two dead owners. She hesitated, but knew the detective wouldn't be so timid. However, she remembered one question she could ask. "Ricky said you called him. When was the last time you talked to him?"

Angela moved to the side, obviously avoiding the question. "Is that what Ricky said?"

"Yes." An uneasy feeling crept across her as she watched Angela continue to walk around the counter.

"That bastard! He told me he loved me, and I trusted him. I was so naïve! I should've known better." Angela had tears in her eyes.

Rachel understood the hell Angela must be going through, but weary at the same time. Something told her Angela wasn't telling everything. She thought if she remained calm, she might tell her more. "I know how it is to fail at your first love."

"Oh really! Do you think you really know what it's like? What it's like to have everyone pointing fingers at you like you're some kind of weird sex toy."

Apparently, Angela needed much more counseling. "I'm really sorry for all of this you're going through. It will all be over soon."

Angela continued to pace around the counter. "I need to know what all Ricky told you before he died. Did he talk about me?"

Rachel thought back on the conversation and how scared she was. "I don't think Ricky was in his right mind when I saw him. He was very upset."

"I understand that–" Angela yelled, "–but . . . I need to know what he told you about me!"

"What he wanted to know was who turned him in. Apparently he thought the owners of the condo here turned him in.”

“Good.”

Rachel couldn’t understand where Angela was heading with this. Angela had told Ricky before he died she had turned him in. Since Ricky had acted like he really loved her, this information would naturally be tough to take. *Did Angela know the information would push him over the edge? Is she that cruel or did she hate him so much for what he did that she wanted to push him to the point of taking his life?*

Since Rachel remained quiet, Angela pushed on. “What else did he say?”

“His words rambled, but apparently he was, at least he thought he was, still in love with you.”

“He ruined my life, that’s what he did.” Angela’s eyes dance around wildly. “Yes, I had sex with the owners of the condo here. I wanted the news to reach Ricky. I wanted him to pay for what he did to me.”

Rachel raised her hands to her mouth. Until now, she thought that part of the past was a lie. “You didn’t really–”

“Oh yes I did. They loved having their way with me, and now they also received exactly what was coming to them.”

“You can’t really mean that.”

“Yes, I can. The police think Ricky killed them. Detective Lindstrom came to see me yesterday and told me the murder investigation was closed.”

“Yes, hopefully Ricky’s death will put an end to all of the murders and endless questions. We can all put this behind us.”

Rachel watched Angela breathe easier. “I want this condo sold now. Are you sure he told you nothing else about the owners deaths?”

Rachel’s phone rang. She retrieved it to see her office calling. “Hello, this is Rachel.” She paused for a second, listening to a message where Carlos had been trying to call her. "Listen, I need you to do me a favor and find the Margie Lakeland file for me and have it ready for me ASAP. Yes, I need it ASAP, do you understand?" She clicked the phone off.

Rachel turned her attention back to Angela, thinking she still hid something. Angela confirmed her fears as she opened a door beneath the counter and retrieved the gun Rachel had purchased. She remembered the last time she saw the gun stored in a bedside drawer at her condo. "What are you doing?"

"I'm finishing the very last of my list. Mary Jane is in the psych ward, and from what I hear, she may be there for life. The only other woman that was part of the cougar pack is you, and with you gone, no one else can tie me to this." She grinned in a sarcastic way. "You know they say suicide is painless." She continued in a musical melody for the old M.A.S.H. TV series. "It brings on many changes . . ."

Rachel's heart beat hard. *Was Angela a killer? Had she killed the others?* "Angela we need to talk about this. Don't be crazy on me."

"You know the room I want you in–the same one my sister died in."

"No. You can't be serious."

"Move it!" Angela leveled the gun at her.

Rachel stood her ground, attempting to ask more questions. "What's wrong with you?"

"I think I've told you everything I need to tell you. However . . . I will tell you what you're going to say on your suicide note."

"My what?" while she had no intentions of signing any such note, she needed to stall and hope the coded message to the office would be understood. She thought about how she had been forced to memorize the name of a woman, a Margie Lakeland who had been abducted a few years ago and brutally raped and murdered, and how to refer to her if she ever became threatened by a situation when she was showing properties.

"Don't worry about it too much, but I think this letter will become exciting reading for some people. All I need you to do is sign it." Angela opened the drawer to the side of the counter again, removing a piece of paper. "You can read the letter if you want." Her smile became more sinister as she shoved it over to Rachel.

Rachel reached for the piece of paper. She needed to stall as long as possible. She had to think, to find some way to talk some sense into Angela's head. She decided to laugh. "This doesn't sound like me at all."

"It'll do. Sign it."

Rachel slowly read the letter, saying nothing.

"I know you must have all kind of questions now. Perhaps, you would like to hear."

Rachel smiled and really didn't want all of the details, but reading the letter would buy her some time. She stood and listened to the story over the next thirty minutes, hoping she had made her message clear to her broker's office secretary.

Suddenly, the front door crashed in with an explosive sound as Detective Lindstrom stood behind a large gun pointed at Angela. "Drop the gun now!"

Shock registered on Angela's face, but instead of complying, she turned and fired. The bullet missed the detective, but hit Rachel's arm. Several other shots came from the area of the door knocking Angela backwards. The detective rushed at her, grabbing her gun. "Call an ambulance now!"

Several other men followed him into the room as another officer rushed over to Rachel. The wound to her upper arm hurt. The blood scared her more. "Ohmigod!" The sight of the blood made her head spin. She knew the feeling many times lately as the world around her vanished.

Chapter 39

The sights, smells and sounds of the hospital revived her. She quickly realized that she was in a hospital bed. While her arm still hurt, her dizzy feeling confirmed some kind of painkiller they must have given her. "Nurse." *How long have I been here?*

A warm hand touched her forehead. "Easy, you're going to be okay." She knew it had to be Carlos.

"Ohmigod. I got shot!" She tried to isolate the feeling in her arm. How bad was it?

"You're very lucky. The bullet barely nicked you, but I know the wound must hurt like hell."

The voice sounded different. She glanced around to find a male nurse standing beside her. "I thought you were Carlos." She watched the nurse smile.

She soon watched another man stand beside him–Detective Lindstrom. "How are you?"

"I feel like shit. I got shot." She glanced around the room to see if anyone else was in the room.

"I understand, and I'm so sorry. It's a good thing you used the distress code when your office called."

Thoughts returned concerning the conversation. Yes, she owed the receptionist a large thank you. She glanced toward the detective again, as she remembered him crashing into the condo. "I think I need to thank you for arriving in time to save me."

"You're welcome. I do have some questions for you, if you can answer them for me."

Rachel glanced at him sideways. "I know you have

questions."

"Yes, but first let me tell you you're going to be fine. In fact, they'll let you leave in a few hours."

"That's good to know." She wondered how she would drive home. *Where is my car?*

"I'm not sure you saw Angela being shot or not." He paused. "She's in serious condition, but we think she'll make it. She has some other serious problems facing her, however."

"I understand. Her sister was a good friend of mine, and I want to help her if I can. She has no family."

He again paused as he appeared to gather his thoughts. "After Ricky shot himself, we all thought he was the one responsible for killing the owners, and perhaps Jody also. But now . . . we know he was in another state until recently. We suspect Angela lured him back here to pin the murders on."

"Okay, but why did Ricky shoot himself, knowing he wasn't the murderer?"

"Love is a strange thing. I think he realized Angela had killed them, but he would be blamed regardless. I think he made the ultimate sacrifice, and he gave his own life to protect her."

"So, you're telling me after everything, he still loved her?"

"Who really knows?" He leaned forward. "Now, I want you to tell me what I don't know. What did Angela tell you?"

Rachel's stomach hurt. She knew Angela's confession would make the case against her for murder irrefutable. "You don't really expect me to answer you on this, do you?"

"Yes, I do."

"Then, I think we're going to have a problem and I need to talk to an attorney."

Rachel watched him smile. "I know you're under a lot of pressure now, but we'll talk again soon."

She knew he was right. "She needs help."

"That much . . . I'll agree to. I think she'll have more than enough to cover an insanity plea. It's hard to imagine after her trying to kill that you you'd want to help Angela, though." He smiled.

Rachel refused to say any more. She switched to her large smile, the one she remembered how Carlos had confronted her on before. Where was he, anyway?

Chapter 40

True to Lindstrom's projection, the doctor came by shortly. "How are you? My name's Dr. Lowenski." His friendliness and bedside manners, apparent from a doctor used to making many bedside visits, didn't surprise Rachel.

"It hurts." She nodded at the bandages.

"I'm sure your arm does. You're lucky the bullet hit nothing extremely important. The wound should heal without many complications. As soon as you feel like it, you can leave. Do you have anyone who can drive you home?"

Where is Carlos? "I'm not sure. I also still don't know where my car is."

"You won't be able to drive with the medicine in you. We'll see what we can do about finding you a ride."

"Thanks." She ran through some names in her head, but she still had a hard time fully focusing. Perhaps she could call her broker. She reached for the phone as the doctor padded her shoulder and left.

The receptionist answered the phone on the first ring. Rachel knew she owed her a big thank you for saving her life. "Hi, this is Rachel."

"Hey, everyone here is asking about you."

"Thanks, I appreciate it. And thanks for remembering the distress code."

"You're welcome. I'm so glad you're okay."

"Me too. I need a ride home and someone to retrieve my car. Who's not busy in the office?"

"Are they letting you go home so soon?"

"Yes, but I can't drive."

"I'm surprise Carlos isn't with you. You did call him back, didn't you?'

Rachel had forgotten about the reason for the call which saved her life. "No, I haven't. I forgot all about your message until you mentioned it."

A long silence ensued. "I hate to tell you this, but he's planning on leaving soon."

"Leaving where?"

"He called yesterday and said to tell everyone goodbye. He's planning on moving to Italy as soon as possible. I thought you knew."

"No, not completely. I've been trying to call him for the last few days. Do you know where he is?"

"I've heard he has a crazy plan of driving his boat to Italy by way of Iceland. I think he's in no hurry to get to Italy."

Not now, not after all that's happened. She needed to talk to him. "I need a ride. If no one can come now, I'll call a cab." She called for the nurse. She had to hurry.

***

After running out of hospital and hailing a cab, she forced herself to concentrate as the cab raced toward the marina. Her heart pounded harder as she quickly located his boat. "Oh God–please be here."

As she started to run, the pain in her arm increased, but she pushed forward. Finally, she saw the front of his boat. He hadn't left yet. Good, good, good, she thought. Since the boat looked unoccupied, she stepped aboard. She knew it was his boat, but she had never been onboard before. Why, she didn't know. She walked forward, hoping he was on board–somewhere–anywhere.

Nothing–nothing but silence greeted her. But, at least, he had not left yet. She sat on the side of the boat, and prepared to wait for him–forever if need be.

An hour passed, then two. She closed her eyes, allowing

her mind to reminisce about the times with him. They had some good times together–they really did. She thought about all of the times she had wished she could control him, and about the times she knew she must've hurt him. Especially the last time they had dinner. She had to talk to him and explain.

The words of the banker, and more importantly, his laughter haunted her. He apparently thought it was amusing she had no clue as to who he really was. In fact, she still didn't know who he was in full. A model–he was a model and apparently not simply any model, but a very famous model. *Did he still work as a model?*

A gentle rock on the boat made her think that another boat was making its way around the marina and causing the commotion. Since the medicine hadn't cleared out of her system in full, maybe she needed to go home and rest and try to find him later.

"Hi, are you looking for me?" Carlos's voice sounded firm and smooth.

As she opened her eyes, the sunlight blinded her as she squinted. "YES! Where have you been?"

"I've been busy." He walked over toward her and stopped. "What happened to your arm?"

She smiled, realizing he hadn't heard. "I got shot."

"Shot! What are you talking about?"

Carlos placed his hand on her shoulder, as she explained. "I'm surprised you haven't heard. Angela talked me into coming to see her this morning. She's the one behind the murders."

"Angela? What do you mean?"

"She admitted everything to me. You wouldn't believe what she has been through, or what all she has done."

"How did you get shot?"

"Angela apparently wanted to make sure no one would

ever discover the truth and what she had done." She watched Carlos react to the news. His expression indicated he had many questions for later.

"Yes, but how did you get shot?" He persisted as he examined the bandage.

"I was lucky that Detective Lindstrom arrived in time. He shot Angela before she could hit me with a good shot. She's alive, and in very bad condition, but they think she'll make it. Mentally, she has some serious problems."

"Wow, I'm so sorry. I didn't hear a thing." He continued to rub her shoulder.

"I've been trying to call you for several days."

"I know, and I'm sorry." His puppy dog eyes confirmed his sincerity.

"I received a message this morning from our receptionist. She said you called." She studied every inch of his face, hoping what she heard was wrong. She didn't want to lose him now.

"I did call you, but first, let me ask you if you went to the bank yet?"

The words of her banker echoed in her head. How could she had been so blind and not see this? "I did. I can't let you do this for me. That's a lot, lot, lot of money."

"Don't worry, I know when you're ahead again we can work on refinancing. I've taken a lot of your time and you'll be back in shape soon with me gone."

"I don't understand. Why do you want to leave?"

"You know, there's much about me you don't know."

"You mean about you being a model?

She watched him glance at the floor. "That's a part of my past I've wanted to forget. Hiding my old life is why I moved here, but I should've known the bank would do a complete background check when I asked to buy your notes." He walked over to the side of the boat and looked around.

She quickly rose and walked behind him, slipping an arm around his side. "Why is it so important to hide it?"

"I started modeling when I turned twelve, and I've had people treating me like a kid all of my life. I quit working as a model four years ago to go to college. There are a few times I take on assignment, but not often. That's why I went to Italy a few weeks ago. I wanted to see my friends who are also models. I think you saw me with them once."

Yes, she remembered them–the skinny French girls. Only, she remembered now, they weren't French. "This is nothing to be ashamed about."

"I told myself I would never be treated like a toy again." His voice sounded extremely strong and determined. She could feel the emotions in him coming out.

"I'm so sorry. I'm older, and I thought I knew best on how to handle things."

He laughed. "What I heard is that you wanted me for a boy toy–nothing more, nothing less."

"Okay, yes I'll admit it. When I first saw you I was attracted to you physically. You have a great body and I was–"

"–fat."

"Well, that's not exactly the word I was going to use. And . . . by the way, I don't think you ever complained about the sex." She had to fight back.

"Yes, I never said I didn't enjoy the sex, nor did I ever say anything about your weight. However, what I've finally learned is that this is all you wanted or ever wanted."

"Wait, we had some good times also." She studied his questions, hoping to stay ahead of him in the discussion.

"Yes, at times." She watched him lower his head, apparently in deep thought. Damn, she wished she could read his mind.

"Are you really leaving?" Her heart beats pulsated throughout her body.

"Give me one reason why I shouldn't. I have a great chance to re-enter the modeling industry in Italy. And at twenty-three, I'll be perceived much differently."

"What about us?"

"I'm sure you can find someone else who can take care of you, and be available for you to spoil."

"That's not fair." She accepted the hurt he had intended, and which she knew she deserved. "I'm not nearly as bad as you think I am."

"I'm not saying you're bad . . . what I'm saying is that I'm not what you're looking for."

Her stomach quivered. Carlos must have made up his mind before they talked. "How can you say that?"

"To me, life is much more than sex and designer clothes."

She studied his face. *What is he talking about? What does he want from me?* "I know that. I'm not that vain."

He turned toward her. "I really wish you the very best." His face had a pleasant relaxed smile on it.

"Carlos, I don't want you to go." She hoped her words didn't sound like she was begging, but she wanted him to know she simply didn't want him to go.

"Why?"

"I think you know why!"

"Why?" He repeated the question, definitely not wanting to add to his reason for asking.

What is he looking for? Did he want to talk about commitment—about love? The deep concentration in his eyes begged for the truth. He moved closer to her as his eyes bored into her soul. His smell over-powered her as the scent often did when he moved in this close. He waited for her, remaining completely rigid in front of her.

She froze–too scared to talk–too scared not to. Time moved in slow motion. She didn't want to lose him. She wanted to kiss his lips and moved slightly forward only to see him withdrawal. She couldn't speak.

He released any connection to her and backed away. "I think I received my answer . . . just now."

"What answer?"

"Love is a very magical word that creates a passage to a dreamland which makes all of the madness worth it. Love is something I think you're scared of. After all, love means giving up control and revealing your inner thoughts, and which we've never discussed in any form. All we ever had was sex."

He backed away again as she pushed forward. "Do you want me to tell you I love you?"

"I told you from the first day that I'll never ask you to do something you didn't want to do. Do you remember?"

She thought back to the first night they had sex and him using those exact words. She thought he meant about sex. Had he been waiting on this all of this time? *Had he . . . loved me . . . all of this time? How can I be such a fool?*

He opened his mouth to speak, but she couldn't allow him to say anything else. She forced her way to his lips, kissing them with a fiery passion to stop any more words from escaping. "Okay, okay, I'll admit it!"

"Admit what?"

"Something I've never told anyone in my life."

He stood still, waiting on her. The timing was now or never, she thought, as she breathed in deeply. "Carlos, I love you. Not as a boy, but as a man, and one I've underestimated all the time I've known you."She waited for a response. *Would there be one?*

He pulled her closer and whispered, "Right answer . . . Rachel, I love you too."

THE END